CHRISTIAN WALLIS

VELOX BOOKS
Published by arrangement with the author.

With Teeth copyright © 2024
by Christian Wallis.

CONTENTS

ANNEDALE

I'm not homeless.

I have a home. I just don't own it. But it's mine and I work to keep it. Every city has its fair share of abandoned buildings to squat in, but usually you gotta deal with either cops or shitty neighbours. The Annedale High Rise has neither. Police stay away, so do the locals. As a stranger from out of town, I stumbled across the place on my first night in the city and thought it a little strange that a 28-story tower block had been left to rot. Every window black. Every light in the courtyard smashed. No cars in the lot. No booth for a guard. Not even barbed wire on the fence. Barely half-a-mile from a playground filled with shouting drunken teenagers, but none of them strayed in the direction of Annedale. No fires or music or bottles hurtling through the air. It was silent.

Inside, I found that the lobby had been torn to shit. Double doors ripped open and left that way for what looked like years. Easy access for the curious, but I was the only one there. Most of the first story had collapsed. Waterlogged ceiling tiles turned to mulch by shitty British weather. I know water is invasive, but it had practically fucking colonised the place so bad algae was growing up the walls. Even the elevator shaft was flooded. My own reflection looking back at me as I peered through brackish water and caught a glimpse of the old rusted carriage just a few feet below. I couldn't help but think about standing on top of it, waist high, and reaching down to pull open the emergency hatch. Only natural to wonder what was down there. Little metal box soaking in pitch black water for years and years. I thought about pressing the button, calling it up and seeing the elevator rise in spite of all logic. An image I still think of from time to time.

Meanwhile, the empty shaft loomed above, cables whistling in the wind. I've learned not to linger by it. If you look up, you'll sometimes see something ducking out of the way, pulling its head through the doors before you get a good look. It finds it awfully funny, even tries to make a game out of it, like peekaboo. Play too much though, and it starts to pop up elsewhere. Any open door becomes an invitation. Sent more than a few people running for their lives in the middle of the night, but bad news for them. That thing is more than free to leave this place if it's part of a game.

If you ask about Annedale most people just shrug or laugh. Kids'll talk about it the same way they talk about any haunted house. Difference is no one dares anyone to go up there. No one uses it to get pissed or high. No one sneaks into the basement to have a risky little fuck. No one hides their stashes there. It has all the hallmarks of your classic urban legend, only people *actually* stay away. They'll laugh and joke and tell scary stories, but they treat the soil it's on like it houses a radioactive leak. And the council, I'm surprised they haven't knocked it down but they, out of everyone in the city, have the most to lose by talking about it.

They built it in the mid fifties as government housing. Only a lot of the young mothers who moved in there found their children's health taking a turn for the worse. Started with newborns. Babies that wouldn't wake after a peaceful night's sleep. The kinda deaths that got written off as either negligence or abuse, screaming teenage girls hauled off to prison on the words of doctors who didn't give a shit. It's always the mother's fault in some people's eyes, and these girls had no one to stand up for them. Two in the first year, four in the next, and they kept on coming for every year until it closed.

Wasn't until 1982 that someone traced the source of deaths to tainted water storage on the roof. Toxic metals leeching into the supply. Not enough to kill an adult, but bad news for anyone with weak immune systems. Thirty-eight women had been imprisoned by then. Another twenty-three had killed themselves before they could be sentenced. And those are just the ones accounted for. Not all the deaths were from the water. Annedale has a way of being bad for any child's health, no matter the circumstance.

More than a few toddlers starved to death as their parents rotted in the tub from an overdose. Even more were lost when they found their parent's stash, little bodies wracked with agonising fits as their panicked mothers screamed for help. One tripped down the elevator shaft because the doors opened as if the carriage was right there. And those are the ones who were found. Plenty more went missing, written off as runaways. In the end, Annedale's reputation as a cursed place got so bad the only way out was to shut the whole thing down. Board it up. Erase it from the records. Pretend it never happened and just forget.

But Annedale kept on killing even after the doors were officially shut. If anything, it only got nastier. Talked to one cop who told me he found a guy dead from sepsis on the sixth floor a couple years after the place was shut down. No one could fucking believe it. They reckon this guy scratched himself on a nail and caught gangrene like it was the 1800s. Never went to the hospital. Just laid there and died slowly and painfully as the infection spread, but not before he took every last bit of furniture in the room and shoved it against the door. Strange enough on its own, but it was the flag he'd made out of his own clothes that freaked everyone out. He'd scrawled *HELP* on it, like he wanted to get someone's attention down below even though the lock was on his side. He could've left anytime he wanted.

Cop I spoke to said he was there when they kicked the door down. Still remembers the look in the dead man's eyes. He was glaring at the door two days after he'd passed, white-knuckled fists gripping a blanket that smelled sickly sweet from all that infection.

There were others too. Lots of people falling, many of them without a good reason. Got so bad they bricked the roof door, but by the time I arrived someone had cleared it all away with a sledgehammer. I still don't hang out up there. Not after I first went up and saw pale fingers gripping the ledge, like someone was hanging off it and holding on for dear life. I reckon a lotta people see something like that and think a person needs their help. They go rushing over to offer a hand. But when I saw it something about those grimy nails set alarm bells off in my head. Fingers looked all wrong. So I took my coat off and used a broom handle to move it closer to the ledge. Sure enough, those ugly hands snatched at the coat and ripped it outta my hands, sending it hurtling to the parking lot below. I've thought about taking a closer look from time to time, but I got a thing about heights and could never bring myself to investigate it much further.

You'd think I'd leave, but it's my home. I own it as much as it owns me. People even refer to me as the caretaker now like they forgot I wasn't always here. Police treat me the same, can you believe that? Any reports of a break in and they call me on my number to go take a look, like I'm some sort of official. Only other guy who was here as long as me was the philosopher. I don't know his name, just call him that because of the books he left behind. He came here back when the block was still just a place to live and he stuck around for a few years after its closure. Lots of notebooks in his flat. Thousands of pages talking about child sacrifice made to gods who don't like being named, along with pictures of strange things frozen in ice and medical photos that look fake.

At first I thought he came to document the curse. He has dozens of books just recording all the strange things he saw, like birds with too many wings or milk that turned to clotted blood in the bottle. But after going through everything he owned I found letters to a wife who'd died in childbirth. He kept her death certificate way at the back of an old looking box filled with the letters he'd kept writing her long after the date.

Another box, just a row over, had the letters she'd written back. Awful things scrawled on random scraps, shit and blood for ink. He dated them himself and sometimes wrote notes about how they came to him.

Delivered by a rat that was cannibalised in front of me.

Pulled by my dentist from a cavity in my mouth.

Written in the web of a spider with thirteen legs.

Anyway, he gives away the real reason he moved to Annedale in one of the letters. Says that Annedale was the key to helping her, that he was weeks away from figuring out how to open the door. Told his wife he'd bring her back. Told her he knew how. I've never figured out where he went next or what happened to him, but his apartment was locked when I found it and likely would've stayed that way if the key hadn't turned up in my inside pocket on the first morning. Now I live in his old place. It's safe in there. He's written things on the wall that keep everything well behaved. Symbols that I don't understand but which are easy to trace so that's what I do. I go over them every couple of months and so far they've kept me safe and sane.

Because you do need protection in Annedale. I don't know when in its history the curse went from something mundane to something very real and very dark. It wasn't all just bad luck or poverty, not by the end, and certainly not anymore. You can't just go strolling around Annedale, certainly not at night. It's dangerous. For one thing, it attracts a constant rotation of the deeply unwell who are likely to attack on sight, if you're lucky. They usually turn up dead in the halls come morning, although sometimes it's just bits of them that I come across. Strips of skin floating on the brackish water that floods the basement stairwell, or bloodied fingernails embedded in the ceiling plaster. Weirdest one was a single tooth in a lightbulb, bloody gum still attached to the root, the glass all around it somehow intact.

Many of them come here with business, something a little like the philosopher's. Rituals. Bargains. Things like that. It's not a good idea to interrupt them, or to give them even the slightest hint you might be a problem. Every night I lock my door and wait for Annedale's business to finish and come morning I do a sweep, floor by floor, and clean up whatever's left of the tower block's strange pilgrims.

Most of the rituals don't look real to me. In fact, I reckon a lotta people who come here just end up as victims of something or someone else. There are a *lot* of reasons to stay out of Annedale at night, and most of its visitors strike me as a little naïve. Most of what I see looks like it got stolen from a bad death metal album. I once found a book called "Satanism and Witchcraft in the 21st Century". It's hard to imagine that the secret inner workings of the universe can be found in something with an ISBN number and 3000 Amazon reviews. Of course, not all attempts at exploiting Annedale's energy are so hackneyed. I had one guy turn up at my door and pay me three grand in cash just to show him the darkest corner of the building. I wasn't sure what he meant at first. Thought he meant light and shadow.

"Sort of," he replied when I explained this to him. "Darkness like that can be part of it. But I'm looking for a corner, has to be a right angle or more acute. Ideally, more acute. You understand that term right?"

He'd seemed arrogant and that last sentence confirmed as much. Good looking guy in his late twenties, nice suit. Looked like the stereotypical banker. Acted like one too.

"Plenty of places like that," I said. "Lots of funny rooms in Annedale. People trying to make the most of limited space. Sometimes the walls meet at tight angles, sure. But I don't know what you mean about dark. There's the basement. It's flooded. Can't think of anywhere darker than that."

He bit his lip and hesitated for a second or two, as if he was actually contemplating it.

"Not a bad suggestion actually, but no, too difficult to reach. And I don't just mean dark as in the absence of light. I mean dark like under the bed. Dark like that one chip in a wall that leads to a hollow space between the bricks and, as a child, you couldn't help but wonder what lives there. Somewhere that just inexplicably feels… like it's not got as much of God's attention on it as every-where else."

I thought about this for a second. His words were vague, but damn if I didn't know what he meant.

"A corner?" I asked. "Has to be an acute corner?"

He nodded.

"I think I know the place," I said, and he smiled like a real creep.

I took him to a flat on the eighth floor. It was rundown like everywhere else but there was still enough of its old furniture lying around. You can pull open random drawers in there and still see the cutlery people once used. There's even an old analogue TV on an old stand. You can perch on what's left of the sofa and stare at that TV and get the feeling you knew the people who lived there once. Run your thumb over the dials on the toaster, the handle of the fridge, or the yellowing plastic of a light switch, and feel an aching loss that creeps up on you out of nowhere.

Look up and you'll see that the light fixture has been torn out of the ceiling, like someone had tried swinging from it.

Not a big place, by the way. Three rooms. A bedroom with a double bed all rumpled up. A living room slash kitchen. And a tiny little spare room that looked like it once would have been used for storage, or a washing machine maybe, *if* you were single and childless. A slither of space, a triangle carved out of whatever room was left over when other more important walls had been put up. That sofa I mentioned, the TV, they were all placed so whoever was sat down could always keep an eye on that room and its contents.

You see, they'd put a cot inside and it's still there, bluebottle flies circling overhead. You can't see inside the cot, not unless you went in and actually pulled the blankets out, but it's been decades and no one has managed it yet. It's dark behind those old blankets, a heavy shadow that dissuades a closer look, like there's something in there no one needs to see and it's spent a long time sat there eating what little light there was. Even with a window in that room, daylight doesn't really filter down.

"Perfect," the businessman said when he saw it. He gazed around the flat one detail at a time, his head pausing for a moment and a smile creeping across his face as he laid his eyes on the broken light fixture. And the cot, the sight of it, the flies that still circled above faded Winnie the Pooh blankets, it made the breath catch in his throat.

"Oh, this is… *yes* this is good," he told me. "Dark like under the bed. You've earned that money. I could have had a dozen men sweep this place and they wouldn't have understood the brief as well as you have."

"Thank you," I replied even if that wasn't really how I felt.

Quietly the man sat down and began to unpack his leather satchel. No pentagrams to be found, although he did unpack seven strange looking candles. He caught me looking at them and smiled.

"Home made," he said. "Each one shaped by my hands. I'm not a good artist, but it's the effort that counts. Took forever to rend the wax. Of course that was the easy part. The hard part was getting the fat to make it. Did you know there can be a surprisingly high level of security around a hospital's medical waste department?"

"I didn't," I replied as he took out some flimsy bits of wood and a few small nails. He oh so carefully began to nail the splinters of wood together into what looked like random shapes.

"Oh well," he sighed after a few quiet moments, his fingers nimbly gripping the tiny hammer as he tapped away. Already he'd put together at least six of the strange little wooden polygons, and with each new one I felt a strange sensation. "Would you like to stay and watch?" he asked.

"Absolutely not," I answered.

He stopped tapping and smiled once more.

"Oh, you're clever," he said. "That's the correct answer, by the way. And if I'm to respect it, I should inform you that now is the safest time to leave."

I made my way to the exit just as he lit the first candles, but not before I looked towards the cot one last time. I was surprised to see a hollow blackness that extended beyond the doorway, like a curtain had been draped across it, only there was depth to it that drew the eye. The businessman paid it no attention, but after a few more seconds he eventually looked up at me expectantly.

"Can I ask what is it you want?" I said. "Everyone who comes here, I don't get the sense it ever works out for them."

"I'm looking for a new kind of afterlife," he replied.

"Do you need one?"

"We all need one," he said with a wry chuckle. "But only those of us willing to take a few risks will get a better deal. Everyone else…" He grimaced. "It's worth the bother. But look who I'm speaking to."

He looked to the darkness that enveloped the doorway. Shapes could be seen floating past.

"You should leave now," he said.

I pulled the door shut and, noticing that the sun was rapidly setting, ran to my apartment where I knew the walls would keep me safe.

When I returned the next day, the man's satchel was still where I'd last seen it, propped against one arm of the sofa. The candles had burned down to the very end of the wicks and left a lingering smell that's still there all these years later. And of the man himself, well in the room with the cot—which still has bluebottle flies orbiting overhead—there is now a shadow burned into the wall. It's blurry and diffused, but vaguely recognisable as a man on his knees, his head pressed to the floor in a gesture of supplication.

I've known it to occasionally move, to turn its head and look towards me at which my point my temples throb, my ears pop, and a darkness begins to encroach upon the edges of my vision. I never exactly considered that flat to be Disneyland before, but now I avoid it like the plague.

Still, it could be worse. Not every ritual ends so cleanly and at times I've had to personally intervene, something I hate bitterly. If people want to go poking around in the universe's undercarriage that's their business. It's one thing if I've got to sweep what's left of them up afterwards, but at least that's a one and done job. Sometimes it isn't so clean. One guy turned up and told me he'd be a new "resident", my neighbour, and we'd get to know each other. A bumbling old man with an upper class accent and the look of a professor who was down on his luck. He set up in the room next to mine and no matter how little I spoke to him, he never really got the hint and kept trying to act like a good friend. Few times I did initiate conversation it was to tell him the place he'd chosen didn't have much in the way of protection. He pointed to some funny little rashes and told me *they* were his protection.

Over the next few weeks I'd bump into him from time to time, always on his hands and knees, scraping some dank corner or mouldy pile of bumpy growths. He collected fungi, told me on the first day, and I'd often see him wiping his samples onto petri dishes that he whispered quiet words to whenever he thought I wasn't around. I don't think he was sane, but he probably wasn't completely barmy because he lived long enough to get a sense of Annedale and only come out in the day. Meanwhile, his apartment filled up with a growing collection of chittering terrariums and pickle jars, their specimens hidden by murky fluids. All over, he planted and cultivated strange mushrooms and moulds. Encouraged them to soak up the darkness of Annedale and set them to grow in the rife conditions he'd cultivated.

Towards the end, his living room had mushrooms growing out of the walls. Plaster crumbling beneath microbial armies until there was only concrete and rebar, and even then mould continued to grow and thrive. A few times I peered in and found him feeding meat to the frilly growths that exploded out of the old furniture. During this time, the symbols on our shared wall would often grow hot, and I found myself having to replace them on a nearly daily basis as he tinkered away on the other side. I asked him once or twice to tone it down.

"This is important work," he growled, an unseen darkness creeping into his voice. "I'm not some ditzy crackhead trying to summon the Baphomet! I'm not looking to get *high*. This is science. Progress! That is what I am working towards."

"Yeah, well, your progress is trying to eat its way into my flat. Can you ask it to stop?"

He stopped, froze in mid-gesture like I'd said something either profoundly stupid or insightful, or likely a bit of both. He looked at the rashes on his arms that had, by now, started to sprout some of their own strange fruit. When he finally spoke again, it was sly, like a lecherous old man propositioning a nurse.

"This fungi," he said. "They had samples of it in the university for thirty years! Can you imagine? They never even realised what they had until I found it and unlocked its potential. Now I've finally found the source and I can do things no one else thought possible. This entire time, my thesis has depended upon the idea that the fungus has… a capacity for information processing way beyond anything we've considered before. And your idea is a good one, you know? Asking it just might be an option…"

He scuttled off without another word and for the next few days he set about the building like a furious little honeybee in spring. Poking and prodding, setting trap after trap and cleaning them vigorously of any rats or mice he caught. When I did my morning sweeps, I'd find him hovering over Annedale's latest victims, scraping what was left of them into transparent bags for his own purposes.

"Don't mind me," he'd mutter. "It's worthless to you, but these poor souls could help me achieve great things."

This persisted for another month. He no longer scraped mould or mushrooms off old apartments. He became interested only in meat, and by the time it came to an end I can say confidently that I have never smelled anything worse than the prickly musty odour that wafted out from under his locked door. It became so bad that I began to wonder if I might have to ask for police help and have him removed when, finally, he simply disappeared from Annedale's halls. One morning he was there, annoyingly shooing me out of the way as he lowered jars into the flooded basement, and then the next he was gone and Annedale's halls were silent once more.

But that didn't mean he had moved out. Far from it, actually.

It took two days before I decided to just go ahead and break his door down. I kicked at it with a short sharp blow, only to find my leg immediately disappeared through wood that had the texture of sodden cardboard. I freed my foot and tried a different tactic, grabbing the handle and pulling so hard that it simply *popped* right out of the rancid wooden frame. Free to move, the door swung open with an eerie creak and fetid air, hot and damp, blew out of the room.

Inside, I found that the man's specimens had gone wild. Terrariums had shattered, their contents spilling outwards. Frogs as large as footballs glared at me from behind furry fronds, and insects with human eyes scuttled away before the amphibians could snatch them up. In one corner rats had built a hive out of old cardboard, their backs covered with fungal growths that resembled human fingers and other appendages. In another corner something that looked a little like a black rubber sheet slapped furiously at passing vermin and it took me a few seconds to realise it was a slime mould. When it finally caught something, it dragged the strange creature squealing into the dark corner where it grew and constricted around its meal like a fist. I stared at it horrified until one-by-one black orbs unveiled itself from within the strange mass and I realised it had eyes to stare right back at me.

It was a cacophony of God-awful terror, so gripping that it kept me from hearing the muffled noise of a human struggling to speak. Eventually it did reach my ears, and I used my torch to light up the far wall without having to actually step inside.

I found the scientist half-grown into the wall. Algae and moss coated him head-to-toe so that he was no longer recognisable, but I had to assume it could be no one else. Wide eyes glared at me with terror and pain as nasty little critters nibbled away at what was left of his shins. Meanwhile strange tendrils probed at his ears and head, never resting for a moment. He kept trying to speak, but the algal growths kept driving their way into his mouth until, one-by-one, they pushed too far, and something snapped. His eyes went wider still, his squeals became hysterical, and his jaw slowly slid further down his chest until it hit the floor with a sodden thump.

"Finally made contact?" I asked. "An awful idea if I've heard one. What would a mushroom have to say, even in the best of circumstances? Let alone one that was grown in the ruins of Annedale? I can only assume you never got around to telling it to stay off my wall, did you? No, you probably had your own reason or doing all of this and that's what took priority."

That made me wonder what it was he'd asked for. As the thought entered my head, I took a quick look around and tried to see if anything particular stood out to me. Something was growing on the sofa that looked strangely human-shaped. It might have been just my imagination, but in the dark it seemed to turn towards me. Meanwhile, the scientist continued to shiver in agony, his eyes focused on me and begging for help.

"I'll see what I can do," I said before slamming the door. Something about that strange pile on the sofa had deeply unsettled me.

I put the word out, asked for a gun, but got a crossbow instead a few days later. A nervous looking sixteen-year-old boy ferried it to my door. I was surprised he'd entered the building, but who knows who'd ordered him to do so. I've acquired a strange sort of respect amongst the locals, and it comes in handy. This boy looked like he would have stamped on my head and robbed me blind any other day, but when he spoke to me, he did so with more respect than I ever imagined I deserved. I thanked him, took the crossbow, spent an afternoon practicing with it, and then used it to kill the scientist the next morning.

Took a few hits, but in the end one thumped into his forehead and shut down his whimpered moans. I didn't see anything on the sofa this time, at least not anything human-shaped, which I was thankful for. After that it was a simple case of calling the police and beginning a long chain of events that ended with half-a-dozen men in hazmat suits spraying the room with noxious chemicals. For a while there I'd been worried that they'd find a corpse and ask questions, but by the time someone actually entered the room there was nothing left of the scientist save a splotch on the floor.

I never did figure out exactly what it was he was after, although it is not uncommon for my morning sweep to turn up a body (or part of) covered in fungal growths. And I have been known to occasionally catch glimpses of a strange person lowering themselves into the floodwater of the elevator shaft. Of course, I might just be making connections that aren't really there. All sorts of things live in that water. The entire level is flooded and if something was down there, it'd have free reign over quite a large space.

It's a strange world down there. I should know on account of one visitor who gave me a very bad time. I'll call him the fisherman since he came to Annedale because of the flooded basement. Saw a photo that's been circulating around for a while now, if you know where to look. God knows who took it and how, but it shows the flooded stairwell leading to the basement and beneath the brackish surface is a hand that's all out of proportion. Fingers splayed with perfect symmetry like a starfish, it is reaching up out of the depths and resting gently on the third step below the water.

When I first met him, he was sitting happily with his feet over the edge of the flooded shaft, water up to his knees, with a rod and line set up beside him. It was quite a surprise at first, seeing him there with a little fly-fishing hat. A chubby but healthy-looking man in his forties with an egg mayo sandwich in one hand and a phone playing candy crush in the other. I called out to him as I approached because, in my experience, startling someone in Annedale is bad for your health no matter how sane the visitor appears.

He looked up when I caught his attention and smiled amiably.

"Hello," he waved with his sandwich. "You're the caretaker?"

"Yes, I am," I answered. "And you are?"

"Just a tourist," he smiled. "Care to join me?"

The sun had risen only moments ago.

"You weren't here when it was dark, were you?" I asked, more than a little suspicious.

"Oh, no, you've only just caught me, been here barely ten minutes before you showed up. I was told you'd be willing to help in exchange for a small fee."

"What sort of help?" I asked.

"Oh, just give me a nudge if any of the lines start moving," he said while pointing to a rod he'd set up beside the basement stairs. The door was propped open, and the line led down into the darkness below, water gently lapping just out of sight. Another line had been set up in a corner of the lobby where the floor had been torn away, revealing a hole straight down into the basement. "I can't keep an eye on them all at once, you see. I have bells ready, but, well, two heads are better than one."

"What is it exactly you're hoping to catch down there?" I asked.

"Are you familiar with the primordial ocean?" he said. "The abyssal waters that God split into light and dark, all that? It's not a physical location, per se, but it does connect to certain bodies of water depending on the time and place. Last recorded manifestation was in a glass of old whiskey underneath a forgotten bar in Mexico City. Some poor fellow knocked it over and didn't notice until the following day when half the bar was suddenly underwater. Quickly rectified, but some of the things swimming in that water were something else, and all from at the bottom of a glass no wider than my wrist. Imagine what we can do with this!?" he said while gesturing at the water by his feet.

"You think there could be fish alive down there?" I asked.

"At least," he replied. "I'd be willing to pay for any reliable information, of course. Do you have any idea what might be down there?"

"Not really," I shrugged. "But I'd guess it wants to be left alone."

"Hmmm you might be right there," he said while looking at his other rods. "I didn't exactly put down any old lure, you know?"

He reached into his pocket and took out a strange tuft of fur and ivory, holding it up for me to squint at.

"A tooth from a man who drowned in the sea. A drone collected it off a shipwreck near the Norwegian coast. The fur is actually red algae that was found growing on his bones. I have plenty of these and, well, other things that might appeal to what's on the other side. My research was thorough and expensive. Come on, take a seat. Flat fee, one thousand, just sit here until the sun starts to set."

"I just have to sit?" I asked.

"And let me know if you hear or see anything."

I groaned and sat beside him, folding my legs instead of letting them dangle in the water below. Despite my reticence, we stayed like that for several hours. He'd brought lots of food, good homemade stuff, along with plenty of cold beer. We sat there and spoke very little, but we did eat and drink a tremendous amount. Not the kind of thing I do normally, but I was being paid to be there, and I didn't really have anywhere else to be. It was, all in told, a very pleasant afternoon.

Until I fell asleep.

When I awoke, it was with a terrible gasp. My chest was tight like something had been sitting on it, and judging from the terrible giggling and scampering feet I heard running off into the darkness, it might not have been *just* a feeling. Already panic was setting in as my eyes darted to the open doors and saw that the moon was out and had been for hours. I fumbled for my torch and, turning it on, saw that there was no sign of the fisherman. All his stuff had been left behind, yet all that remained of him was his hat that still floated on the water. Even as I watched, a smooth glistening shape curled beneath the water and plucked it off the surface.

I recoiled and crawled away from it as fast as I could. This was bad. I knew deep in my heart I'd never been as at risk I was in that moment. The open doors that led outside were tempting, but just beside them were the stairs that led downwards, and I swore I could hear something approaching. I couldn't help but picture the fungal man I'd seen in the scientist's flat. Then again, that basement was huge and who knows what lay down there.

I decided to go for the stairs. The entire time my heart was in my chest. I had never been caught outside my room at night, not since my first night when I'd slept in the lobby with my coat pulled over me. You don't get lucky twice, not with Annedale, so I knew had to be careful. I had to be quiet. My only hope was to go unnoticed. I took to stealth, climbing each floor in perfect silence, hiding in well known spots at the slightest hint of footsteps, human or otherwise.

Annedale comes alive at night. Whispered mutterings from strange children who descend from air vents, living there for God knows how long. Other times I saw apparitions. One, a toddler, made my stomach growl with an insatiable hunger that hurt just to contemplate. She stared at me with pleading eyes as I slunk away from her open door. I might have been tempted to help her were it not for the sight of the moon peering through her translucent image.

And yet, despite all this, I somehow made it to the fourteenth floor alive. Only it was there right at the final hurdle, so close to safety, that I came across something out of my worst nightmare.

A woman stood outside my apartment door. Silent. Pale. Dirt covered fingernails. It was all too often I'd open my door and find muddy impressions on the floor made by a woman's bare feet. Now I knew who left them every night. I couldn't see her face from where I hid, but something about her seemed profoundly familiar.

When she finally turned towards me, I remembered. I recognised her, even though most of her face was missing. It was the philosopher's wife. He had succeeded, it seemed. But I couldn't imagine at what God awful price, because the woman who stared at me had clearly weathered some years in the grave. It was only the poor lighting and her long hair that had covered up just how bad a state she was in. A lipless grin stared back at me below sunken cheekbones and hollow eye sockets. And yet, I could tell that in another life she had been beautiful, which only made the sight all the more gut-wrenching.

"My darling," she whispered, and there was something about her voice that I found hard to stay sane in the face of. I don't know why. Over a decade in that place and I'd borne witness to living nightmares, but it was *this* walking corpse that pushed me to my limits. The inescapable feeling of loss weighed me down and without realising it, I found myself taking steps towards her even as my knees buckled. By the time I reached her, I was crawling until I could clutch her grimy icy leg, and that was the last thing I remember before I woke up in my bed the following morning.

Everything seemed normal, so completely mundane that I could've written the whole thing off as a bad nightmare. But there were footprints leading from my bed to the door. And later on I found the fisherman's things much as he left them, although when I finally reeled his lines in I found the lures gone and replaced with bits and pieces of the man who'd first set them up. I threw it all into the water below and decided it would be best to forget him.

Every now and again, of course, I can't help but check my peephole at night. I never did before that, but now I do. I see her every single time. She looks sad. Hurts me to think of her out there. It ought to be terrifying, but it's more like someone's ripped out my stomach and heart and let all my insides fall out the bottom.

Each time I see her I wonder what exactly it was he did to bring her back?

He leaves only one hint. A final letter, I think. It's not like he dated them. In it he says he would give everything to have her in his arms once more. Not only his life, but everything he's already lived. Every sunset. Every good dream. Every nightmare. Every victory. Every loss. Every little memory that makes him who he is, he'd give it all just to save her.

Sometimes I wonder about him, figuring we'd probably be about the same age. I'd like to think back and imagine what it would have been like for the two of us to meet as young men, but for some reason whenever I try to remember what my life was like before I came to this city, before I woke up with that coat pulled over me… well, I don't know…

It's just hard, that's all.

It's almost like there's nothing there. Like something reached in and took all the years away. I guess it's just one of those things I'm better off not dwelling on.

THE BUNKER

Dr Daniel Vance was a smart man. Too smart for his own good, maybe. Forty years old, a lecturer in fluid dynamics with a mind made of shapes and numbers. No one knows why, but one day, on a whim, he crunched the numbers on the apocalypse and came to a troubling conclusion. He didn't share exactly what it was he'd deduced, but given that he immediately quit his job and liquidated his many assets, it's fair to say it wasn't positive. Swept up in the wake of this tremendous upheaval was his wife, a twenty-four-year-old PhD student who had grown infatuated with Daniel some time before. She loved the strange bear of a man who could just as easily build a log cabin as he could explain the idiosyncrasies of an asteroid's orbit. Speaking to Daniel always left you with the profound impression he was right, so when he told her what he wanted to do, she agreed.

Fifteen years and five children later, the Vances were living in the distant woods just beyond my hometown. They were enigmatic, richer than the Pope, and extremely serious about their prepper lifestyle. But they were also funny, easygoing, and incredibly compelling to speak to. Larger-than-life survivalists who swept into town with bizarre requests that thrilled local businesses. Vast quantities of cement, iron, lead, and steel were all shipped through the remote mountains so that the Vances could build their shelter. The advanced methods they used to keep it secret were legendary. Daniel had once spent six months earning the licence necessary to drive HGVs up to his compound so that no one else would lay eyes on it. And on one occasion, when a company had refused his request for GPS tracker-free vehicles, he bought them out whole-sale so that they had no choice.

So, when they stopped appearing in town during the pandemic, when requests for food and goods stopped and all contact was dropped, most attributed it to lockdown. They had a bunker and had spent their entire lives training to be self-sufficient in the face of civilization's collapse. Even Alexander, the youngest at just three, was already collecting firewood as a chore, and learning what local plants were edible. Most of us just assumed that if anyone could ride out Covid without breaking a sweat, it would be the Vances.

The reality turned out to be something else.

When the worst came to light, we discovered that Daniel had used the pandemic as an excuse for a dry run. The family intended to spend six months in lockdown and essentially beta test their fallout bunker. Three months in and the Sheriff received a distress call on the radio. Coordinates were provided by the hushed voice of a sobbing child that most assumed was Alexander, even though that's never been proven.

The police arrived and found the bunker still sealed. It took hours for emergency responders to cut into the door, all the while efforts were made to contact the family within, but to no avail. Once inside, police were left dumbfounded. There was no one to be rescued. No bodies. No survivors. There was evidence the door's locking mechanism had failed and trapped the Vances inside with no way out, but if so, where had they gone?

Beds and cots lay everywhere with mouldering yellow sheets, buckets close to hand with stains all around them. Some doors were barred, others smashed to pieces. There was even evidence of makeshift quarantines, and, in places, what looked like violence. The police, usually a fantastic source of gossip, were not forthcoming until the town demanded answers and the Sheriff was forced to offer only the barest of outlines.

An outbreak of a waterborne illness had struck the Vances down not long after they were locked inside and unable to seek help. Rumours of contagion were overstated, fuelled by the unrelated rise of Covid. Whatever contaminant had killed the Vances, it was non-organic in nature. No need to panic. The Vances loved ones had been notified. The bunker was going to be demolished, and we could all put this terrible tragedy behind us.

Of course we still had questions. A thousand of them. Why hadn't the family called for help? They had radios, computers, smartphones too. They were survivalists, not Amish. And where *were* they? What had happened to their bodies? Why hadn't they simply left? We shouted these and more at the town meeting, but the police simply refused to comment. For most of us, the excitement lasted another week or two until we realised we weren't getting answers any time soon. Besides, the pandemic was in full swing and most of us had other things to worry about. The tragic story eventually faded until it was just one of those awful things in the town's history that we didn't talk about. I was as guilty as anyone else of just forgetting about it.

I certainly never expected to find the bunker out there in the woods, faded police tape still on the open door that hung wide open with scorch marks around the lock. It stood out in the woods like someone had cut a hole right in the fabric of reality, the darkness so deep and black it almost ached to look at. The sight of it made my heart drop into my stomach. It radiated pain. Does that make sense? I think some part of my lizard brain picked out details that wouldn't become apparent to me until I got closer, like the bloody finger streaks that stained the handle from where someone had scrabbled furiously at the lock without success. And the tiny viewing window had been smashed with a hammer that still lay nearby. I needed only to glimpse it, to imagine the family taking turns to stand there and scream into the woods desperate for rescue.

Under any other circumstances, I would have run.

But I'd gone there looking for my dog, and my light revealed a few wet paw prints making their way down the dusty concrete tunnel. Half Bernese and half collie, Ripley is the sort of dog who trembles in my arms when a storm buffets the windows and needs his paws held when we brush him. I love him. I do not have much of a family, or a wife, or even many friends. But I have Ripley, and I could no more have turned around and gone home to an empty apartment where I would have to sob my grief away than I could flap my arms and fly. He was my dog, and I'd raised him since he was a puppy, and I wasn't going to leave him out in those woods.

I went in after him.

I didn't know what to expect, but I knew it wouldn't be good. Whatever the police had found, they'd not only kept most of the morbid details to themselves, but they had also lied. The bunker was not demolished, or even sealed off. In fact, looking at the occasional blue latex glove tossed aside and the one or two broken police-issue flashlights, it seemed like the last people inside had been in a hurry to get out. Given this was where seven people had presumably died, I assumed it was *someone's* job to clean it all up. But the corridor looked largely untouched. Just a few metres in and manic writing started to cover the walls, the desperate scrawls of a lone survivor left there to be rediscovered like cave paintings. Most were deliberations on how to get out. Diagrams. Blueprints. Equations and formulae. All focused on the door and the circuits responsible for its faulty lock. I instinctively assumed they belonged to Daniel and that he'd been the last to die. What a God-awful fate for a man to outlive his children. And yet it got worse. Slowly the writing changed from equations and plans to a desperate scrawl. The same few phrases repeated over and over.

Five doors. Five. Not six. Six. Didn't make it. Didn't make it. Six doors. Six.

It seemed like the kind of thing you'd find in an asylum. A psychotic rambling punctuated only by six paragraphs right at the end. Each letter was impeccably neat, and each small paragraph was topped with a beautifully drawn Christian cross.

Elliott Vance aged fifteen. A gifted guitarist. He liked boys even though he thought I did not know. I loved him with everything I had. He would have made a great man.

Alicia Vance aged fourteen. She liked to paint and to shoot. She had her mother's mean streak. It would have served her well in the future.

Elijah Vance aged eight. The smartest of us all…

These were Daniel's memorials to his family, and seeing the words lit up by my torch was a haunting insight into the overwhelming despair he'd endured. He must have realised he wouldn't get the chance to speak at his family's funerals or to write their obituaries. This was his last desperate way of making sure the world might one day know them as he did—as real people.

The words marked the end of the tunnel, standing adjacent to a trapdoor in the ground. It was not open, but the tunnel came to a dead end immediately afterwards and Ripley's prints disappeared at the hatch. I feared he might be in danger, but still I stopped and looked at the bunker door twenty metres behind me. The once gloomy forest looked so bright, even on this cloudy day, the air dotted with rain. A part of me felt like I was leaving the whole world behind as I began to climb the ladder down.

I entered a large circular living space that was packed with furniture and little nooks and crannies. The walls were covered with folding beds and tables, and every inch was multifunctional. A dining space could become a sitting space, which in turn might be where someone slept, or even exercised. It all depended on what particular bit of furniture you unfolded or unclipped or unfurled. Seven people in close quarters, nowhere near enough privacy, it made sense they went with this cluttered overlapping use of space. But it was still a large room, bigger than most studio apartments. And there were a few corridors that led deeper into the Earth, telling me the bunker had unseen depths.

I looked for some sign of my dog and soon found his trail, but this far from the rainy copse Ripley's prints were starting to fade. After barely a few metres, they petered out vaguely in the direction of a nearby door. I wanted to follow, but stopped myself from rushing onwards. It was unlikely Ripley was getting out any other way, and I'd do us no good getting hurt myself. I decided to take a look around and quickly spotted a dinner table.

If I needed proof the police had not bothered with a cleanup, this was it. The plates were still out, the food rotten to a strange, blackened husk. A child's hat lay across one place-setting, the once-creamy fleece turned a sickly green and yellow. The chairs had their backs reinforced with wooden beams fitted with long grooves so that something the width of a nail could slide into them. And on each of the cushions were foul smelling stains that looked oddly like an ass print. I touched one with gloved hands and the material crackled audibly. Whatever it was, similar stains were on the cutlery and plates, and there were even handprints of it placed firmly on the tablecloth. At first, I thought it was blood, but that wasn't quite right. It was too contained to be from leaking blood. On the back of one of the chairs a stain tapered exactly where a woman's waist would be like a near perfect silhouette. I shivered as I remembered that Miranda Vance had always been a slim woman and wondered how she had left her imprint on the grey fabric.

Using my torch, I saw that these stains repeated in the oddest of places. Yes, there were some on beds and blankets and even patches of plain floor exactly like you might expect in a room full of sick people. But why did one stain on the floor bear such a strong resemblance to a child huddled in the fetal position? And why was the same stuff all over the tv remote, and on books on shelves, and board games too. Everything from sofa cushions to DVD boxes to piles of dirty laundry were covered in the same dried brownish material that gave off a foul coppery miasma.

I found the jigsaw particularly baffling. Someone had set up another table with four chairs, all modified with the same back support as those by the dinner table. And a jigsaw had been lain out with four separate piles, but only one was depleted. The rest looked largely untouched, almost like someone had portioned out pieces for three other people who had absolutely no interest in going along with it. Maybe Daniel had tried to keep up morale while the family were sick? God help me, if that were true I couldn't help but imagine the poor man sat there with his loved ones close to death, desperately trying to encourage them to click their own pieces into place while they faded in and out of consciousness.

Something about that room emanated madness, and the longer I stayed down there flicking the bright disk of light of my torch from one detail to another, the more I wanted to leave. One door had wooden beams nailed across it. One sofa had been partially disassembled. Multiple beds had been burned. And all the light bulbs had been removed and put in a box on the kitchen countertop. Looking up at the ceiling, I finally had some insight into why the police were so confident the Vances had not survived despite never finding their bodies. Someone had jammed a human finger into one of the empty sockets, almost like they'd expected it to glow with the flick of a switch.

What was it about this place that had caused the police to leave and never return? Not to even take that finger and test it for signs of illness, or even just to confirm who it belonged to?

I decided it was time to hurry up and find my dog. People had died in that place, and while I'm not superstitious, I can't be the only sceptic who has done the calculations in his head and realised it costs nothing to be respectful of ghosts. That bunker was cramped, terrifying, and the air stank so bad I started to worry I'd get sick myself. It served no one any good to linger. But I'd be damned if I'd just walk away and leave Ripley to rot down there. It's not like he could climb a ladder and get out on his own (even if I wasn't entirely sure how he'd gotten down there in the first place).

Summoning what little bravery I had left I called out and broke the silence, something which felt like a terrible taboo in that God awful place, like screaming in a graveyard.

"Ripley!"

I waited and hoped to hell I'd hear the pitter patter of his paws, but for the longest of moments there was only the kind of silence that makes you wonder if someone or something in the darkness is holding its breath trying to look like just another patch of nothing. Biding its time until you finally turn around and show it your back…

The TV came on with a blurt of white noise that was so loud and so sudden I cried, threw my arms up, and nearly fell backwards onto a rolled-out sleeping bag that looked like it had spent a week in the sewer. By the time I realised what had caused the noise, I could already hear a tinny rendition of Daniel Vance's voice.

…I realise the issue here. I need to emphasise just how little I understand anything that's…

I frowned at the screen as I approached. It showed a greenish infrared view of the bunker with Daniel upfront, and the dinner table behind him. It was grainy and hard to see, but I could clearly tell that his family were sitting in those chairs.

…Miranda was first to fall ill. Looking back, it makes perfect sense. Miranda often went into storage to fetch food for cooking, and we found it behind one of the refrigerators. So that's–ah shit…

One of the figures in the background slumped onto the table with a loud *clank* and sent a plate spinning off onto the ground.

Shit shit shit, Daniel muttered as he got up and grabbed the woman by the shoulders and sat her upright. *Miranda never did like my cooking!* He snorted a laugh as he fussed with something at the back of the chair. *The rods are much better than tape. All those hours spent taping them upright to the chairs. Never worked. But the rods… they fit right into the spine and, with a little modification, I can just slot them into the chairs. That way everyone is able to join in for dinner. I'm working on something similar for family game night.*

Daniel wandered over to the camera and with a grin he lifted it from the tripod and scanned the dinner table. What I saw nearly made me drop my torch.

His family were long dead. Gaunt faces. Missing noses. Lips that had receded to reveal awful grins. These were corpses, plain as day, even when viewed through such a low resolution image. The only thing that made them seem remotely alive was the way their eyes still reflected the infrared back so that they glowed in the dark. And yet Daniel seemed oblivious to it all. He tousled Elliot's hair. Kissed his wife on the cheek. Run a hand across one young girl's shoulder. He even picked the young Alexander up from his highchair and, I assume, he coddled him. I don't know for sure because I looked away, unwilling to see the poor boy up close.

Eyes averted from the screen, I couldn't help but pan my torch across to that same dinner table and shiver as I finally realised what all those stains were. Not quite blood. But close. *Liquefying flesh.* Left alone for months, Daniel had not put his family's bodies to rest. Instead, he had moved them around from place to place and puppeted them, living life as if nothing had really changed. Looking at where those stains had settled, I saw a clear pattern emerge. He had put them to bed. He had set them dinner. He had propped them up to watch TV, or gave them their favourite books. They even sat there as lifeless husks while Daniel waited for them to complete a fucking jigsaw. The idea horrified me to my core.

...back to work. It's obviously not part of the original designs. No room on the other side, not on the blueprints. Elliot didn't believe me, and why would he? I made every inch of this place, but I did not install that door in storage on the bottom level. I checked the cameras and some of the photos I took during the build and the wall is just blank. But the door is there now, and it must lead somewhere. I don't know when or why it opens, but it does and the next time I'll be ready. Because I have to know what's on the other side, and why it did this to us. Alone down here, often all asleep at once. Anything could have slit our throats and been done with it. But it didn't. It took its time and I have to know why!

It took our radios and computers and phones. One by one. None of us noticed until it was far too late. I kept telling the kids they needed to take better care of their things, and even as they complained I just assumed the phones were lying behind some shelf. Where else could they go in a locked bunker? But it wasn't the children at all. Looking back, there are so many signs... who kept taking away the lights? Who kept draining the batteries in our torches? How long did we live with it before we finally realised we weren't alone? Was it here every step of the way?

A door out of nothing that leads to nowhere, at least most of the time. Because I know for a fact it does not always open onto a blank wall. There is something behind it. I can hear it shuffling around in there, wet breath rattling in its lungs, a horrible sound I hear roaming these halls when it thinks I'm asleep...

I listened to Daniel, fascinated by this strangely compelling rant, when movement caught my eye. An infrared camera running in the dark, its image a roiling mess of uniform noise. What was it I'd seen? I paused the tape and rewound. Squinting, I saw two pinpricks of light in the darkness just over Daniel's shoulder. Slowly, the image resolved itself in my mind. I knew what I was seeing, and it turned my blood to ice.

Miranda Vance had turned her head, and her lifeless eyes glowed as she fixed them on the back of Daniel's head.

...not even any point leaving at this stage. I'm no doctor, but that door is giving off enough radiation to... well, to kill a family of seven. If none of us had touched it... Being in the same room is risky, but not lethal. But given how sick we've become, it's pretty obvious our curiosity got the better of us, one by one, and we all got too close. Or maybe not. Maybe that thing on the other side came through and did this. I don't even kn... wait... what was that?

Daniel turned, and the camera stopped recording. The image it froze on was of a lone man, bright as a star in the camera's lens, facing off against unknowable darkness broken only by six pairs of white, glowing eyes.

I became painfully aware of my position relative to the table and I had the painful premonition that if I turned, those chairs would not be empty. I would see the Vances, all of them, Daniel as well, waiting for me. Heads turned. Bodies left to rot for years in the dark. Behind me something shifted. It breathed. Loud. Quick. I knew what it was. *I knew.* It came at me so fast that when I felt something hot and wet touch my hand I screamed, only for the presence to suddenly recoil. But then, without hesitation, it leapt at me and bore me to the ground.

I wept as Ripley licked my face. He was shivering and, worst of all, silent, which was not normal. He was not a quiet dog, not when greeting me and not when excited like he was now. But whatever he'd seen down here, he clung to me and dug his paws into my shoulders like he wanted to be cradled over the shoulder, something he has been too big to do for years.

"Oh you fucking idiot," I cooed in a soft whisper and even in the dark I could feel his tail wagging. Joking aside, I felt nothing but relief at finding him. "Let's get the hell out of here."

I picked him up, straining a little under the weight but refusing to give into tired muscles, and made for the ladder. It wasn't easy climbing the three or four rungs to the hatch, but I managed it and gave the hatch a shove. First one hand, then two. Again and again, with everything I had, but still that hatch refused to budge.

"Shit!" I cried while pounding at it with my fists, but all I achieved was a sore wrist. The hatch had jammed when, somehow, the handle had been snapped clean off. Now I'd need a pair of pliers or something to cut through the metal bar, locking it shut. My fingers couldn't move it, nor could I brute force the hatch open. The metal bar was an inch thick and, at the very least, I'd need some tools to get at it from this side.

At least it's fixable, I thought as I climbed back down and caught my breath. On one wall I noticed a simple diagram of the bunker made in chalk. It had three floors. The bottom was storage–Daniel had mentioned that before, and I noticed that he had drawn through it with a large red X–and the top floor was labelled *Quarters*, where I stood now. But the middle floor was labelled workshops, and it was there I realised that I'd find what I needed.

There was one door that opened onto a concrete stairwell and, standing at the top, I shone my light down the spiraling guard rails unsure of what it was I hoped to see. There were only harsh shadows and the sense of something foul rising up on the air. A smell that tickled my throat and burned a little in my lungs. Had the police even gone down this far? Had they seen what I'd seen on that TV and just left? Somehow I thought it was unlikely that had been enough to send the entire Sheriff's department running, so was it something else that had done it. Something that had been enough to terrify dozens of armed men. Something that was almost definitely down there.

The door…

I went down quietly. At first I considered leaving Ripley behind, but after losing him the first time I decided I'd rather risk it just to know that he was right next to me. Besides, he was being quieter than I was, and I didn't feel much like going down those stairs on my own. He accompanied me with only the quiet click clack of his paws on concrete, a sound I found deeply comforting as I barely managed to keep my torch from shaking in my hand and my breathing steady.

Down one floor and I found the workshop exactly as you might expect. A large space filled with generators and fuel and water tanks and boilers and heaters and pretty much anything and everything that you'd need to survive but which you couldn't put outside due to fallout. Wires, pipes, and tubes ran from one end of the room to the other and even years later, most of the machinery still hummed in the pitch black emptiness, an idea I found deeply unsettling. Taking one look at that strange tangle of harsh shapes and industrial figures looming out of the walls and floor, I shivered and looked around, quickly finding a small area Daniel had cordoned off for his own use. About a fifth of the total floor space, there was a large workbench and some seriously high-end machining equipment, all very well used. Lathes. Buzzsaws. Drills. Belt sanders. Welding torches. Everything a man needed to do-it-himself.

And Daniel had been busy.

I'm not sure exactly what it was he'd been working, but there was an arm on the bench. It sat atop a pile of papers that had slowly turned brown over the years until the whole thing looked like it had been soaked in tobacco spit. On the whiteboard was a faded but still visible diagram of what looked to me like a ball-and-socket joint. I thought of the tape, of Daniel's little mechanism to keep his family upright, and then looked at the arm and suppressed a momentary gag reflex. I don't know if Dan had been working on posable limbs, or just a way to put the decomposing remains back together after they'd started to fall apart, but the size of the arm suggested a pre-teen child, and he'd left it out on the surface like it was a disassembled clock. It was also missing a finger. *Just how fucking crazy was he?* I wondered as I pinched my nose with one hand and began overturning boxes looking for a hefty pair of pliers, or maybe a hacksaw. Ripley backed away from the noise, but once I made sure he wasn't going anywhere, I carried on grabbing and pulling at box after box, hoping I'd find what I was looking for. Anything to break that fucking metal bar.

In the end I managed to get a pair of bolt cutters, a crowbar, and a heavy-duty pair of pliers. One went in my pocket, one went down the back of my jeans, and the other was clutched in my fist, too large to be tucked away in my clothes. The bolt cutters felt hefty in my hand, which was a bit of comfort, but that feeling didn't last long.

Something moved in the darkness, out there in the twisted jungle of shadows cast by all those pipes and wires that ran from one machine to the next. A figure moved. Thin, but unmistakably human in its outline. I couldn't help but remember what I'd seen on that tape. Surely it couldn't have been real? Maybe Daniel had rigged something up. Some fishing wire and a motor, maybe? The idea that those bodies had been moving on their own… I couldn't be sure of that, could I? It was a frightening idea, one my mind had latched onto out of sheer panic. That was all…

And then I saw them. A pair of white pinpricks reflecting back at me from the depths of that cluttered room. Ripley, already behind me, head nuzzled into my leg, pushed even closer against me and let out a barely audible whine under his breath. The behaviour of a dog who was terrified, close to pissing himself with fear.

Just a bit of metal, I told myself as the light shook so violently in my hand I struggled to see straight. *Just two shiny bits of metal…*

They blinked and began to come towards me. If I had any doubts left, they were dispersed by the sight of a pale white hand emerging into the light.

I ran straight to the stairs and went to climb them, but only one or two steps in and I saw something gripping the handrail on the top floor. A mouldy clump of flesh only just recognisable as a fist, the flesh withered until the fingers were basically bone. Without meaning to, I brought my light up out of habit and I saw the bloated face of a hairless corpse glaring down at me. I couldn't even tell you if it had been a teenage girl or the sixty-year-old Daniel. Either way I instinctively turned and found another body shambling towards me out of the workshop. I was trapped. Nowhere to go. By the feel of warm fluid on the back of my leg, I could tell Ripley had finally pissed himself. An adult dog, tail between his legs, shivering like a puppy and desperate to be picked up. God, I needed him to just stay together for a little longer. I couldn't take him in my arms, but I couldn't leave him behind either…

With nowhere to go, I ran down and entered the storage. There was the temptation to stop once I hit the bottom. Down here the air was thicker, and the sounds of my breathing were muted, somehow distant. But I only had to look back up to see three pairs of eyes glaring down at me, so without giving any of it much further thought I barreled down the corridor and stumbled onto a door at random. Opening it, I saw what looked like your standard storage room. Only most of the shelves had been overturned, and the food left to rot on the floor. One or two shelving units were still upright though, and their shelves were covered in tall opaque boxes that made them a fantastic hiding spot. That, I decided, would have to be where I crouched down and turned off my light.

I was already inside when I realised that wasn't all that was in there…

The door *almost* looked normal. I could see why Daniel must have been confused by it because it looked a little bit like all the other doors down there, but it was different too. It was too tall and too wide, about a foot and a half off the ground, and the metal rusted in its entirety like it had aged out of sync with everything else down there. All around the jamb was a profusion of wet soppy moss like the kind you find hanging off trees in a swamp, and every few seconds the door would leak something strange and oily, like the kind of thing you find in a parking lot on a rainy day. Of course that wasn't too strange in itself, but the leak was horizontal, defying gravity so that every few seconds a large glob of the stuff would whip across the room and *slap* into the wall opposite creating a puddle about the size of a man that defied all reason.

Remembering Daniel's words about radiation, I instinctively inched away from this puddle and the door on the opposite wall, backing myself into the darkest quietest corner I could while I pulled Ripley behind me and hoped to hell he wouldn't give me away. Once I was in there, I turned off my light and waited.

I must have taken longer than I'd thought to hide because it was barely two seconds later when a few figures entered the room. It was pitch black after I'd turned off my torch, but they made enough noise to let me know that at least two of them had stumbled in after me. I stayed there, unable to see anything, not sure if they were heading straight for me or just getting ready to leave, forced to hold out and let luck decide my fate. When I finally heard something scrape against the wall barely two feet from where I stood, I gave up and switched my light on, desperate to know what was coming for me.

The sound had been terribly misleading.

Daniel Vance was no more than six inches from my face.

"Get out," he hissed from a toothless and cracked mouth. A living corpse just like the others, somehow a flash of intelligence remained in those wide, terrified eyes.

And then I heard it. The creaking of a door. And without even thinking I turned on the light and saw it on the wall. I saw *it* open, and behind the strange steel there was more than just plain old concrete. Much more. I saw a raging gullet of flesh. A ringed tube of pulsing muscle lined with teeth the size of hands. A spiralling descent into madness. Hot fetid air washed into the room, buffeting me and the rotting corpses, all of us paralyzed by what we were seeing, even if for most of the figures beside Daniel and myself, they didn't have eyes to see with.

"What the fuck…?" I muttered, unable to take my eyes from the flesh tube beyond that doorway.

"It's coming," Daniel whispered as he grabbed me with one fist and hurled me out of the room. I hit the floor and skidded along a slick fluid left by the Vance's footprints, the smell of which turned my stomach. Perhaps the worst detail was that it was cold. I don't know why; I'd just expected whatever oozed them off them to be feverishly hot. But it wasn't. It soaked my shirt like I'd fallen into a muddy puddle.

"It's coming."

This voice wasn't Daniel's. I couldn't say for sure, but it sounded like a child's whisper. One by one the bodies shuffled over to the open door and knelt before it. I don't know why, but I got the impression the others had lost pretty much everything left of their minds, but Daniel remained aware. He looked back at me once more and spoke before he pressed his head to the floor in supplication with the others.

"The only thing we did wrong was being *here* for it to torture. It didn't need a reason, just an opportunity. Leave. It won't let us go. It won't even let us die. And if it catches you, it won't let *you* go either."

His forehead kissed the dirt.

And then something reached through the door and gripped his head in its palm the way you or I might pick up an apple.

In full panic, I ran over and grabbed my dog and the bolt cutters and I ran like my legs were pistons, machines whose signals of exhaustion and fatigue could not slow me down or cause me to fall. I had to move. I had to leave. The hand that had grabbed Daniel… the sight of it flushed my mind clean like some kind of enema. It hurt to see the image replay in my mind but there was nothing else in my head echoing around except the sight of fingers with one too many knuckles, and nails as large as a smartphone.

I reached the top floor and nearly collapsed from breathlessness, but I wouldn't let myself stay down for long. I crawled over to the ladder and climbed up and immediately went to work trying to cut the metal lock. It was hell with just one hand, the other clinging to the torch that I kept frantically pointing at the door behind me, and it wasn't long before I fumbled one too many times and dropped my only source of light.

"No no no no…" I mewed. But there was no time to look for it. I had to get out, and I had to get out fast! I couldn't see, but I was sure I could hear something climbing up those stairs. Not the steady *thump thump* of human feet. No, this was different. This was a rapid pitter patter of a spider, maybe. Something with hundreds of feet or hands, or God knows what, skittering along the floor and walls and ceiling, pulling itself along with a body whose mere shape would offend God.

Using all my strength I leaned hard on the bolt cutters and, at last, the bolt gave. I threw the hatch open and got just enough ambient light to see Ripley hovering at the bottom of the ladder, growling ineffectually at the doorway. I crouched down, scooped him up, and fled up the ladder so quickly that my muscles turned to jelly at the top and I fell over onto hands and knees. But still, I was out. The long corridor covered in writing was ahead of me, and at the very end a doorway capped now by the tired blue light of a full moon.

Ripley needed no encouragement. He whipped down the corridor with canine speed and I followed at a broken and stumbling crawl, eventually shouldering past the open door and collapsing onto the forest floor.

For a few seconds I drifted in and out of consciousness, but when I looked up and saw the canopy overhead moving–the branches backlit by a full moon–I snapped awake and glared down at something gripping my ankle. The hand had reached out of the dark and seized me and was slowly dragging me back into the Earth below. Whatever it was, most of its body lurked out of sight in the shadows behind the doorway, but the hand that crushed my leg was the size of my torso, with an arm that looked like it belonged to a mole rat.

I struck it with my own fist. I dug my nails in. I cried and kicked and screamed, but nothing could stop it. From behind the door, something like a face grinned and leered at me with joy. It was taking its time, sure enough, pulling me in so slowly that it gave my mind all the time in the world to appreciate the nightmare that awaited me. I think if, in that moment, you'd given me a gun, I would've shot myself because God help me I couldn't escape the look in Daniel's eyes, how he'd knelt to worship this thing like a man who knew that hope or pride or joy or anything with even a hint of goodness to it was so far out of reach for him it might as well be a dream. How long was this thing going to keep them down there? How long did it intend to keep *me!?*

I wept like a child, feeling like my mind was slowly cracking as I tried everything to stop that fucking pulling me into the shadows. I kicked at the earth. I dug into it using my hands, looking for a root or a pipe or anything to hold on to. Nothing, *nothing* I did would slow it down.

I was no more than a foot from the doorway when Ripley re-appeared.

A dog afraid of hoovers and plastic bags and doors that move on their own. A dog who once got stared down by a particularly feisty rabbit who stopped mid chase and turned around, baffling the predator on its tail. A dog you couldn't even watch scary movies around…

And he lunged at that arm like he was a wolf, like he'd always been one. And while he didn't quite break the skin, the pressure was enough to make the thing's grip weaken, and I slid my leg out. Unable to stand, I knelt and grabbed the dog and pulled as hard as I could and now that fucking thing bled at last as the pressure of the jaws and the sliding teeth ripped into its flesh. Together, at last, Ripley and I were let go and sent rolling backwards head over heels.

I wasted no time waiting, looking, or processing. I heaved the dog to my chest and crawled until I passed out, making it maybe half a kilometre away. Only when I could no longer see the door did I let myself fall to the ground face first and gave up consciousness.

***

The doctors said I had pneumonia, which I suppose made some kind of sense. I might have even believed them were it not for the Sheriff's visit, asking strange questions of me as I lay in bed about what I may or may not have seen. I dismissed them to the best of my ability. I wasn't interested in chasing that particular nightmare down, figuring out if it had been real or not, at least not while I lay there half-drowning in my own infection. To be fair, I had at least some sympathy for why the police had done so little to seal that place off. I have, on occasion, thought about going and doing the job myself, but to this day I still have nightmares about being pulled into the dark beyond that door. Not just the bunker door, the one I narrowly avoided at the end, but the one *below*. What I saw was a kind of madness, I'm sure of it, and I often think of Daniel's words.

It didn't need a reason, just an opportunity.

Somehow, the Vances were that opportunity. Maybe they built their bunker on a ley line, or a weak spot between dimensions, or the site of former Satanic rituals. I'm not sure it even matters. They went into the dark thinking it'd be a safe place to wait out the world's troubles, but something had been down there waiting for them, waiting for a chance to get at a family of seven people, to lock them in and deprive them of escape and slowly take from them everything it could.

I've moved since then. Couldn't help it. It wasn't just the memories you see. It was the short-wave radio I kept in my basement. Something my father passed onto me when I was just a boy. God I'd forgotten about it… at least until I woke up one day to the sound of it blaring white noise down in the dark.

And buried in that sound was the faint whispering of a man, his voice barely recognisable, but unmistakably *his*.

…let them go let them go let them go let them go let them go let them go…

PRETEND PLAY

When he told me he wanted to play "pretend", I thought it was something to do with sex. And the funny thing is, if he'd whipped out a Wonder Woman costume, I would have gone along with it. Things had been cold between us for years. One word replies and tense conversations had become the norm. I was prepared to do what was necessary to try and patch things up. When he clarified he wanted to pretend to be young, I felt a lot more hesitation. If this was a sex thing, I thought, it could get pretty weird. Even as he explained it all, I just kept waiting for it to turn in that direction. I figured that's what it had to be, right? But he said it wasn't like that at all. He just wanted some time, now and again, when he could behave like a child. Nothing too weird, just sort of therapeutic roleplay.

I'll admit, it wasn't what I thought. He wanted me to pack his lunches and kiss his cheek before going to work, he said. He wanted me to give him the kind of things you'd give a kid, so I packed him a yoghurt, a ham sandwich, and an apple. There was also a small carton of juice, all tucked neatly into a brown paper bag. His whole face lit up with joy when he saw it. I came up with the brown bag myself and he told me it was a nice touch. I remember thinking it was the first sincere compliment he'd paid me in years. I felt a rare pang of pride at that.

After that I got the gist pretty quickly. He wanted me to run him baths and sit there beside him while he played with toys. He wanted to ask me for permission before going out to play in the yard. He wanted spaghetti and hotdog for dinner, and jelly and ice cream for dessert. I did it all with a smile. He never really looked at me all that much as a wife. But as a caregiver? It was like every little gesture was the greatest thing to him. I thought it was messed up, sure. But I don't know, those first few weeks were actually quite nice. One day he came home, and I had the telly set to old cartoons from his childhood and he just burst into tears. I'd bought the DVDs as a little surprise but didn't expect that kind of reaction. I ran over and held him and we stayed like that, huddled on the sofa, for hours. I'd never felt that kind of closeness or vulnerability from him or, well, anyone else I'd ever met.

It was… confusing. But I liked it. We'd always been each other's closest friends, and now he was spending more time with me than ever before. And he cared about what I had to say and genuinely paid attention to me. I once baked him a cake, and he sat on the counter, kicking his legs, asking me questions the whole time. I told him about the recipe, about how my grandmother had brought it over with her when she emigrated, about how it'd been passed down for generations, and I could see that he wasn't play acting. He really was blown away by the whole story.

But the requests just kept coming, as did the amount of time he spent roleplaying. It started out as something before and after work, but he soon quit his job and without notice, it became an all-day activity. Like I said, it was part of the fun, and I didn't put any limits on it. He did what I imagine most kids do all day long. He watched TV, played with toys and video games, ran around making silly noises. He also wanted to do the less fun stuff, so I had to set him chores, bathe him, brush and cut his hair, make him eat vegetables. He even asked me to start organising him "homework", so I bought some old exercise books for low-level maths and English. He was never "naughty", but he did like to make a fuss when I told him to do these things, but sometimes I'd catch a sly smile or a twinkle in his eye and I knew he really liked it. There was something inherently bizarre and actually kind of funny about watching an accountant sit there and struggle when carrying the one. Still, it was a far cry from the very guarded and deeply arrogant man I'd married.

I guess I'm just trying to put it all in order for you, but I'm not sure I can. There were times it felt… wrong, I suppose. All my attraction to him went right out the window, but I didn't care because we didn't have sex that much as husband and wife, and even when we did, it wasn't very good. Maybe if you understood that I'm not a social person you could see why I let this all happen.

I don't have friends, never have, not even when I was in university. His company, his placid warm and adoring company, it worked a kind of magic on me. I think, also, that I actually quite liked looking after someone. In hindsight, I probably should have just got a cat. At the time, I just liked the change of pace and I always suspected there was some dark secret lurking beneath him—my mother had warned me about this with men—and I was just glad he didn't like killing hookers.

This seemed safe, harmless… at least at first.

As we settled further into a routine, I started to feel lonely again, only it was different. This wasn't the bored listlessness of a day spent at home trying to look busy. It was more like standing over an ocean and looking down. I think it was the way he started to change, physically. I thought they were all deliberate changes, things he did to *look* less like an adult. Sometimes he looked at me and I didn't like it. It was a hungry look. I met a boy once when I was teenager, and he looked at me like that and I liked it. But that was different. Coming from my husband in blue pajamas with a pacifier in his mouth and a rattle in one hand… God, I could have been sick.

And come night time the house started to feel different, larger and colder than usual. I started drinking for some reason, I think partly just to unwind. When things broke, it was up to me to fix them, or to answer the phone, or deal with bills. We had plenty saved up, so don't get me wrong, it wasn't like we were in dire circumstances. But there was no one else to share the endless responsibilities with and I felt it like a weight on my shoulders. Come morning I'd have to go through the motions with a pounding headache and I found that the days started to blur. Months passed, maybe even a whole year. It's hard for me to remember any of these events in a straight line, and that's not all my fault.

I remember thinking that he was a *growing boy*, but that wasn't true at all. We ordered new shoes for him online and they were a different size to the usual. Smaller. He'd said it was because he wanted the light up ones, but he'd been a size 11 as an adult and the ones we bought were for a young boy. I don't know how, but he wore those new shoes just fine. I pinched the toe and told him he'd grow into them.

I have vivid memories of watching him struggle to put a stuffed toy on the top shelf, but he'd always towered over me at six foot three. Even now I'm putting it all back together in my head and finding little surprises. There was always the sense that if I stopped too long to think, then everything would rush past me, and I'd miss it. Even trying my best to just go with it, I found myself feeling like a stranger in my own house. Things moved, rooms were rearranged, and new toys just appeared, all without me knowing how. A whole swing set was installed in the garden without me remembering, but when I checked, my signature was on the invoice.

At one point he began wearing diapers, and I didn't even notice until days passed. It just kind of made sense somehow? In the moment it had felt so natural and, looking back, I seemed to remember my husband as a child, not a fully grown man. I'd been feeding a toddler, hugging a toddler, watching a toddler play games. But at the same time, it wasn't any of that... it was my husband sitting there with his long legs crossed and crumbs in his beard.

One morning I woke up to a dog, and the next day it was gone. I searched for hours, feeling like I was going insane, but sure enough, there was a bowl and dog food right by the kitchen door, so it wasn't like I'd imagined it. There was no dog in the house though, nor in the garden. Exhausted and beaten, I went into my husband's room for a final check when, at the sight of him, this strange apprehension came over me. I couldn't get the thought out of my head that he'd done something. After all, if he was a child, he was a bit odd, wasn't he? He didn't play with other children, he didn't misbehave, he barely spoke. He was a good little boy, sure, but not necessarily all that normal.

And of course, he *wasn't* a child. He was... he was something else. Standing there, I appreciated just how odd he had started to look. His hair was thinning—not just falling out, mind you. It felt downy to the touch, soft, like a newborn's peachy fuzz. And, good God, the smell. It was *like* a baby's smell, but foul like sour milk. And it clung to him no matter how much I bathed him and washed his clothes. There were days when it felt like I could choke to death on it, and I learned to breathe carefully through my mouth whenever we were together.

His pupils were huge, too large for those small sockets. His eyes had always been spaced far apart. But placed on a child-shaped head, he looked like he was wearing a bad Halloween mask with doll's eyes instead of his own. Sometimes I'd catch him staring at me from around a corner, or at the bottom of a long corridor. Sometimes that meant him standing there in the dark, audibly breathing as his shoulders rose and fell while some unseen thought excited him. Other times it meant glimpsing his grey head disappearing behind a wall or door the second I turned. He drooled almost constantly and wiped the excess on his sleeve, but a lot of it landed on the floor anyway. There were times I'd find small puddles of spit in locked rooms, often just behind where I'd been standing. Other times I could hear his difficult breathing inches from my back, but he was never actually there when I turned around.

I was afraid of him, I realised. And I nearly cried out when, standing in that dark and quiet room, he rolled onto his back as he slept in the crib. He opened a gummy smile, and I saw that all his teeth had fallen out, barring just a few. And the closer I looked, the more certain I became that even those were not his original ones. They were too white, too small, too peg-like to be an adult's incisors.

I secretly hoped I was going insane. The alternative was somehow even worse.

***

I was on the toilet when the doorbell rang. It was a shrill screech that grated, and I jumped so badly I dropped my phone. I quickly finished up and waddled over to the window with my pants still down. There was a van just outside the front gates which were open, but there was no sign of anyone walking around down there. Normally, this kind of problem would just go away, and they'd leave the package on the doorstep. But something felt wrong. I couldn't hear my husband anywhere in the house. No footsteps, no babbling, no clacking toys or rolling wheels.

That van looked strange. The driver-side door was still open, the engine still running. I tried to digest what it all meant while running downstairs, stopping only when I saw the front door open. A gust of wind blew through the main house, drawing out all the homely warmth. I had images of our roleplay being found out, and fears of humiliation and embarrassment filled my head. There was something else muddled in with all the thoughts as well. We'd spent so long locked up together, my husband and I, safe and far away from the rest of the world.

How would he react to this intrusion?

As if in answer, someone cried out from the living room. I ran down the last few stairs and pushed open the door to find a small man shaking where he stood, brown cardboard box clutched to his chest for protection.

"Wh—wh—what," he stuttered.

I put my arm around his shoulder and started to move him towards the door. I couldn't see my husband, but he was never too far away from me and I couldn't help but notice one of his favourite toys lying on the floor.

"He let me in," the man continued. "Looked just… looked just like a…" Suddenly he turned to me and gripped both my arms. "What's wrong with him?" he asked. "I've never seen anything like that before."

I don't remember what I said, but I kept pushing him towards the front door, out of the living room and into the kitchen. A quick turn of my head and I saw my husband ducking back down beneath the sofa. He was the wrong size to be so quick and sneaky, but he had a way of hiding and moving around the house so that you almost never saw him unless he wanted you to.

"Come on," I muttered, but the deliveryman's feet were slow and cumbersome. It was like his head was all muddled up.

"It was just a child," he cried like it had just dawned on him. "Oh no! I frightened him, didn't I?" He tried turning back, but I stopped him. "No, I didn't mean to scare him. I just… I just… his *face*." He stopped resisting and his shoulders slumped back down. "What's wrong with him?" he asked. "Why do my eyes hurt?"

"He's sick," I answered, finally pulling him the last few feet to the door. I shoved him back past the threshold and stood, panting, to catch my breath. "He's just very unwell," I said, stifling a sob— part lie, part truth. "It's a condition."

The delivery man looked as if he still was trying to sort his own head out, but it seemed like he bought it. He went to leave, putting one foot down on the porch steps, before suddenly deciding that he needed to make amends. "Please don't report me!" he cried, and I jumped a little. "I didn't mean to come off as rude." My heart started to race. I could smell my husband, the stench nearly overpowering. He was so close I could practically feel him, but where he was, I couldn't say. I just needed to get this man away before something terrible happened. He was babbling endlessly about offending me.

"Please," I said, on the verge of tears. "Please leave."

Did he understand? I wonder. Sometimes, when I think back, I see a flickering of understanding in his eyes. It looked like empathy. I can't be sure because it all kind of just blurs together. The shock in his eyes as my husband's arm grabbed his ankle cannot be understated. Neither of us expected him to be down there. I still don't know how he did it. But he *was* down there, giggling in an unhealthy falsetto rasp. Before anyone could speak, he yanked so hard the deliveryman fell down backwards and his leg disappeared into shadow. With one hand the crying man clamped down on the thigh as if to soothe some unseen pain, and with the other hand he tried to push himself back out from between the wooden slats.

But my husband was always a big man. And now he had a strange air about him. A quiet, crackling power that followed him from room-to-room. The struggle was one-sided, and the deliveryman screamed and howled. He gave up holding the one leg and tried using both hands to pull, or push, or drag himself away. I didn't know what was happening out of sight, but his face drained of blood and his screams just kept getting worse. I've never heard a man make a sound like that before, not an adult man. It was scary in a way I wasn't prepared for. I think he asked me to help at one point. I contemplated calling the police, but never did. I was so terrified; I couldn't even bring myself to move. Occasionally, one of my husband's thick-knuckled hands could be glimpsed as he pulled more of the man inside. Those hands looked so large, so pale, so deeply unhealthy. I could hear what he was doing, but that didn't really come to my attention until I unpacked it all mentally long after it was over. But yes, I could hear bone crack and something like paper being torn.

Was it an hour? Or just a few minutes? I don't know. The man just kept crying and pleading and my husband just kept pulling.

And pulling.

And pulling.

The stairs started to buckle, but the wood was thick and strong. The final question came down to what would break first, a pelvis or a post? The deliveryman's cries told me what he thought would happen. He was right. With a tremendous yell of joy—just like a child on their birthday—my husband latched another fist around the man's other leg and pulled so hard there was a sudden *crack!* And his victim fell limp like a toy losing power. What followed was a silence so heavy it hurt my ears, broken only by the faint wet sound of my husband dragging the rest of the man into the dark. The space between each step couldn't have been more than six inches, but brute force won out. The last I remember of the man's face, he was pale with bulging eyes. The arrangement of his arms and legs didn't even make sense anymore. He looked like a spider after you stepped on it.

I stayed there for a while longer, hoping to hell and back I'd hear an ambulance or police siren. But like I said, we lived far out of town. By the time it occurred to me that no one would rescue the man—or me—the blood on the steps was congealing. My husband was still just out of sight, giggling and clapping like a kid making mud pies.

"Come on," I finally managed to say, speaking like the doting mother I was. "Put your new toy away. I'll make you some lunch."

***

I was washing dishes and staring into the yard. It resembled somewhere I'd seen before, but I couldn't remember where or why. My husband was somewhere upstairs, and I was alone. I'd often hear him thunder around up there, doing God-knows-what, his bare feet slapping on hardwood floors he'd once picked out in a turtleneck and chinos. That seemed like a different person's life now. Hard to believe it was the same man who brought me something just days before that made me sick. He'd made it himself and it had hung on the fridge for a whole afternoon like just another piece of macaroni art. *Was that thing where the dog ended up?* I wondered, running a dishcloth over the same plate for the second hour in a row.

Movement caught my eye. Out in the garden, something floated down past the tall hedges that walled our yard and landed plainly on the overgrown grass. It was a bright, luminous yellow that glowed like a safety vest. For some reason I held up the plate in my hand and looked between the two. God, I was so out of it. It was like a worm in my head. I could feel it, maybe even reach out and grab it if I could just focus on it for long enough. But each time I closed my mind around it, each time I started to feel out the shape of this intrusion, this rewriting of my own brain, it slithered away.

"Frisbee," I muttered.

And then, just like that, she was there. She was maybe nine or ten. How had she wound up here? I wondered. Maybe she was lost.

She was looking around like she didn't know where she was. I could see she was scared, and my heart sank as I realised how awful our home must have looked to her. There was a time I was house proud, but now we lived in decrepit filth. Of course, the little girl looked scared, I thought. This was the scary house every child feared, with broken windows and overgrown bushes that choked a yard filled with rusted swings and abandoned toys. And this poor girl had lost her frisbee and...

"No," I said, first to myself and then once again to the room. "No!"

But it was too late. I could hear him scuttle around before the house fell into quiet. From outside, the girl started to say something. A greeting perhaps?

There was a knife in my hand that I didn't remember taking, and I was outside before I had time to even think. The little girl looked to me and instantly burst into tears. I was sprinting towards her with a knife in one hand and a murderous look straight out of a horror film. But before that, before she'd seen me, she'd been looking towards a thicket of grass with disgust on her face.

"No!" I screamed, not at her, but at him.

I picked her up in my arms even as she batted me away. I didn't care if this girl thought I was Satan himself, if she ran back home and told her parents about the mean creepy lady and they called the police and this all ended with me safe and warm behind bars. I didn't care. I clutched my arm around her waist and willed it into a band of steel to keep her safe. She squirmed but could not break free and I ran towards the gate as fast as I could carry her.

"It's okay," I cooed. "He won't get you."

I was half-way there when her screaming and wriggling stopped. Her head was over my shoulder and all of a sudden, she gripped me like I was a life raft. The change was instant, and it made me falter. For a brief moment, I heard his feet pulsing towards me. I turned, brandishing the knife like a torch against the darkness, but nothing was there. The girl started screaming again, the sight of my husband sinking, and she held onto me for dear life.

"Not the baby!" she screamed. "No no no! Not the baby!"

"Not the baby," I repeated. "I won't let him."

I backed up to the gate carefully and began to wonder what next when, out of nowhere, he leaped into sight and grabbed the girl's hair, yanking her head back while she screamed so hard her face turned beetroot-red. He jumped up and down, hollering and crying like a giddy toddler with a Christmas present. His misshapen face was grinning, his gums black and bloody, but his hands threatened to tear the girl's scalp right off. I started to feel nauseous at the sight of him. His size seemed to change with every glance. I couldn't make sense of it, and I felt that worm inside my mind wriggle and dislodge more of my thoughts. Sometimes he was waist-high, sometimes a full-grown man. But always those hands were too large for his frame and the brown flakes of blood still trapped beneath his chipped nails reminded me exactly what he wanted.

"No!" I screamed and lashed out with the knife. The motion that came to me in the moment was a downward thrust, and the knife was left embedded in my husband's right shoulder.

He let go immediately and started to howl and sob. He seemed to shrink before my very eyes, and I quickly set the girl down and pushed her through the gate. I pulled the bars shut, screamed at her to run, then quickly turned back to my husband, who was sucking his thumb and trying to pull the knife out with his remaining hand. After some awkward fumbling, he grabbed the handle and threw the knife to the ground. It clattered to the floor, blood glistening in the sun.

"You're just like her," he said, his voice breaking and returning to the calm authoritative man I'd once known. His beady eyes bored into me, and I could've collapsed under that stare. The change in cadence was as sudden as a sheer drop off a cliff. "I just wanted what she never gave me. But you're all the same."

Suddenly his whole face bunched up into a twisted infantile smile and he declared with joy and delight in a voice identical to a child's,

"I'm going to crawl inside you!"

***

Dinner was cold. It was the first meal I'd made him after our little fight. I'd fidgeted over it for hours, filled with doubts and fears. But it all came to naught. He was too smart to fall for that, whether he'd seen the rat poison or not. He hadn't come for dinner. Now I was left with a problem. I'd stayed fixed to the spot in the kitchen, working away with endless looks over my shoulder, and night had fallen. The only light was in the kitchen, and it was a big house filled with inky black shadows that swallowed entire rooms and corridors. Often, I would glimpse a sliver of movement, like a shark's fin cresting a wave. I might see a blue piece of fabric catch the moonlight before disappearing back into the dark. He was out there.

I had a new knife, at least. And something about the adrenaline in my veins helped me think more clearly. When I looked back in my thoughts, I no longer saw a child, but something twisted and deformed with delusion and malice. A disease had festered not only in our heads, but the space we shared and the world we lived in, spilling out into reality like a migraine aura made real. I didn't know if it was an intruder or just something dark that had spread from within, but it belonged to me one way or another.

I couldn't let it live.

"Dinner's ready," I cried. "Come on!"

There was a shuffling somewhere out front, by the stairs. I don't know why I bothered saying anything. He must have seen me. I cried out again, my voice faltering from fear and exhaustion. I picked the plate up and put it by the threshold of the kitchen, its edge just inches from the darkness. "You must be hungry," I said, doing my best to smile. "Please eat it," I added. "For me?"

A single chubby finger peaked through the doorway and slid the plate across. It was so loud in the silence, grating across tile. Something felt wrong, but in the moment, I just hoped it was the sheer panic trapped deep within my chest.

The plate whipped out of the darkness and struck me in the face. My nose cracked and my head snapped backwards and before I knew it, I was on the floor, the plate rolling to a noisy stop a few feet away. It was whole, but one edge was coated in blood. I became aware of a coppery taste in my mouth and realised it was mine all over that plate. It felt like I was lying there for a good few seconds, agony ringing in my ears while I opened and closed my jaw in disconcerted shock. Slowly, layer by layer, things started to right themselves. There was a sharp pain in the back of my head, and I realised I must have hit it when I fell over. And there was a weight on top of me, pressing down, making it hard to breathe. Had I broken a rib? I wondered. But it didn't feel much like that. It felt like something was moving around, something sharp and painful.

I looked down and saw my husband's cabbage-shaped head bobbing away at my breast. I screamed and pushed him away, but he clamped down hard, those nasty little peg teeth burying themselves into my flesh and refusing to dislodge. I was overcome with disgust and started beating away at him, scratching deep gouges in his scalp and shoulders. Only when I buried a thumb in his nasty little eye did he relent and let go. He sat up and my thumb slid out of the socket with a *pop* and, for a moment, he looked overcome with naïve sadness. But then hatred washed over his face and his remaining eye glared at me with murder.

He started to choke me, those terrible fists clasping around my throat like bands of iron. I struggled, lashing my hands out at the floor and furniture, desperate for something, anything, that might help. Thankfully my hands alighted on the knife, and I drove it hard into the soft flesh of his armpit. For a moment he carried on as normal, but by the time I drove the blade between his ribs, once, then twice, the blood had already drained from his face. It soaked us both, and to my horror it stank of sour milk and talcum powder. I watched the realisation of his wounds dull the fire in his eyes. He stumbled backwards, his face scrunching up as he let out a horrific bawl.

Pink foam seeped from his mouth, and he gasped and choked. His lungs were filling with blood, and I watched him die slowly before me. By the time it was done, he was a man again. A strangely dressed, emaciated wretch of a man, but nothing more. I touched my throat and it felt sore, and my chest was a ragged mess.

"Was it good for you?" I asked, a laugh rising unbidden from my lips. The sound of my own voice scared me. I sounded deranged. But I couldn't stop laughing at the joke I'd made, and before long my breath became short and consciousness slipped away in its entirety.

***

It's been some time—how long, I don't know—and I still wonder whether he was ever real. I burned the house down and I finally got to hear the sound of sirens coming to take me away. It was a weird problem to explain to the police. They had evidence of a child living in the home, but no body. They thought I'd offed a kid and burned the house to hide the evidence. Later on, they found one adult body, but it was the deliveryman's, not my husband's. And I was arrested just a few short weeks later.

Of course, I told them the truth, just barring a few of the weirder details. My husband had gone insane, I said. He'd snapped, started acting like a child, killed one man, then tried to kill me. Unfortunately, there are no records of my husband, nor our marriage, nor our life together. I lived alone, unemployed because of a wealthy trust granted to me by family. The mortgage was not paid by my husband, but rather the trust.

All of this was news to me.

He was real; I know that much. I still have the wounds to prove it and they found that little girl who testified, somewhat, in my defence. She really had seen a man dressed as a baby, she said. Although when asked to give a description of what he looked like, she broke down screaming and had to be sedated. I knew what that felt like. I couldn't tell you my husband's age, his eye colour, his birthday, or even his name. It's all worked against me. I think I'm on my second appeal, but my lawyer told me to lower my expectations. No marriage certificate, no wedding invitations, no relationship status on Facebook, no photos, no plane tickets for the honeymoon, no official documentation. Every conceivable trace of this man's life simply doesn't exist.

I managed to get a brain scan and they say my brain should belong to a dementia patient, except I'm just 36. It's all full of holes. Lesions, they call them. That's a good name for it. I said there was a worm, didn't I? It was eating through my head like an apple core. Not a literal worm, of course. Well, I don't know that for sure. But still, I think he did something to my head because even now just the thought of him can give me a nosebleed. I don't remember much of my life before. He wrote over it like a computer file and deliberately blotted out whatever didn't suit his purpose. And of course, they never did find his body, did they? Bit of a cliché, I know. I think it was childish of me to ever believe that a few holes in the torso would kill him.

It, I should say. After all, he was "playing pretend" at being human just as much as being a child.

THE DEALER

It starts with people needing some help. It might be a girl you like, or some guys you're trying to impress, or even just an old buddy you bump into on the street. The important thing is that you've got a reputation for smoking weed and they'd like some. Maybe they're new to town, or they want to throw a party and want to impress someone as a one off, but they need you. They need your help. So that's what you do. You start to "help" them out by buying weed on their behalf and then you start charging extra because it soon becomes regular, and it's more than just a favour, and then you realise you're putting so much time into it you need to find someone who sells large amounts at a discount.

Eventually, you realise weed won't cut it. The margins are too low and the work's too hard. By now you have four phones, way too many friends on Facebook, a day job you fucking hate, and so much of your time goes into being a dealer that you've given up hopes of it just being a hobby. Oh, and of course, you have your own addiction to take care of. Most of the time you'll be lucky to break even, but selling weed helps. Maybe the guy you buy off mentions mushrooms, or MDMA, or something else that's common.

But the important thing to remember is that it's a surprisingly short road to heroin. It pays the most, weighs very little, and you don't have to worry about spreading yourself too thin. Now you'll be able to get a little book of really valuable repeat customers. And, if you're like me, you might just have had enough sense to never try your own product. But it's still a problem. Every person who buys is a ticking time bomb, a walking liability. And every day you work this job, you're not doing something else, something with prospects. And it only takes one arrest to fuck it all up, and it only takes one idiot to lead to that arrest.

See, what I did was I went after a certain kind of client, someone who, through luck and opportunity, is rich enough to hide their addiction. Someone who doesn't "look" like an addict, if you get what I mean. They're hardly immune to the effects of addiction, but consequences are a lot less severe for the upper classes. Good thing that applies to their dealers too. It's nice to have clients who don't die every few years. That's not to say their health is my number one priority, but I've known most of them for going on eight years. I've helped them move, fix broken-down cars, find dates, rehearse presentations, pick up deliveries, and on one occasion I even baby-sat one of their nieces while they got high in the garden shed.

Sadly, I would have to admit that they're my closest friends.

And about a fortnight ago, something bad happened to each and every one of them. Normally I like to sell all my goods on a Sunday, no open door policy and no phone calls. I keep a consistent routine and it avoids trouble, but last Tuesday I had one of them knocking at my door. I was pretty pissed to have this guy, Rolo (don't ask, not his real name), turn up out of the blue. That's not how I like to do things, and I was pretty damn close to not opening the door. But, as you might guess, junkies are resistant to denial, and he wasn't going to go away out of politeness. So, in the end, I let him in.

But to my surprise, he wasn't there to buy. He came straight in and put a brick of the stuff in my hand, leaving me totally speechless. He then went on this winding rant about his childhood and the things his mother did to him and the scars she left and after a long, long time, he eventually got to the point:

"I found it," Rolo told me. "I found it in a gutter on the side of the road. Way, way out in the middle of nowhere. I was driving home and my wife she'll... oh, man, I just spotted it. What a weird thing, right? My headlight caught it, and I was like 'wait was that... no fucking way!?' But it was. Just a brick of the stuff waiting for me in a ditch in the middle of nowhere and..."

He paused and bit down on his thumb so hard I thought he was going to snap it off like a baby carrot.

"I'll kill myself if I have this much," he said. "I know it, you know it, everyone fucking knows it, man. You can't give me all of this. You can't. I looked at that brick and I realised I'd be dead within a day. And you… you've been so good to me. How much do I owe you? Like, seriously? All those times?"

"You don't owe me anything," I said. "You've been paid up for years."

"It's not about that though," he replied. "It's about the gesture. You helped me. So… here's what I'm thinking. You take this and you just… you sell it? And any money you split with me and then I use that money to buy more stuff off you when I need it. That way I never have enough on me to just… go crazy. You know? I can't even tell you how much strength this took, by the way. I've been driving the streets for like 5 hours just thinking this through carefully. I took the elevator up here three times. But… I know it's what I need. I can't… I can't leave this place with that brick.

"I'll kill myself."

I weighed it up in my hands. It was easily worth a grand, and I had to admit, what he said made sense. There was no way any addict could be trusted with that much, least of all him. And, just to reiterate, it was worth a shitload of money.

"You found this?" I asked, clearly incredulous. I glanced at the gold leaf symbol stamped onto one side, failing to recognise it but feeling an intense anxiety in its presence.

"In a fucking ditch," he said, his face elated. "Someone must have just chucked it! Whoosh, straight out the window."

"Alright," I agreed. "This is… this *is* a good deal," I added, hesitating for reasons I couldn't say. But I decided I was just being irrational because, by all accounts, this was a fucking good surprise. Free money is always a good surprise. "Come on," I told him. "I'll weigh a little out for you."

Instinctively he reached into his pocket and started counting notes.

"It's *your* stuff," I snapped, and he laughed at himself. But I just shook my head and took it to my scales, where I began taking off just a little to give to Rolo. Pretty soon I was left sitting in my flat on my own staring at the brick with a sense of confusion, partly at the preceding events, partly at the strange pit in my stomach, and partly because that symbol made my eyes hurt.

Over the next week that brick was sold in pieces to each of my customers, slowly whittling itself down until about half was left. Bit by bit I sold it to all eleven of my regulars and then, bit by bit, none of them came back. When it came to Sunday—a day where my phone is normally lit up and my door's a fucking tambourine—there was silence. I tried calling them all, but there was no answer for each of them. I cannot stress to you just how weird this is. Heroin addicts don't skip appointments with me. It just doesn't work like that, not unless they're dead.

And that was a harrowing thought to have.

All of them?

Man, even back then I took a long hard look at that brick. Something about it had bothered me the entire time, and now I was truly worried. Do you know what they'd do to me if I sold bad drugs to eleven different middle-class Londoners? One of them is a blonde girl in her twenties. *Fucking blonde.*

Do you have any idea how bad that would be for me?

My first stop was the news. At least three of the people I sold to were Oxbridge graduates with banking jobs, and I figured if they died it'd be in the papers somewhere. People love those kinda scandalous stories, so I started Googling names until I got a hit. It was… not what I expected.

That blonde I just mentioned. I'm gonna call her Milkybar, anyway she turned up in one paper having gone missing, last seen a few days before. It was a plea from her husband and parents, asking for her to come home. The paper mentioned her addiction and there were worries she'd relapsed or worse, died. Well, I was worried too, but what I knew that they didn't was that Milkybar had a small flat she rented in a friend's name where she smoked before going to work. I also happened to have a key from a misguided attempt at seduction (long story).

I had an address and access. And I rushed there hoping to God I'd find her partying her tits off or handcuffed to a bed deep in withdrawal.

If only.

I entered quietly only to find a dingy shithole in a high-rise apartment that was a huge step down from the last time I'd been there. Somehow, there were signs of decay. I mean, ten plus years of rot and decay. Wallpaper was peeling, the ceilings were yellow, pipes had rusted, plaster had chipped, the windows had faded. I'd been there just a year before, and it had been a newly decorated flat. It wasn't squalor that had done the damage, no. It was derelict, broken down the way old houses are. Nothing about it made sense to me. I triple checked the address but, sure enough, that was the right place.

So I kept looking and eventually I found Milkybar. At least, I figure it was her because of the clothes. Really, I guess all I found was a pile of bones in a sundress with some faint straw-coloured hair. Her skull, her mouth, was wide open and the sockets empty and it just looked like she was in pain. And the porcelain tub was all stained a dark red, looking an awful lot like a puddle of blood. I felt like I'd stumbled into a crypt, the way her bones looked brittle with age, with little teeth marks from rats.

Was this a bad attempt at faking her death? I wondered.

After a little more poking around, I found some papers stuffed between her pelvis and her dress. I pulled them out and unrolled them, recoiling from the smell, and read. I don't wanna put it all up in print, but she wrote about some fucked up stuff. Real nasty messed up things, like "I just saw Se7en" messed up. It nearly made me sick and, struggling to understand anything in the moment, I put those crazy words down to her having a fucked up troubled mind.

After looking around a bit more and not finding anything, I took the notes and left. At the bottom of the last page, she'd sketched the symbol from the brick in my flat and that freaked me out. None of the people, aside from Rolo, could have possibly seen that symbol, and I did not like it being there one tiny little bit. It left me shaken, not just because of the potential trouble it might bring, but because I was worried that it really was Milkybar in that tub, and that something awful had happened to her.

So, I decided to check up on the others. It wasn't easy, but I managed to visit at least two others before morning.

The first of the two was a guy I'll call Snickers who, if you can believe it, was a professor of English Literature at KCL. He was something of a tortured artist when he was younger, and while he later grew up and let go of the "artist" part he guarded the "tortured" part like a tiger protecting her cub. When I first knocked on the door of his own personal little fuck-pad, I heard what I'd best describe as a kind of quiet sobbing and some shuffling. I wound up banging at his door for a good ten minutes before someone finally let me in and it wasn't Snickers.

The guy didn't even greet me or look surprised. He was a young man, early twenties, and I'd have bet my life that he was one of Snickers' many student hook ups. Not that it mattered, but I followed him carefully as he held both his arms and shivered violently, tears streaming down his cheeks. Both of us sat down opposite one another and the first thing he said was not what I expected at all.

"What the fuck happened, man?" he said, stifling a sob.

"What?"

"Where am I?" he asked. "I don't. I don't... what the *fuck* happened, man? Where did we *go*?"

"Where's Snickers?" I asked.

"What the fuck? We were all there! You saw exactly what happened, man. They *made* us watch. All of us, me especially. You saying you don't fuckin' remember?"

"I think you've mistaken me for someone else," I answered. "What happened here?"

The kid stopped and stared at me for a long minute before sniffling and pulling his knees up to his chest, holding them close while he rocked back and forth. His eyes were distant, and when he spoke next, he didn't talk to me.

"I thought you were Dan," he said. "Who are you?"

"I'm a friend of Snickers," I answered. "I was worried something had happened."

The kid laughed and for a brief moment I saw a network of cuts leading down his neck onto his chest.

"I don't know," he answered, a quiver in his voice. "We were here, we got high and then... Jesus Christ," he broke down, holding his face in his hands and crying. I waited patiently until he could resume. "Oh, it was fucking *awful* man. You don't even know. They just... they didn't even come, we went to them man, floating through... through... I don't even fucking know, the sky? We just all wound up there washed up on the shore and then they came and they took us and I thought it was just a trip, y'know? Just a bad trip, but it weren't like that at all. Oh fuck, man, my mum, oh my God how am I even going to explain this to her? We've been gone so long..."

I looked around for a moment and took in the state of Snickers' apartment, noticing the strange dust that coated everything and the peculiar person-shaped imprint on the sofa.

"How long were you gone?" I asked.

"You should know, man, you think they let us keep fucking clocks? Where are the police? Where are the ambulances? It's been a year at least..."

"Nooo," I said. "I saw Snickers just a few days ago."

"No..."

"Yes," I answered.

"No, they kept us for years, man…"

I stood up, and the boy flinched. But I happily showed him my phone and the date and even let him scrawl through BBC News for a good few minutes.

"No no no," he mumbled before looking up at me, pleading. "It wasn't just a dream, man, we fucking lived it. We lived it every day for years, all four of us. You don't know what it was like, the things they did to us. What they did to Snickers…" he burst into tears and this time I realised he wasn't going to recover quickly. I asked him if anyone else was around and he feebly pointed towards a nearby bedroom door.

What I found inside that room was not what I expected. You could have hung it in a modern art museum and no one would have noticed. Milkybar upset me, but I'd done a good job convincing myself it was like a big elaborate ruse. It's easier to believe that than God knows what. I mean, what was the alternative? That those things she'd written were true? Years spent taken away and subjected to humiliation, degradation, and unspeakable torture?

But that room… I couldn't convince myself that was a ruse. I couldn't rightly say if Snickers was in there. But whatever it was, it had been a person once, and now it knelt on the bed in a position of supplication. Their face… it didn't really exist anymore except for the mouth that had been cut so far back into their head I could glimpse vertebrae. The rest of the skull was just smooth, pitted wrinkled skin, like a person's thumb after a long bath. The skin of their armpits, where the arms and torso met, had started to melt together, forming a broken webbed joint that forced their arms into prayer.

All along their abdomen and back, human teeth had been implanted only to keep on growing into strange bones that broke apart stitches and surgical staples, turning into grotesque hairy, toothy tumours that covered their midriff like barnacles on a ship. They knelt in a pool of crimson liquid that looked much deeper than it was, rising to their belly button. The strange lapping water gave off the strange sensation of looking down onto an enormous blood-red ocean. At moments it looked as thin as water, other times it looked as viscous as slime mould. Rising up out of it were ten different limbs, each one thinning unnaturally until it terminated in a single lonely toe. New joints had been added to them, seemingly at random, so that this person was hunched over their branching legs like an immense mangrove tree rising out of a blood-soaked swamp.

And marching up out of the waters was a forest of mushrooms no bigger than my thumb, tiny and identical like neat, orderly buttons, their caps opening and closing in a rhythmic dance that made my skin crawl. And then something twitched in the water, looking for the world like a breaching fish. And I was out of there, unable to even think or reason what had happened in clear terms.

"Look what they did to us, man," the boy screamed as I stumbled past him, tearing open his shirt to reveal a single large black equine eye embedded in his chest. "It took years to grow us into this. Fucking *years*," he screamed, his shrill voice following me all the way down the hall.

And with that, I was back in my car shaking, barely able to think. At this stage I was doing mental back flips to explain what I'd seen and somehow, I got it in my head that what I needed to do was to check up on the others. It had to be fake, I told myself. The only way I'd prove it was if I followed things up. I had to know, it's the human condition and I couldn't walk away. I couldn't retreat. I couldn't possibly accept living in a world where anything I'd seen in that flat was real.

I drove away from that block way too fast, but eager to get on and find answers. The closest place next on my list was an office run by a man I called Aero. He fancied himself as a sort of Gordon Gecko, Wolf of Wall Street kinda guy, but he was the richest man I knew and whip smart too. I hoped to God he wasn't in on all this bullshit and could offer some kind of help or explanation.

Earlier that year he'd given me a security card for his building, and I luckily fished it out of my dash before going in. He had a floor or two in this massive high-rise and I got the card out ready to explain why I needed to enter the building at 2am to some bleary-eyed security guard only to find the front desk empty. It was a simple flick of a switch to call the elevator, but I couldn't stop staring at the half-drunk cup of tea waiting for the guard.

Probably gone to the loo, I thought, before briefly touching the ice-cold cup and calling it into doubt.

Man, it was dark in there, and unsettling in the way that night-time offices always are. Any place that goes from busy to quiet has that air about it. The sense that once everyone goes home something comes slinking out of the shadows to stretch its legs. I felt like I was intruding, but I couldn't bring myself to leave it yet. I was secretly trying to tell myself I'd been hallucinating in Snickers' place, and I desperately wanted someone to reassure me that was true.

I used the card to get access to Aero's floor and walked out into an otherwise dead office space. Even though the sky in London isn't very clear, I could still see a full moon hanging over the skyline, following me like an eye as I walked along the enormous windows.

Aero's office was easily found. It was the only one with the blinds pulled shut, unlike the others that were as clear and transparent as a scientist's beaker. His name and title were on full display, and I could have walked right in, but something about the silence unsettled me. There was the sense that someone was moving around in those shadows, ducking and scuttling below cubicles and desks, just out of sight, whenever I turned. So, I tried to peek through the blinds of his office first without going in, just to get a sense of what was in there.

All I could glimpse was a desk chair facing me, and the dark outline of someone sitting in it. Steeling my nerves, I forced myself to open the door and found a desiccated corpse waiting for me. Although the skin was leathery and dry, pocked with peeling blisters and signs of decay, enough of the features remained that I could easily tell it was Aero. Unlike the others, he looked asleep, peaceful even. For a moment I stared at him, lost in the silence, when something behind me fell over and I whipped around, heart thundering.

It was Aero, looking a little younger than when I'd last seen him. I was shocked to see him after I'd convinced myself of the corpse's identity, and for a moment I looked back and forth while he stumbled in, stopping to take a breath with his hands on his knees, before looking up at me and smiling.

"Oh, thank God you're here," he said, panting.

"What happened?" I asked.

"How long has it been?"

"Huh?"

"How long has it been?" he repeated. "I'm amazed any of this is still here."

"Not long," I answered.

"I spent so long wondering if I'd have to come back," he said. "I thought I'd never see this place again."

"What happened?"

"Oh, who knows," he said. "It's been so long I can barely remember my own name, let alone…" Aero stared at me, his face wrought with confusion and his eyes pleading. When I told him my name, he looked deeply thankful. "That's right," he said, nodding. "Yes, I remember you now. And my… did I have a wife?"

"No," I said, shaking my head. I almost said something else, standing there so close to him. Looking back, I'm glad I didn't. Instead I asked, "Aero man, you gotta tell me what the fuck is going on? Who is that in your chair?"

"I guess I um, I wound up going somewhere, you know? It was beautiful. You should see it. They gave me everything. Everything I could ever want. Even eternal life. I was there for a lot longer than just one lifetime. That," he said, pointing to the body in the chair. "That's the old me, my old shell, before they gave me a younger one. They can do incredible things. It was beautiful. But now I'm home!"

He laughed with relief and gently caressed the carpet.

"Home sweet home."

He smiled at me, turning into the moonlight for the very first time, and an inexplicable wave of revulsion washed over me. I had to swallow it, trying hard to ignore the bile rising in my throat. It was hard to see, but something about his pallor unsettled me.

"Come on," I said, let's get you back to yours. Once more a look of confusion briefly flashed across his face, his eyes flicking to his surroundings before landing back on me.

"Of course," he said, nodding slightly. "Home. This is… this isn't…" I reached down and pulled him up, trying not to wince at the slick feel of his cold palms. Leaning down when I did, I couldn't help but notice a speck of blood across his shoes.

"They gave you everything?" I asked.

"Oh, everything," he said, suddenly gushing. "A human could want for nothing. Oh, the food, the clothing, the knowledge. It was divine."

"And the women?" I asked.

"Magnificent," he smiled.

"Good," I said, trying to hold back a cry.

Aero was gay.

"Let me go get my keys," I said, my voice just starting to break. "I dropped them a while back." I turned and went to leave, stopping for a moment in the doorway to look at the doppelgänger. He was staring at me, his eyes overcome with a frightening intensity. At that moment, I dropped the pretense and ran, making for a twisting path through the office and doing my utmost best to ignore the sounds of wet footprints behind me. I don't know if he was breathing or panting, but it sounded like a gale wind passing through a beehive. I was desperate to put something between this thing and myself, and for a moment I almost ran to the elevator but at the last moment images of me slamming my finger into the call-lift button as he shuffled out of the darkness burst into my mind, and I went for the stairs instead.

The first thing I saw when I opened the door were the remains of the security guard. Unlike everything I'd seen so far, something about him bent over, blood pooling around his shredded entrails, grounded me. He hadn't been altered or butchered. It wasn't like some crazy nightmare. He'd been assaulted and, from the looks of it stabbed, repeatedly. I nearly slipped in his blood, but I was careful, managing to shuffle around it before bounding down those stairs, leaping three or four steps at a time, almost willing myself to fall just in the hope that it'd get me down quicker.

Above me, that thing burst into the stairwell. I half expected it to taunt me, but it just made these shrill, almost birdlike cries of joy. It wasn't far behind me, and it closed the distance fast. It was barely a single flight behind me when it spread its arms, let out a swine-like squeal, and jumped headfirst in my direction.

It hit the concrete barrier hard and broke its neck immediately, falling into a broken pile of muscle and bones just a few feet away. It was like it didn't even know the limits of its own body, and I shuddered at the thought of what it might once have been. As it lay there, a small pool of that crimson fluid slowly oozed out of every orifice and from that strange blood rose thousands of little brown mushrooms, unfolding their caps with the smooth grace of a dancer. Barely a minute later and the flesh within had started to crumple and hiss, leaving loose skin hanging off bones like clothes on a washing line, the slackening mouth leering at me like a drunken idiot's grin.

I don't remember much else from that night. I awoke in the driver's seat of my car a few hours later, engine idling at a green light as a van driver went caveman on his horn. I drove home, ready to write the whole mad night off, eager to pretend it hadn't happened. It was something I might have managed were it not for the brick waiting for me in my flat. Now I've finally caught up with my rest and I'm left wondering if it's worth checking out the other eight people. I have maybe a night or more before the police realise I'm the common denominator for a lot of carnage and misery, and maybe getting ahead of it is the only chance I have of knowing what the hell to do.

But today, when I finally collapsed in my bed, I dreamed. I dreamed of a city on a coast with blood-red waters, a collapsed moon hanging in the sky. I dreamed of things that live there, filled with ambivalence and cruelty. I saw dungeons and torture chambers filled with people toiling away, and amongst them I saw Aero, Rolo, and Milkybar, old and frail, beating rocks with stones while shadow-covered figures grow ready to satisfy strange and unspeakable desires.

And when I awoke, I was screaming, that strange brick burning its symbol into my palm.

A PRIVATE EXHIBITION

"She looks like you."

The old man nodded towards the painting, one of many that adorned the halls of his stately home. It showed a young woman being flayed from the hips down, her skin trailing behind her like a cloak as she carved a path through a crowd of desperate peasants. She looked peaceful, content with basking in the people's admiration, even as they peeled the skin from her legs with notched blades and scalpels.

"It's... odd," was all I managed to say.

Mr Brynshaw smiled like an amused father. I'd expected him to be some trust fund creep after reading about the job, with slicked back hair the colour of straw and teeth too big for his gums. But when I met him, I was surprised to see that he was quiet and dignified, even a little affectionate. Somehow, he was all the scarier for it.

"The artist was very close to my heart," he said. "I was his patron, but it can be hard for people to get what they want, especially money. I thought I was saving him. He died before the millennium, twisted all out of shape on some hospital bed, begging for more drugs."

"I'm sorry to hear that," I said.

"Don't be," he replied. "He wrote some remarkable poetry. Revolutionary stuff that would have introduced us to a new age of spiritualism if he hadn't burned most of it. He also gave me this painting and, in doing so, he led me to you."

"You mean?"

"Jenson brought it to my attention." He was referring to the strange-looking assistant who'd petitioned me at my door three weeks before. "He was the one who brought your application to me. I took the resemblance between you and the painting as a sign."

"I thought that you hired me for my experience as a professional—"

"Oh, we have all those types here already. The educated and the qualified," he said. "But it's not always about qualifications, or even talent. Sometimes I simply like to give people a chance at getting what they want."

"Like your artist?" I asked. "He got what he wanted."

The old man smiled again and this time it wasn't so fatherly.

"I suppose that's up to you."

***

We were expected to wake at 5am and spend the day preparing. Costume fittings. Practice runs. More costume fittings. More practice runs. Hours and hours spent sitting still. Standing still. Posing. Smiling. Crying. Purring. Roaring. Growling. I was sexy, vulnerable, dignified, angry, fierce, quiet, cold, warm, hot… by the end of the first day, just as the sun began to set on the shores of the private island, I was exhausted and ready to collapse.

Only the show hadn't even begun yet.

I'd known we weren't alone, if only because the other performers never shut up about catching glimpses of Prince So-and-so or Senator This or Baron That. Each night we would be displayed for whatever wealthy guests Mr Brynshaw could fly in. But I had to shut that out. I just had to. I couldn't think of princes and oligarchs, of people with the power to change my life, to raise it up out of the dirt, or to stamp it into nothing if the feeling came to them. I couldn't even think of the people next to me. Lithe and tall and hauntingly beautiful, the other performers gossiped endlessly and wore the day's stresses with effortless grace. They were professionals, not like me, but instead like the people I had aspired to be when I was younger. They were performers and dancers and models… human clay to be turned into works of art that inspired and enlightened. There were photos of them in galleries worth more than my entire life's possessions.

For our first piece we were dressed in graduation gowns, only instead of caps we wore old-school military helmets. They were spiky looking German things that I'm sure made some commentary on violence or education or something else. I can't say exactly what because the artist who organised it would not talk to me, would not even look at me. I listened, but did not speak, for twelve hours until the moment finally came, and we were herded onto a stage where I was told to stand in the corner and look forlorn.

There were thirteen of us set in various places around a central podium. A young woman, easily six foot three with the frame of a Victorian ghost, was then guided to her place at the focus of the piece. She tried not to smile as she climbed the steps, but her eyes alighted on me for the briefest of moments, and I felt her smug superiority overwhelm me. I began to shake, to flush hot with sweat and embarrassment, but before I had time to compose myself, the room suddenly burst into frantic alarm and every black-shirted assistant, choreographer, and costume designer fled into the distant corners of the room where they disappeared behind secret doors. Only the artist remained, and he made some final adjustments before the guests arrived.

"Katherine," he said, and God if I haven't heard that exact same phrasing of my voice a thousand times before. "Katherine darling, can you just scootch down, just a little?"

I bent my knees ever-so-slightly, getting a face full of a young man's back. I was effectively hidden behind him.

"Brilliant," the artist said and clapped his hands.

And then the guests poured in.

***

I stepped down from the podium, gold paint flaking from my armpit and crotch. It was the third week. The twenty-first show. Each day, we spent six long hours posing or performing like we were taking part in a ritual. No two shows were alike, and every day brought strange new instructions. Today's task was to remain perfectly still. I was exhausted, shivering, and drained from the sheer physical exertion of holding a pose for so ridiculously long.

Ilanna floated past me, a full head taller than I, not even looking down as she hurried on towards the adoring artist. Other dancers broke away from their conversations and surged out to greet her, and a timid-looking man who I knew to be a guest lingered awkwardly, waiting to make her acquaintance. His movies dominated the box office every year, but he fidgeted nervously like a chubby teenager at comic con.

She was painted silver, only on her it looked platinum. The rest of us were like shabby copper figurines in comparison. This was our first nude show, and I didn't feel like sticking around with all the others who seemed so comfortable in their own skin, so I hurried from the stage and made my way to one of the corner exits.

"Oh Ilanna!"

I turned to catch Mr Brynshaw, flanked by the lanky Jenson. He shuffled up to the precious metal debutante and took one of her hands into his. His eyes looked at her with pure admiration, like she was his favourite daughter and mistress rolled into one. Whatever he said to her, I couldn't make it out, but it looked like a secret shared between two lovers. It hurt to see him talk to her like that. It was childish and stupid of me. I knew it even then. But it still hurt like hell.

I looked down at my legs and saw the paint flaking away and I felt so irritated that it would do that for me but none of the others. I got ready to hurry back to the changing rooms only for my attention to be caught by Mr Brysnshaw. He was talking and laughing, and he had swept his eyes across the crowd in a way that I mistook for his turning in my direction. Only his eyes didn't stop to linger, not even for a second.

He simply did not see me.

***

"Not looking for Prince Charming?"

It was Jenson, smiling awkwardly as he sat beside me on the step where I smoked. We were behind one of the many kitchens that opened onto a gravel-filled bit of yard. Big houses… really big houses, I knew they often had little openings like this. It let natural light fill rooms deep in the centre of the building.

"A lot of the models have been gagging to meet the guests outside of the performance. Mr Brynshaw finally relented," he added.

"For Ilanna?" I asked.

Jenson smirked. I think he was trying to be sympathetic, but it didn't seem that way.

"Didn't realise I'd be coming all this way to be hidden at the back," I added. "It's been three weeks and ever since the first I've been out of sight the entire time."

"You're trying your best," he said with a limp shrug.

"Do I stand out that badly?"

He laughed. "It's a weird job," he replied. "Mr Brynshaw likes the arts. He always has. But he's fickle. He won't have Ilanna at the centre every time. I'm sure there'll be some opportunities to be up there."

"I'm not some teenage girl in need of approval," I told him. "Why don't you get up there and flash the CEO of GE your balls if it's so easy?"

"Oh God, no!" he laughed. "I couldn't get up there and do what you guys do. There isn't a single mature hairline up there." I don't know if he realised it, but he rubbed his hand across his head as he spoke. "For what it's worth," he said, "one of the guests left this for you."

He handed me a small card, my name written on one side in flourishing cursive.

You are a force to be reckoned with, it read. *Shine brightly.*

"Mr Brynshaw?" I asked.

"It's not his writing," he replied. "But someone saw you up there and liked you. I know you feel a little out of your league, but you're not hopelessly outclassed. We hired you for a reason. Just... just keep at it."

***

That night I could not sleep, so I decided to take my restlessness and exercise it a little with a walk around the house. Most of it was open to us, and in one of our first meetings Mr Brynshaw encouraged us to roam the halls and galleries so that we could take inspiration from his private collection. Most of it was a little mundane—obscure blocks of colour and black and white photographs of naked women alongside ugly caricatures and unsubtle statements on all kinds of isms. Any one of the pieces would be worth millions to the right person, but none of it spoke to me. Or at least, *most* of it didn't. Sure, a lot of it was rote, exactly the kind of thing you'd expect to find hanging on the walls of someone with too much money. But every now and again I'd find myself stopping at a painting with a cheap frame, hanging awkwardly over a bathroom door or tucked away in one of the endless hallways, and it would seize my attention.

I saw turquoise oceans with bone-coloured spray, the sky a writhing pattern of fractals that hurt my eyes. Another showed a cacophony of dissected eyes and broken bones. Beside it was a tableau of poisoned men collapsing at their table as the skin sloughed from their body, and they clutched at purple faces. One of the most beautiful showed an endless field of ice broken only by a spatter of bloody fur.

I walked until just after midnight, honing on these baroque paintings that had been so clearly and deliberately understated. Slowly, I came to realise that they formed a kind of secret exhibition, one that threaded between all the others. The paintings were diverse in their content, but all possessed a singular sense of taste that I knew must belong to the collector. If he'd bought the other paintings out of some pretentious need to impress, he'd at least bought these out of a genuine interest. He liked them.

I liked them too.

My favourite was an image of puckered lips, flushed red with matte lipstick, pressed firmly against the orifice of a cigar cutter. The tip of the woman's tongue was squeezed into the hole, and the blade was faintly visible at the corner of the rim. It hadn't drawn blood yet, but you could see how close it was to bursting the thin skin. God, the rush of colours was astonishing, capturing the strange lilac complexion of veins that riddle the underside of her tongue with near photorealism. You could practically feel the pressure as a tangible excitement.

"Do you know who painted these?"

I turned to see Ilanna looking nervous, bags under her make-up-less eyes. She didn't look so big out of her frocks, nor did she seem so unpleasant. She looked young, and I softened my expression and tone in order to swallow some of that ugly jealousy I felt.

"No," I answered. "Do you?"

She shook her head.

"They're in my dreams," she said, chuckling nervously. "I find it hard to sleep."

"Probably just the stress. Always being in the centre of it all," I said.

"I don't mind the attention," she replied. "I think it's this place, maybe. Have you explored much? A lot of the doors are locked off but one of them… Do you mind checking something for me?"

She relaxed a little and reached out to take my hand before hurrying along with me in tow. She reminded me of a little kid relieved to find out they're not lost and alone, and I felt some trepidation as her footfalls slowed and we came to a small door set at the end of a very long dead-end.

"Listen," she whispered, before stealthily sidling up to the door and holding her breath. She gestured for me to do the same and I did, pressing my chest against the nearby wall and leaning out so that my ear hovered over the wooden panels.

"There's someone in there," she mouthed silently.

I strained to hear past the rush of blood in my ears. For a few brief seconds, the world narrowed to a fine point as I focused all my attention onto that door. Quietly, so quiet I couldn't say for sure it was even there, I heard a shuffle. Or perhaps a scrape. Or maybe even a footstep. It was so hauntingly still… I became aware that I could be hearing something as subtle as the shifting of bed sheets, or the turning of a body as it rotated silently on one foot.

And what of me? I wondered. What of my clumsy feet? Or the creaking of my bones or tensing of my muscles? Could they hear me?

I looked back the way we came. We were deep in the spider's lair, so to speak, and I made to uncouple from the wall and begin the slow walk back. Ilanna did the same. Only both of us were stopped in our tracks when a single white card slid out from beneath the door. Ilanna was frozen by the sight, her eyes going so wide and her skin so pale she looked like a porcelain doll. I realised I was going to have to be the one to pick the card up.

A small thing to do, I told myself, but the hairs on my hand still stood on end as my skin came closer to the gap at the bottom of the door. I felt a breeze wafting through, only it was hot and damp like someone's breath. It smelled of rotten meat and perfume.

As soon as I had the card in hand, I stood up and ran.

***

Your friend is unpleasant, it read. *But I'm glad you liked my painting.*

"I didn't like any of his paintings," Ilanna said, giggling and giddy from the fright. We had both settled down on one of the many stairways that curled throughout the house. "I don't know why this person thinks I did."

I didn't have the heart to tell her that I recognised the writing. But then again, she had automatically assumed I was the friend, and why not? Hadn't everyone loved her? Hadn't everyone focused all their attention on her?

"Whoever it was," I said, "they didn't like that you brought me along. Maybe next time you should just go alone?"

She nodded in agreement.

***

Everybody was talking the next day, except for me. Ilanna had been whisked off in a sudden flurry of excitement at around five in the morning. People asked if I had seen her, but I always answered in the negative, my hand straying to the card in my pocket with each posing of the question. There had been a struggle, some said. Something awful had happened in the library closest to Mr Brynshaw's bedroom. Some of the other performers even mentioned screaming. That or they'd wormed the information out of one of the staff. Whatever had happened, it had taken place in some far-off corner of the mansion, and it resulted in an orange coastguard helicopter flocking to the private island where Ilanna was lifted away with a face covered in bandages.

With one less performer, everyone's attention soon returned to the task at hand. The artist-of-the-day was practically in tears as she ordered us around and screamed at the costume fitters to do a week's work in an afternoon. Everything was manic, and before long the mystery subsided, and we were all hurried out onto stage. We were ballet dancers this time, each of us slashed with fake blood and covered with prosthetic makeup that made our faces strangely disfigured. It was stifling and awkward, and it took all my energy to focus on the strange procession we made around the stage. A slew of famous guests Mr Brynshaw courted were paraded before us and I'm sure I recognised one or two faces. They looked approving.

For the first time since arriving, I could be seen clearly. I was not the centre, of course. But at least I wasn't being deliberately hidden. I locked form, held position, and in accordance with the prescribed choreography, I would occasionally change from one pose to another or act out some vague medical procedure.

These displays were agonisingly slow and boring, but I suppose that was the point. A living painting was how Jenson had described it, although it wasn't quite that at all. The fact we were alive was in itself part of the brush strokes that rendered the image whole. Us being there, uncomfortable and tired and exhausted with pins and needles prickling up our arms and legs… that was what it was really about.

I was a living decoration.

When it ended I stayed behind, for once. This time no guests were to be allowed, although the performers drank a little. I managed to speak to a few people and to make a few little friends here and there. One of them, a young man, was actually quite charming and clearly somewhat interested in me. By the time we shuffled out and back to our rooms I was tipsy and happy, and all thoughts of Ilanna were long forgotten.

At least until I reached my bed and pulled back the bedcovers to reveal a bloodied cigar cutter. Beside it lay a tiny little cone of pink meat and I realised with great horror that it was the tip of someone's tongue.

Whoever had left it had included a note.

You looked so good tonight! It read. *The competition should watch out.*

***

We were naked and cold. This meant that we shivered, that our skin grew pale and covered with goosebumps, even our breath was frosty. With the money we were being paid, no one dared complain. But there was something about this display that felt particularly dehumanising. I believe it was a commentary on homelessness, perhaps? The artist had mentioned that the room must be conditioned to the exact temperature of a New York night in December. I thought that was funny given the guests got to wear furs and hold heated cups. If they really wanted to learn about suffering, I thought, they shouldn't do so by watching others.

Still, I kept such thoughts to myself. We all did, even after the first performer collapsed. I was surprised to see a cohort of paramedics rush out from behind some curtains and begin attending to him with no fanfare. I wanted to turn my head to look; I knew a few of the others did, but neither the guests nor the staff reacted.

To my right, one of the other performers began to shiver. I could see him struggling to keep it together. His chattering teeth were the loudest thing in that room. But the audience had become riveted by our struggles. The lazy procession of fur-clad women and old men with pipes slowed to a crawl, and as one they turned to face us, all faces on the quivering young man whose skin was turning blue. Eventually he gave up, a cry of frustration rang out and he began to walk away, only for his body to give up. He too collapsed, his head coming scarily close to the hard edge of the stage as he fell over. In my mind, I knew that meant there were ten of us left, and I swore that the room was still getting colder.

Some of the others made minor adjustments, perhaps thinking the same thing I was. This was an exhibit on endurance, or pain, or some similar thing—they just hadn't told us. Still, it was all part of the show. I couldn't for the life of me figure out why anyone would think of this, but I found myself wondering what it would mean to be the last one standing. To be the only person up there? Standing and displaying it all… perhaps not to be admired, not by everyone, surely. But at the very least, to be acknowledged. To be seen.

I like to think we all realised this at the same time. It would be another two hours before anyone else fell. I bet that was down to the sudden spur of determination inspired by the first two. I knew the competition had worked wonders for my endurance, and it continued to do so even as another one, then two, and then three people collapsed or ran off sobbing, unable to bear another second of the freezing cold.

That left six, *one of which was me.*

The audience seemed to change members without anyone moving, or perhaps the temperature was starting to mess with my mind. By now, snot was pouring out of my nose and at times I had to close my eyes to stop the cold from burning my irises. Sometimes one of the performers would have to adjust, to wipe away the snot or to prevent a limb from giving in completely. A few even took to rubbing their arms and chests. After all, no one had spelled out any game or rules. We'd just decided it was up to us to hold out as long as we could, and it appeared the unspoken rule was that you only gave in if you left.

But I didn't want to compromise the display. Unlike them, I remained stock still until the pain was so unbearable, I felt the edges of vision begin to blur.

I was close to giving up when I felt a flush of hot air. It was so deliriously delightful that I thought it was the onset of hypothermia, but that didn't explain the smell. God, it was awful. A stomach-churning mixture of meat and rotten fruit that made me think of buzzing flies and bloated roadkill. But it was warm... it was so warm that I found the feeling returning to my arms, and then my hands and feet, until even my toes and fingers were tingling with heat. An awkward glance at the others showed them shivering, and I watched as another fell into a puddle of tears and cried for help.

But I was warm, even a little comfortable. The fewer of us there were, the more eyes I felt lingering on me. They were impressed, I could tell. Billionaires and oligarchs who ruled the world and there they were, getting to see what I was made of. Far from what I'd first imagined, this wasn't some display of nubile delicacy. They had come here to see some mettle, and I knew I had it in me to be the last one up there.

Of course, in the end it came down to me and me alone. The last one collapsed with a loud thunk that came from behind and I couldn't stop the smile curving across my face. And yet I wasn't done. This was meant to be a six-hour display, and I knew there was another one to go. So why did the audience look at me like I was going to take a bow? A few of them were starting to look a little worse for wear. I could see that even from all the way up on stage. Their furs would only do for so long, but me? I was basking in warmth, in the hot fetid gusts of air that blew down upon me from above, like the breath of a giant.

In the end, the artist came out and announced the display was over.

For the first time ever, the audience applauded one of our performances and I knew with certainty it wasn't for anyone but me!

***

"You know what happened to Ilanna, don't you?"

It was a young man speaking to me, one of the performers. I'm sure he'd told me his name early on. We'd probably even flirted. But I had been lost in my thoughts when he found me, and I could only say that he looked familiar.

"No." I shook my head and turned back to the painting. It showed a teenage boy floating nude in a void, his mouth open so wide the skin began to tear, his head wrenched back like a baby bird feeding. From above, liquid gold poured down into his mouth, flowing over his lips and over his face and shoulders in shimmering rivulets. Something about the brush strokes made the gold look incredibly three-dimensional, like you could reach out and interrupt the flow with the tip of your finger.

"I don't believe you," he replied.

"Why not?"

"I don't know," he said. "I think you know something I don't. You haven't fit in since day one. I asked a friend to look you up and the last time you did any professional work was in 2008. Since then it's been, what? Day jobs? Retail?"

"It's hard for a dancer to be seen," I said. "The going is good for you now, but it won't last. You know how many people graduate from a contemporary dance school and go on to have nice, long, successful careers? It's hard, and it only gets harder."

"But you're here," he replied, "and they aren't. Smells fishy. Ever since that night when they tried to freeze us to death, I've been thinking that this all feels wrong. Wouldn't surprise me if it's one big show and you're part of it."

"So, what do you want me to say?"

"I want to know the truth," he said. "I want to know why someone like you is up there, taking centre stage after a contrived series of bullshit just to, what? Keep us eager? Make us that little bit extra insecure?"

"Why don't you see for yourself," I said, and gestured for him to follow me, leading him quietly to the door at the end of the long hallway. Lately that door had the strangest habit of always being close at hand, but I didn't think about it much. I had no idea what exactly I was planning on doing. But he had seemed so pleased with himself and his little theory, and me agreeing had to show him something had validated all his petty jealousies.

When I stopped and told him to open the door, I think he suspected something, although it was probably hard for him to say what given that even I didn't understand my own actions.

"What's in there?" he asked.

"I think it's whoever all of this is really for."

He took that as confirmation of some idea he'd been ruminating on for a while, and all hesitation left his face. He opened the door and marched in, ready to demand answers of some kind. I stayed back, my mouth dropping open at what lay within the room. For the young man, it clearly took him a few moments before the signals his eyes received actually registered somewhere in that dense head of his. I can't blame him, I suppose. It made so little sense… he shouldn't have been able to walk in there at all.

It was a featureless void of distant blues and cosmic light. It felt so utterly enormous but also somehow intimate, claustrophobic even. I found myself stepping back so that the door framed the open space, and the young man stood in the centre with his feet resting on nothing at all.

"What the fuck?"

With a spine breaking crack, his head flew backwards, and he began to struggle. His body lifted up gently so that his legs hung freely, and he kicked furiously in an attempt to find the floor. His eyes were flickering madly from side-to-side, and I knew that he was looking for me, hoping that I would come to his rescue. But I was paralysed with terror and awe and wonderful anticipation.

He screamed when the gold came down, crashing over his face and eyes in a scolding mess. Up close I realised this wasn't paint, but real molten metal and, God, it was beautiful. He thrashed and howled in agony as the very meat of his face and torso cooked in its cocoon of boiling metal, only for his limbs to seize up and his body to fall still. He was not dead. I could see that from the way he kept trying to turn and look at me. It was as if something had gripped him in an enormous fist, and just like that, his mouth was pulled open by an invisible force so strong I heard his jaw dislocate with a stomach-churning *pop!*

He struggled some more until finally his whole body went limp. He hung there suspended in nothingness as the gold continued to pour downwards in a terrible cascade. It was a perfect recreation of the painting… even the doorway had taken on a strange golden quality, and I realised it was a perfect replica of the painting's frame. I couldn't say if it had always been that way or had somehow transformed before my very eyes, but I had no doubt that what I saw was real, even as the doorway seemed to shrink until it was no more than a foot across.

Without quite knowing why I reached out and just like that, perspective bent in on itself, and my fingers touched canvas. The door had disappeared and now there was only the painting. Still the boy hung there, rotating slowly. When I withdrew my hand, I noticed a trickle of gold running along my skin. Giggling, I licked it off and relished the chemical taste. When I looked back the scene had frozen, and I was faced with a perfect replica of the original painting.

"You know what happened to Ilanna, don't you?"

It was a young man speaking to me, one of the performers. I'm sure he'd told me his name early on. We'd probably even flirted. But I had been thoroughly absorbed by the painting in front of me. Blinking away the urge to giggle or run, I turned back to him. He looked oddly familiar.

"No." I shook my head, unable to keep a wry smile from coming to my lips.

***

I opened the cupboard door and was shocked to see a young woman staring at me. Her eyes were wide, and she backed into the corner like a wounded animal. I recognised her immediately as one of the performers.

"Good God!" I cried. "What are you doing in there?"

"Shush!" he hissed. "I think the others are gone."

"Don't be silly," I grumbled. "Aren't we doing a show to-day?"

The woman looked at me like I was insane, her anxiety momentarily overridden by confusion.

"Do you even know what's out there?" she asked. "What's happening?"

"A house?" I laughed. "Some paintings?"

"Have you looked at the paintings!?" she cried. "No no no no, I won't let that happen to me."

"You should," I said. "Didn't you come here to be part of something special?"

She gave me that look again, like I was a lunatic, but before she managed to throw any mean words my way, something moved in the cupboard behind her.

"What was that?" she snapped, her head whipping from side-to-side.

It moved again, and I realised it was the wall behind her. I decided to calm her, but when I reached out my hand touched something cold and hard, like a sheet of glass. *Tunk!* My finger probed the surface with confusion while the woman frantically pulled the tiny space apart looking for whatever had moved. When the wall shifted again, it finally dawned on her what was happening.

"Let me out!" she screamed and went to shove me aside, but like me, her hands couldn't get past that invisible wall. "W-w-w-what...?" she stammered. "What the fuck?"

Her eyes alighted upon me with burning hatred.

"You!" she screamed. "It was you all along! I fucking knew you never be—"

Her words were cut off when the wall behind her touched her back. All accusations fell away as she was pushed up against the glass and the pressure started to build. Desperately her hands probed the invisible wall, and I noticed that her fingertips peeked out around the edges. I touched it myself and felt that the gap was no more than a millimetre wide.

"I don't think you'll fit through there," I said, only for the wall behind her to come closer once more. This time it was followed by a crack or two, and the girl's eyes widened. She kept screaming, but there was another shunt from the wall behind and all noise stopped. Not because she was dead, but just because she couldn't move her ribs and diaphragm enough to draw in any air. What little was left in her lungs was used to whisper a quiet plea.

"Help."

"I am," I said.

The wall was relentless, and I stepped back as it pushed through her like a pneumatic press. The colours that were pressed up against that invisible surface started to bloom as her body underwent what one might call a post-modern deconstruction. Pinks and purples and yellows and browns and reds... it made me think of pre-mixed paint. I stepped back and started to appreciate the way the door framed the picture, the space that it defined, and for the first time ever I found the image lacking.

But then she started to leak through the gaps in the sides! Oh, that was a delight, like play doh squeezed through a toy. She flowed out of all four edges of the frame and out towards me like a curling wave of ever-thinning material. It hit the floor and began to fold over itself, and I stepped away to let it pile up.

"Much better," I said. "A far more interesting piece."

Near my foot I heard a peep and saw a piece of her looking up at me. Poor thing, she was still so afraid. She was still trying to move.

"Art can be transformative," I said, reaching down to stroke her. From above a hot gust of wind blew across me, stinking hard of rot and meat.

I could tell that *he* agreed.

***

There were multiple paintings on the wall of my room. They all looked so very familiar, the people up there swanning around. That's if they were even people at all. Some of those photos showed bits of people, or their insides. I admired the collection. It wasn't Mr Brynshaw's. It was mine. I had a card that said as much. It was a shame there were so few performers left. I would have appreciated the chance to show it all off.

One of the paintings was sweating. I took a cloth and wiped it down, carefully trying to avoid damaging the precious canvas. It was fast becoming one of my favourites. I leaned forward and blew on it, giggling as its hair rose on end.

"You are beautiful," I whispered.

It moaned.

I stepped back and looked at the others. It occurred to me there would be another show soon, and I decided to go see if anyone was ever going to come get me. At this stage, they really couldn't afford to forget. The whole thing was riding on my shoulders.

"Hello?" I cried, poking my head out of the door, but no one answered. I kept on looking and shouting, but the whole place was deserted. No staff. No butlers or chefs or maids or aides or secretaries or make-up artists or anyone. On a whim, I made my way towards Mr Brynshaw's wing, thinking that he'd be able to sort this all out. And, if he was open to it, I'm sure he'd like to see my own private collection. I really was quite keen to show it off.

I found him in his bedroom. It was a gorgeous four-poster frame made of stunning hardwood oak; the colour so rich it looked almost like opal. His companions were very attractive as well. No one could ever say Mr Brynshaw had bad taste. I just wish I hadn't stepped in him when first entering the room. But the light was off, and he was just *everywhere*. The women were also in a bit of a state. Still, the room was full of giggles and cheers, and I just had to accept that Mr Brynshaw was occupied for the time being. I left and went looking for Jenson.

He was hanging in the atrium, his wrists clearly slit using a letter opener that lay on the floor. He had written a note that was kept in his pocket, and I took it just knowing it had been meant for me. It was pretty hard to read, what with the bloody thumbprints and the messy handwriting, but I managed to make some of it out.

...in our wildest dreams did we expect this to happen. I won't lie to you and say that we had the best of intentions. But never this, Katherine. By now you must be the last one left and surely wondering what all of this was about. The summoning...

I threw the note aside with a cocked eyebrow.

"Me," I grumbled. "This was always about me."

I gave Jenson a playful little shove that sent him swinging.

"Silly goose," I said before walking away. I was at the door when the rope snapped, and his body hit the marble floor with a bone-crunching thud.

***

I like you.

The card fluttered down from the darkness overhead and landed in my hair. It was always dark up there lately, like it followed me from room-to-room. Although I didn't move much anymore. It had been a good few weeks since the last show.

"I like you too," I said.

I see you.

The card landed in my lap. The words sent a warm fuzzy feeling rushing up my stomach, and I reached out and held it close to my chest.

"Thank you."

I have enjoyed my time here.

"Me too."

They are coming.

"Oh, let them," I said. "They were always going to come."

I must go, but we need the final painting.

A part of me wanted to cry, but I also knew this had been coming. After this I wouldn't be seen by anyone the same way *he* had seen me.

"I know," I said.

You were always going to be the best of them all.

A knife fell from the darkness above and landed beside me, blade first. It stuck in the wooden floor and the handle quivered from side-to-side. Without thinking I grabbed it and looked down at my legs.

In the distance, I could hear a helicopter.

I started cutting…

***

I refused to go into detail for them. It was a ridiculous request to tell them "what happened" and it didn't matter how many angry people asked. Maybe if they'd appreciated the exhibit, but I could tell they were disgusted by the collection. I had inspired an unrivalled creativity in *him*, and he had run rampant making and twisting and reshaping, and some of the things they found sobbing in that house were truly beautiful. A few even slipped away into the ocean, but I haven't told.

They put me in this place, and he's gone. Well, sometimes I feel that breath on my shoulders. He keeps an eye on me when he can, I'm sure of it.

One of the other people here, a poor old man without any hair and who always talked to himself, he asked what happened and so I told him that I had shone like a light, wanting to be seen and admired, and something had taken up the call. I told him that if he wants to be seen badly enough and casts his thoughts out far and wide enough, he can be seen too. It was then that the space above me darkened, and he cast his eyes up and that was when the screaming started.

Now they don't let me out of the room, but the staff do always give me what I want. A laptop, the wifi password, cigarettes, even some art supplies… They must think I'm dangerous and don't want to get on my bad side. Such a silly thing to think. It wasn't me who blinded that old man. He did it to himself.

But I thought he should know. And you should too.

If you want to be seen, and I mean you want it *really* badly, you might actually attract *his* attention.

THE WORKSHOP

"When did they arrive?" Maggie appeared through the blizzard like a ghost, her footsteps and profile having been hidden by the sheets of snow and ice falling all around us. I didn't jump, and once I realised she was looking at the cigarette in my hand, I merely nodded and offered her one. She surprised me by taking it and we stood quietly, eyes fixed on the spot on the horizon where we knew the ship was lying perfectly preserved.

"I had HQ send a drone over with more appropriate supplies," I said.

"So, we're definitely staying then? Sebastian must be beside himself," Maggie replied, following it up with a quiet chuckle.

"He's certainly looking itchy," I replied. "But personally I'd be fine never looking another piece of suet in the eye."

"Utter torture," she groaned, shaking her head. "I've been jogging ten miles every morning since I was 17, but these last few days have been something else. He just thrives off it though, doesn't he?"

"It's his schtick," I replied. "What he does. He only agreed because he thought we'd never find the damn thing, and it'd be two weeks of solid trekking through Arctic winter. But he has his own fund-raising to do, and he needs to work up interest with littler treks like this one."

"5000 calories a day," Maggie said. "I don't know how anyone could do it for fun."

"Well, at least the new supplies are better suited to camp-life. Plus," I gestured with the cigarette in my hand as it burned down to the final few embers, "we can slip in a few little amenities now we don't have to haul every last pound behind us."

Maggie took a final draw and handed me the butt when she was done. I had an empty can of coke I was using to keep them in, personally unwilling to throw them willy-nilly onto the ground.

"The ice is safe," she told me, dropping a bomb like it was nothing. "In fact, it's a few miles thick. We've just got the full satellite data through and... well, it's quite intriguing."

"Why's that?" I asked.

"It's not alone. There's something else a day's hike north. Hard, hollow, and big. I wanted to double check before I told you. It's certainly a very odd finding."

"Well, we've got the ship to explore for now," I said. "If Sebastian feels like it, he can burn off some calories checking out the second signal."

I watched Maggie disappear back into the grey wind before returning to my own tent. Sitting down on my cot, I contemplated the news she'd just delivered. My eyes drifted to the horizon again and again as I turned the words over in my mind. The ship was safe to board. The ship I'd spent years writing about, publishing papers on, researching... Hell, there was a scale model of the damn thing in my living room I'd made by hand as a young post-doc.

The Pinafore was lost with all hands during a barely discussed attempt at finding the Northwest passage. Standing at 80 feet long it was a Caravel, and thus one of the first European ships capable of Oceanic crossings. I'd spent years postulating that it was still frozen in the ice, just like the infamous ghost ship, the HMS Terror. A comparison I happily played up after the success of the fictional novel and tv show based on the lost Franklin expedition. One wealthy benefactor later and I was equipped with more money than my whole department had seen in years, along with the testy, but experienced, guide Sebastian. And somehow, against all odds, we found it after a brutal 7-day hike. Ever since I'd first spotted the mast from miles away, I'd been vibrating with barely contained excitement.

Knowing it was out there just waiting, well... I had no hope of getting to sleep. I stood up from my cot and grabbed a torch but kept it off, letting my eyes adjust to the dark as I checked camp for any signs of life. Certain that I was alone, I began my walk. It wasn't a long way to go. We'd camped a few hundred metres away to keep clear in case the ship was at risk of cracking the ice, unlikely as that was. Still, it was dark, and I got turned pretty bad after a few minutes. Even with my torch, I started to feel the first twinges of panic, but I kept at it until, after twenty minutes of nervous fumbling, I finally saw the mast once more.

It was a barely glimpsed shape in the dark, a patch of white overhead that caught my torch and made me jump. Lowering the light brought the rest of the ship into view, and for a split-second I was dumbstruck with awe. The ship was close enough to nearly touch, and while I've seen bigger ships before and since, something about it made me feel breath-takingly small. It was as if the groaning of the ice beneath my feet belonged to the ship, and not the weather, like it was some great nautical beast crying out to me.

This ship had left shore in 1543 and never returned. And yet the word Pinafore was still written along its side, engraved in gorgeous detail on a plinth as long as I am tall. And right there, just a few feet away, was a ladder that enabled entry. I tried the wood and could have cried when I found it held my weight. I got two rungs up before I fell back down and bloodied my lip on the hull. I didn't let it stop me. Even as the weather threatened to freeze me to the spot, I clumsily forced my way overboard and collapsed onto the deck shouting my laughter into the blizzard.

No one would be able to hear me anyway.

The ship was like black volcanic rock encased in glittering ice. Here and there bits of rigging and wood jutted out, so cold I'd imagine it would tear the skin right of my hand if I touched it. I marvelled at the sight of it all and made a slow and deliberate circle of the deck, letting out a tremendous laugh of joy when I saw the helm was still intact, wheel and all. I thought I would stop there, but as the minutes ticked on it wasn't enough. And when my foot caught the trapdoor that leading to below deck, I found my hand moving towards the latch before I'd had a single conscious thought.

It wasn't easy to open, taking maybe an hour or two. But all things considered, it wasn't as hard as it ought to have been. And when the door finally slammed open, landing on the deck with a terrible thunderclap, it revealed a set of steps descending into total darkness. At the sight of it, I felt a small catch form at the back of my throat. The rigging of this ship had been snapped, the beams and masts broken and gouged, the wood splintered...

I was walking into a tomb.

The arctic is an alien place, the geography profoundly different to what we're used to. Great obelisks of glistening white rock rise metres into the air, walls of snow lie ready to collapse, and a landscape rendered in pure blank white appears to the human eye as faintly abstract, almost surreal. The ground is not solid rock, but floating ice, and below it lies one of the most hostile and unknown oceans in the world. An ocean that is forever ever cut off from sunlight.

I took one last look around at the starlit deck and descended into the ship, the roaring wind fading to a whistle as I ducked below. The stairs led to a small hold with a single corridor that carried on to the fore of the ship where I knew I'd find the captain's quarters. My intention was to head right there and ignore the little things along the way, except what lay in wait for me in the hold was no *little thing*.

I screamed when I first saw the head. It was a gaunt, eyeless, leathery thing twisted into a frozen grin of pain. A gnarled hand reached out towards me, and I let out another shriek and fell backwards, sending the torch spinning out where it finally settled on the monstrosity before me. The scream died as I realised slowly that the thing was not moving, and it was not a single thing. A dozen heads lay crammed together, arms and fingerless hands shoved out in awkward angles, as if they were desperately groping for something that lay just out of reach. It was a pile of bodies, their limbs and torsos interwoven in a bone breaking display of torture and mutilation.

I let the mortal terror drain away, but lost all desire to stay for a moment longer. I grabbed the torch with quivering hands and turned back towards the way I came. That was when the hatch slammed shut, and I found another scream of terror rising in my throat.

***

"Couldn't have called me?" Craig said as I sat shivering under a foil blanket. I was clutching a small cup of hot chocolate, which Craig supplemented with a shot of Brandy when no one else was looking. I thanked him with an appreciative nod. "You know I would have given anything to be there with you," he added.

"Then you're as stupid as he is," Maggie said, stepping down onto the ice as Sebastian started to follow her. "If I hadn't wanted another cigarette, I would never have realised you were missing. You'd have been trapped in there all night with that thing."

Craig looked at Maggie and she nodded.

"Holy shit," he said. "I've gotta go look."

"Let him," I said just as Maggie went to stop him. She rolled her eyes but let him go and Craig rushed off, catching Sebastian just as he took the final step down from the ship.

"This could have gone so much worse," she said, expecting no reply. I imagined that would be the end of the matter, and I looked up eagerly when Sebastian sidled up to join the conversation.

"I uh... I owe you a bit of an apology there, David," he said, looking a little too pale around the edges. "When I heard you screaming, I thought it had been the hatch slamming shut, and you were just scared. But Jesus, that is... no one wants to be locked in the dark with that thing. What the hell is it?"

"The crew?" I suggested. "Shame we didn't bring any biologists with us."

"Your toys can help with that, right?" Sebastian said. "You've got drones coming and going so often we could set up a department store."

"We can take samples and return, maybe set up a video feed," Maggie replied. "As a meteorologist, I definitely feel a little out of my wheelhouse. What about you?"

She asked me the last part, and I tried to think of whether anything I'd ever encountered came close to what I saw in the hold of that ship. When nothing came to mind, I shook my head.

"One fucked up Christmas tree," Sebastian said with a dark laugh, and I felt a shiver run down my back at his words. It really had resembled some kind of tree, and I filed the thought away in my head hoping it wouldn't pop back up the next time I put my own tree up in my living room. "Hey," he cried. "Maybe you can hook the drones up to it and just fly the whole thing back to town."

Sebastian really didn't like the drones. If he'd had his own way, he would have had has doing the expedition with dogs and seal-fur boots just like his ancestors.

"That reminds me," I said. "Maggie has something to show you. I think you might like it."

***

We were told the worst thing to do was to touch or move it, so we didn't. The mountain of frozen flesh and withered bone was obscured from view by some make-shift curtains Craig threw together, and we carried on working like it wasn't there. Craig and Maggie took photos and made an inventory of every object we could find, carefully labelling and categorising each tong and blade for later expeditions. I tried to pour through these items to find something that might give a clue to the ship's final fate.

A dozen or so men crewed the ship in its prime including a surgeon, a cook, a smith, and a cartographer. We found faded broken letters that spoke of mothers and wives, small figures sculpted from whalebone, and ancient bottles of homebrewed spirits stashed away under pillows. The ship's surgeon and resident scholar even had quite the collection of shells that he'd carefully labelled. Here and there we also found a patch of floor stained suspiciously in the dark, or a blade embedded in a door or wall, but we tried to ignore the implication of violence.

The captain's quarters were… well they were odd. I concluded that the ship had disappeared close to Christmas given the sprig of holly fixed to the ceiling. A small concession the captain had made to the season. But the desk was smashed in two. Rope and twine lay all around the floor, and drag marks were visible along the wood along with a few scattered fingernails. There was also a discharged musket under the desk, along with a solitary half-gnawed human finger that lay close by. In the doctor's quarters I saw that the cabinets were bare of the usual oils and tinctures employed at the time (useless as they would have been), though his diary spoke of nothing spreading amongst the crew.

There was a lifetime of work, and the details we captured guaranteed more funding than I could have ever imagined. We had our ghost ship, we had our thrilling and creepy details, and we had one great big inexplicable pile of corpses that would boggle some of the greatest researchers in the University. It was a little scary, but otherwise it was good news.

Sebastian had departed the day before and checked in regularly for the first twelve hours or so. After that he went silent, which we put down to the poor weather or his general single-mindedness. At the twenty-four-hour mark, Maggie became a little itchy, and when she pointed out the silence to Craig and I, we found ourselves sharing her concern. We decided to try calling him on the radio and waited silently for his reply.

What came was a discordant series of clicks and heavy breathing.

"Sebastian?" Maggie asked. "Are you okay?"

But there was only the strange hiss of the radio broken by the occasional breath or scrape.

"Sebastian?" she cried. "Please respond!?"

We tried for hours until, eventually, his radio stopped returning any signal. Craig figured it may have died, or maybe Sebastian had turned it off and started ignoring us. But something about the strange noises had left us all feeling a little nervous. Maggie suggested that he'd just activated the radio by accident, and we were hearing the sounds of his walking, but the breathing felt close and ragged, almost animalistic, like a man approaching death. Still, it was the best theory we had, and we agreed to wait a little longer.

The following twelve hours were tense. Eventually we stopped working and returned to camp, where we tried to contact Sebastian with a more powerful radio and updated HQ to let them know. The ship that trailed us along the coast sent a few drones over the area Sebastian was meant to be and reported no visible signs of the man. No big surprise there, we figured, given just how hard it'd be to find anything in the tundra. But the pit in my stomach grew heavier with each hour that passed without us hearing back from our guide.

After 48 hours it was decided we'd have to go look for Sebastian ourselves. We were moderately experienced in hiking and the spot shouldn't have been more than a six hour ride away. It was Sebastian who had insisted on making the journey by foot, always eager to push himself to the limit, and chances were it had led him to some kind of misfortune.

***

"Is that a door?" Craig asked.

"I think it is," I answered.

Maggie was on her hands and knees staring at the door that was no taller than my waist and embedded in a snow bank. I reached out and rubbed away the ice and snow around the doorframe revealing a wall made of crudely stacked slabs of wood as thick as my torso.

"Who the fuck put a door here?" he asked.

"It goes deeper," Maggie replied, hands cupped around her face as she peered through a small window set into the door. "I think I can see stairs going down."

"Are we sure Sebastian was here?" I asked.

"Almost definitely," Maggie answered, holding up a small shred of blue fabric that had been jammed into the door frame. It was the same unmistakable baby blue of Sebastian's wind breaker.

"He's not the only one," Craig said, reaching into the snow to pull out a wooden knife bearing the Pinafore's seal. "Looks like our ancient explorers came this way as well. And I don't think it ended well." I took the knife and noticed a faint trim of rust brown red spattered along the edge.

"We'll have to mark our path for the future," I said. "And GPS tag this whole area for full excavation at a later date." Maggie nodded and took the knife to add it to our inventory while Craig and I worked on opening the door. It took a little effort, but quickly popped open and swung inwards with a spine-tingling squeal.

The building had a roof so low we had to duck. The beams above us were roughhewn trunks with still-visible bark preserved by God-knows-how-long spent in the arctic tundra. It was a like a makeshift cabin, the kind of thing you'd find in the Canadian or Nordic wilderness. It had the sturdy appearance of Viking con-struction, and Maggie noted a few strange runes stitched across the inner doorway that I couldn't translate or properly recognise, but they seemed faintly familiar, nonetheless. The room itself was a good twenty by twenty metres with a worktop that ran along three of the walls. Maggie shuffled over and picked up one of the stools that was tucked neatly under the countertop, and holding it up, she showed it to be no bigger than my forearm.

"What the fuck?" she muttered.

"Is this a fucking joke?" Craig cried, calling our attention to a small wooden object he held in his hands. It was a hedgehog, or a carving of one, with little wheels instead of legs so it could be rolled along the ground.

"Could be some kind of fetish," I mumbled, swallowing a knot of anxiety in my throat.

"It's a fuckin' toy!" Craig cried, laughing at the ridiculous-ness. "Is this some kind of prank, Dave? Is this some fucked up PR stunt by the University because if it is, I'm not going to be happy."

"I don't know what this is," I said. "But I'm not in on it, and if any of you are, I'd appreciate you saying now."

"Sebastian, maybe?" Maggie said, a quiver entering her voice. She was holding up one of his shoes, the fabric half torn, and the insides splashed with still wet blood. "Maybe this is all his doing? He *was* assigned to us by the University."

I knocked a fist against the wall, and I realised I could shatter my hands against that wood and not put so much as a dent in it.

"Seems elaborate for a prank," I said. "We should work on the assumption that Sebastian needs our help. And if this is a joke, we can kick his ass afterwards."

"Amen," Maggie replied, and together we walked towards the nearby stairs. Footprints were visible in the thin layer of snow that had drifted into the building over the years, and we knew that if Sebastian was near then he must be somewhere below.

***

"I haven't seen this before," Craig said. "This kind of material."

He was holding a toy horse crudely put together out of basic cylinders and squares. The material that covered it was a velvety sort of leather that was strangely soft despite the ice cold temperature. He turned it over in his hand and we both noticed a faded blue patch. I watched him squint at it for a few moments, and I reached out and gestured for him to put it down.

"What is it?" he asked, ignoring my suggestion.

"It's Erasmus," I said, my voice a little hoarse. "The patron saint of sailors. You should put that thing down."

"Why would someone paint that onto a toy?"

"They wouldn't," I replied. "But they would almost certainly have tattooed it onto the arm of a 16th century sailor."

His eyes went wide, and he dropped the toy with a disgusted cry.

"Fucking hell!" he cried.

"That's not all," Maggie said. "I think this is bone." She held up a small carving of the baby Jesus, no larger than my thumb, made out of a yellowing ivory. "Any guesses as to where it may have come from?"

"Many arctic cultures make carvings out of seal bone," I suggested.

"How many of them make fucking toys in a workshop built for hobbits!?" Craig cried. "Am I the only one who wants to pin the tail on the donkey and make the connection here?"

"Do you have any ideas?" Maggie asked, looking over towards me.

I shook my head.

"Maybe an old European colony," I said. "Someone came out here to try and… I don't know. Some religious fanatics maybe? Someone who wanted to recreate the myth?"

"Out of human skin?" Craig asked. "And where the *fuck* is Sebastian?"

The floor we were on was a lot busier than the last, crammed full of desks and tools for woodworking and carving, many of which lay strewn about the floor. Somewhere below us the walls must have collapsed, and that was where the ice was coming from, as the snow that covered the floor was noticeably thicker here than above. We found no obvious sign of Sebastian except for some signs of disturbance amongst the snow that led, once again, to another set of stairs descending into darkness.

***

"That bodes poorly," Craig muttered.

Sebastian's icepick was embedded in the floor up to the hilt. A few strands of hair were still threaded around the blade, along with some coils of rope identical to the kind in the Pinafore.

"As does that," Maggie said, gesturing to the Christmas tree. Not only had the toys in this part of the building grown more demented, depicting men with huge phalluses and women tearing their breasts open to reveal ribs and lungs and hearts, but an ancient, withered tree stood dominating the centre of the room. Its limbs were decorated with withered black prunes and charcoal rope that would have been familiar to anyone who's seen what centuries of decay can do to frozen human remains. The baubles were organs, the tinsel intestines, left out to freeze dry over centuries of exposure. One of the baubles, however, was fresh, making red velvet slush of the ice below.

"What is it?" Craig asked.

"I think it's a kidney," I said. Steam was rising from the dripping piece of offal that sagged from the tree branch. "It's still warm too."

"The eyes on that doll," Craig said, swallowing nervously in the cold. "Do they look familiar to you?"

I turned to the toy he was staring at, its haunted face lit up by the intense beam of his torch. Its expression was remarkably well carved, seeming almost life-life were it not for the obvious colouration of hardwood. The eyes, however, were far too human, and the irises a crystal blue that was, indeed, quite familiar. Unable to ignore his curiosity, Craig reached out and gently poked the glassy orbs.

Only they weren't glassy. They were soft. And Craig's finger came away with a faint trickle of viscous fluid that lingered on his skin.

"They're still warm too," he gagged. "Oh God, they're his. They have to be!"

***

We did, eventually, find Sebastian. He was alive in a sense, although on his very last breath. He had been cracked open like a turkey and left to air in the freezing cold. His skin and bones were pulled apart with expert precision, his face a pallid mask of terror. He was conscious, but could only wail and cry. Blinded and terrified, he initially tore his hand away when Maggie reached out and took it. He was naked, seconds away from freezing to death. And Craig almost draped his coat over him instinctively but stopped at the realisation it would be resting directly on top of his exposed chest cavity.

He was alive for no more than a minute as we crouched there. He did not speak, no matter how often we asked our desperate and frightened questions. The only sense we got of what he was going through was the relief that passed over his face when he finally died, as if he had awoken at last from a terrible nightmare and was free of the terror.

"I thought ol' Nick was a saint," Craig said, wiping the snot and tears from his face after we'd all had a good cry. "If this is his workshop, it's a pretty fucked up place."

"Could be some lunatic who's settled up here," Maggie said. "Some serial killer with a demented Christmas fixation?"

"Doesn't explain the sailors," I replied. "The knife by the door, the tree, the toys so clearly made out of their remains. How could that be a serial killer?"

"So, what are we saying exactly?" Craig asked. "Santa's elves went off the straight and narrow? Is that it? What the fuck does any of this even mean?"

"Does it matter?" Maggie replied. "We need to get Sebastian back to base camp and then we need to get out of here ASAP."

"Sebastian might not be an option," I said, looking over the still steaming remains of his corpse. "I don't know about you, but I don't want to spend another second longer in this place. And as awful as it might seem, we have to weigh up our responsibilities to the dead against our responsibilities to the still living."

"You mean us," Maggie said.

"Yes." I nodded. "I mean us. We won't help him by hauling him up four floors and across fifteen miles of open Arctic tundra. But we can at least make our lives a little easier by getting on with it and calling in help as soon as possible."

"What are we going to tell them?" Craig asked.

"We'll figure it out," I replied.

* * *

We returned to camp a few hours later, taking a few of the less-terrifying artifacts for testing. The ride back was a silent and eerie affair, and Craig mentioned more than once he was thankful it was still light. We managed, with some effort, to get back just as the sun was setting. Watching the approaching night cast a dreary gloom across the magnificent tundra, I found myself agreeing with him. All of us wanted to be somewhere safe, somewhere secure. And the thin tents of our camp offered little enough protection against the elements, let alone whatever else may lie beyond. But they were the best that we had. As if to emphasise this point, when I arrived I noticed them flapping in the wind and dreaded the night I'd spend in here.

"How long 'til the secondary team arrive?" Maggie asked.

"A few days," Craig replied. "We could ride out ourselves using the snowmobiles, but I don't fancy my chances without Sebastian. Not to mention…"

He left his words hanging in the air. I knew what he wanted to say. *Not to mention whatever else may be out there.*

"It's going to be a long wait," Maggie said.

"It is," I replied.

***

We all spent the night in the same tent, listening to the storm pick up until it felt like we were an island alone in the endless dark. At one point, we were woken up to the sound of something outside, and we waited carefully until it stopped. I don't remember when I fell asleep, but it must have been late. I couldn't have slept more than a few hours before Maggie was shaking me awake to the blinding light of morning.

"David!" she cried. "Craig's gone! He's gone! I can't find him anywhere!"

I threw myself out of my sleeping bag and crawled out of the tent. In one swift movement, I took in the destroyed equipment and torn open tents. Something had come sniffing through our camp, and it hadn't stopped looking until it found what it wanted.

"Do you think it was a bear?" Maggie cried. "With the ice shelf melting, they're coming farther and farther in land every year and there have been more than a few—"

She stopped when she saw me bend over and pick something up. I held it up for us both to see—a piece of rope made of rough-hewn twine unlike anything we'd brought with us. It was an exact copy of the kind I'd found lying around the Pinafore and the floor of the workshop, except this one was stained with a bright red patch of blood.

"Fuck," she whispered. "Where do you think he went?"

The storm had cleared up and the morning air was so crisp we could see the mast of the Pinafore all the way from camp.

"You don't think…?"

"I do," I said. "Look, the snow is disturbed along the path. Maybe if he was lost or confused and got lost, he might have relied on the markers we left to find his way to the ship.

"You know what Craig would say right now, don't you?" Maggie asked. "He'd say that's bullshit."

"Let's hope he'd be wrong," I replied.

***

We were half-way there when we found the box. It had been gift-wrapped and left alone in the middle of our path, its top clear of snow. Small footprints, the size of a child's, led away from it back towards the Pinafore.

"This is too weird," Maggie said.

I bent down and noticed the name tag etched with meticulous cursive. *Wilcuma Géowineus,* it read.

"Welcome, old friends," I said, doing my best to translate. "It's Old English."

I pulled on the twine that bound the plain brown paper around the box, and the whole package unwrapped with elaborate ease. Each face of the box fell down one by one, and Maggie let out a terrible cry.

"Oh God!" she shrieked. *"What the fuck!?"*

It was Sebastian's head, his mouth stuffed with blood-sogged straw while his hollow eyes glared at us with terrible pain.

***

"Craig," Maggie cried, her hands cupped around her mouth as she yelled into the open door of the Pinafore's deck. "Craig!" There were no more gifts lying in wait for us aboard the ship, and no sign of our friend on the deck. At one point, I nearly told Maggie that he was probably in the hold, where it'd be safe and warm. But the words died in my throat. I couldn't keep clinging to such a hopeless idea.

"Come on," I said weakly. "Let's head down."

The hold was unchanged since we were last aboard. The pile of corpses entwined in a desperate orgy of violence still stood over everything else in the room. Something about the eyeless faces burned its way into my skull, and once again I wondered how exactly they'd suffered such a horrible fate.

Maggie and I were silent in our search for Craig. I couldn't bring myself to cry out for him, and neither could Maggie. It felt useless, and some small part of me kept telling myself to stay small and quiet, hidden from view. *Don't call attention to yourself,* it said. *Don't cry out.*

We checked each one of the ship's rooms—every quarter, every hold, every cupboard and closet. Until at last we both converged on the captain's quarters, and our breath caught in our chests as we noticed the door wide open. Craig's clothes were in a pile a few metres past the threshold.

"Craig!" Maggie cried, rushing forward. I nearly joined her, but at the last second some flicker of motion stopped me. Before I could warn her, Maggie was on the other side, reaching down. The door slammed shut and by the time I reached the door, a distance that was barely two metres, she was screaming in unspeakable pain. It was a gibbering howl of terror and agony that filled me with such horror I could feel the corners of my vision blur and turn black. My muscles became weak and my stomach damn near fell out my ass. As it was, I could feel a warm stream of urine trickle down my thigh and calf. I wanted to push on. I wanted to slam into the door with all my rage and strength and rescue my friends. But my legs betrayed me. They screeched to a halt and before I even realised what I was doing, I had turned on my heels and was fleeing the other way.

The strangest plan formed in my head. I can't say how or why it came to me, except that in the end it was probably the only one that saved me.

The pile of corpses, as horrifying as it was, was large enough to allow entry in some places. One place in particular came to mind. A small nook, barely large enough for a person. But I went for it, sprinting into the room and crawling on my stomach back-wards so as to slide underneath the mountain of rotten bodies. The feel of ice cold fingers sliding along my trouser leg, hooking on pockets and poking my chest and back, was enough to nearly make me cry out. And when one of those fingers broke off and lay resting on the back of my neck, turning moist and clammy from the warmth, I had to fight to keep myself from vomiting.

I managed to wrench a few arms free of their place and cov-ered myself as best as I could. And then I lay there, suddenly aware of the terrible deafening silence of the ship. The weight of my decision to flee settled in during the long seconds, and I was forced to reflect on the piss that was still soaking into my under-wear.

I could have been there hours, or maybe just minutes. In the scheme of things it was but a moment, although it didn't feel like it. Eventually something sounded out from the corridor, and I heard the terrible squeal of a door swing open. Awful voices spoke in an ancient Germanic form of old English, turning my stomach with the sound of phlegm and inhuman cadence. Whatever I saw move past was not a human, I can say that for sure. But neither was it in my field of view for long enough for me to say what it was. I think there may have been two. I'm not sure. I may have blacked out because the next thing I remember was Maggie's face glaring at me with terror. She was gagged with straw, just like Sebastian had been, and her eyes had been brutally carved out. Except, unlike Sebastian, she was sweating and shivering, occasionally letting out a small trembling cry of confused pain. I know it's impossible, but I swear she was looking at me. I swear she knew I was there…

She started to thrash, and it amused her captors. One of them approached her seizing body and, still laughing, bent down to stick a small red bow to her forehead. It muttered something to its friend and together they hauled her towards the ladder. I couldn't see what happened next, but I never saw her again. There was no sign of her on the ship, or anywhere else. There was some rope lying on the deck, and I imagine she was bound and hauled up to be taken back to the workshop.

I was in there for two days and eventually hypothermia got the better of me. By the time the second expedition arrived and pulled me out—screaming in terror when I'd first cried out at the sound of their voices—the bodies around me had started to freeze to my skin. It tore away like duct tape, leaving long stretches of black necrotic flesh lying beneath. Two fingers on my left hand were gone, two on my right. I still have respiratory problems and my remaining fingers have lost all but the most basic coordination. Which, at the very least, has put an end to my smoking habit.

My story wasn't exactly met with the warmest reception. The official story is that Sebastian became lost hiking to the second signal—which was determined to be nothing more than a fluke according to later scans—and without a guide the rest of us succumbed to hypothermia and suffered severe delusions. Blood-soaked snow along the base of the Pinafore raised some suspicion, all of which was aimed at me. And in the end I had to leave my post at the university after rumours that I'd killed Craig and Maggie in a deranged moment of cabin fever refused to die down. I don't think it helped that when I'd first awoken and pulled my face free of the frozen wood beneath me, I left a chunk of my right cheek behind. I still look ghoulish, scaring even myself when I look in the mirror.

I don't celebrate Christmas anymore, that's for sure. Not that it matters to some people. As we approach yet another jolly season, I'm forced to revisit this terrible adventure again and again. And now, as if to make it worse, someone has been having fun at my expense.

I received a gift—a plain wrapped box with a familiar twine wrapped around it in a neat bow. It was small, far smaller than the one that had contained Sebastian's head. And it opened to reveal one of my missing fingers, quite likely left behind when they tore me out of my frozen tomb. I thought it would stay there, a little piece of me locked forever in that nightmare hole, frozen stiff to the side of some medieval sailor. There was even a little tag.

Êow Winstre Ðês, Géowine.

The words sent shivers down my spine.

You left this, old friend, it read.

THE TEMPLE IN THE LAKE

"You get clearance?" I asked as Kim approached my workstation.

"Some questions about a cousin with a big following on Instagram but that's about it," she replied. "Not the most normal background check I've been through. I don't really the get big deal though. They brought me here. Why do I need further clearance just to enter this funny little place."

"It's about containment," I said. "No one thinks you're going to steal equipment or military secrets, although God knows my drones are valuable enough to the right people." I reached out and patted the sleek black hull of the car-sized submersible laid out on the large workbench before me. "They're concerned about more generalised social media leaks. What they have here... well, it's odd to say the least. Has Alex briefed you yet?"

"Yeah, he did," she answered. "I'm assuming that's..."

She nodded towards the enormous pressure chamber that dominated the room. "I didn't really think it was true when Alex told me," she continued. "They're talking about a possible inland sea that was sealed off 100,000 years ago, right? They say the pressure keeps it liquid."

"That's the official story, but no one knows for sure," I replied. "Unlike Lake Vostok, no one knew this thing was here until they stumbled across it. Alex's team was originally here just doing meteorological work."

"How did they drill a tunnel down to it if they didn't know it was there?" Kim asked as she stepped past me and went to the chamber's bulkhead.

"My guess is they were doing something they shouldn't be," I answered while moving beside her to look through the glass. "You'll probably find the US government is up to all sorts down here and that's why they're keeping it secret. I mean, it's that or what Alex told me is true and that's just... well, it's not possible."

"What did he say?"

"He told me the hole appeared on its own." I shrugged. "The chamber came afterwards to allow access and to stop the water flooding upwards from pressure."

She leaned forward and wiped the condensation off the tiny little window on the steel door.

"Maybe that's why they don't want us telling anyone about it," Kim replied. "Maybe they don't know what's down there yet, and they want to know first before celebrating it as the scientific discovery of the century."

Kim stood on her toes to look through the glass and into the water below. Beyond was a small room with a floor covered in churning black water that never seemed to stay still. The movement reminded me of an ocean in miniature with waves that never stopped. Sometimes, if I stared too long, I felt a kind of vertigo from the warped perspective, like I was looking down on some colossal ancient ocean from hundreds of feet in the air. I couldn't help but wonder what made the water move like that. I figured that it must be driven by forces and currents that originated miles beneath the ice, which was a sobering reminder that I was staring at a direct connection to a primordial abyss unlike any other on the planet.

"Gotta wonder what's down there," Kim muttered.

I didn't respond. She might have continued talking, but if she did it was lost to me. The whole world was reduced to a background hum that barely registered while the water dominated my view with mesmerising force. The currents had changed... I couldn't say for sure, but for the briefest of moments it had looked as if the water had been disturbed by something below. I could have sworn I saw something slithering just beneath the waves.

I shook my head and dismissed the thought.

"Come on," I told her. "We've got work to do."

***

"What's that?"

Alex reached out to the seemingly featureless video feed on the 100-inch monitor. For the last twenty minutes it had shown us nothing but black fuzzy noise as the drone descended into what had been dubbed Lake Saturn. The room stayed silent with anticipation despite the dozen or so people crowded around me as I clutched the joystick with white knuckles.

"I didn't see anything," I answered. "Probably just noise. If anything gets close we'll know for sure. The lights on this thing could cut through brick."

"What are we expecting to see in this water exactly?" Kim asked. "I'd be shocked if life down there is multicellular. It's been cut off from the outside world for hundreds of thousands of years."

A pale thin tentacle whipped past, both languid and lightning fast, as if its size and speed were somehow mismatched. All at once, everyone lurched away from the screens, reacting like the monster might reach through the glass and snatch one of us. For a few seconds we were all dumbfounded until the tension eased and people let out astonished gasps and nervous chuckles. A few scientists even cried out in celebration before scurrying away to a smaller desk to agonise over the recorded footage.

"Well... now we know," I said, utterly astonished. "Multicellular life."

Another tentacle whipped past and the accelerometers on the drone registered a kinetic shock. Not that we saw or heard anything of it. The drone's camera showed only pixelated darkness.

"It's just scoping us out," I said, looking intently at the profile of acceleration on the drone's instruments. The submersible was being nudged a little from side-to-side, but it was hardly under attack. It might even be described as a light cuddle, considering the size of the drone and the monster doing it. The encounter lasted a few seconds at most before the squid retreated back into the deep as quickly as it had emerged.

"Jesus," Kim cried, "the ventral camera and LIDAR instruments measure it at thirty feet long."

"World record for a verified specimen was 22 feet," I said. "So that's the first record broken on this mission."

Kim and I began to laugh like excited children and after a few seconds the others joined it.

"I've never been so happy to be so wrong." She grinned. "Life. Honest-to-God multicellular life. There must be an ecosystem down there. Predators. Prey. Some kind of base to it. Bacteria, fungi, maybe even some kind of plant."

The sub's descent continued. Occasionally the sonar would pick up passing shapes in the void, but nothing else came close enough to register visually. It was unnerving, if I'm honest. Even though I was perfectly safe, I couldn't help but imagine myself down there in that impossibly dark water while unseen shapes glided silently around me, just a few dozen metres away.

It took another hour before we were within thirty feet of the bottom, at which point I slowed the sub's descent and, using downward-facing ventral cameras, looked for some sign of the lakebed. What finally resolved on the smaller screen was a complicated array of strange and irregular looking rocks. There were spiralling ammonites and lifeless shells everywhere, strange bones jutting out of what looked like an endless carpet of bone-white death.

"What…" I muttered.

"Animals must have been trapped in the water when it froze over," Alex said. "Animal graveyards are common when excavating dried up lakebeds."

"This is normal?" I asked.

"No." He shook his head. "Not like this. Not… not so many."

"Talk about an understatement," I said as I began to pilot the drone in an outward spiral. Every camera showed the same thing. An endless plain of jumbled ivory that stretched out in every direction. If there was a floor beneath those bones, we couldn't see it in that location.

"So, what does the squid eat?" Kim asked. "If everything in the lake died?"

As if in answer our port-side camera picked up the sluggish movement of a pale white starfish. Slowly, it crawled out of the nasal bone of an ancient whale and probed its surroundings.

"It's thirty feet wide," I said as I squinted at the readings on one of the dozen screens. "Do star fish come that big normally?"

Most of the biologists were too busy taking notes to answer, which I took to be a 'no', but Alex was polite enough to tear his eyes from the screen and answer.

"Absolutely not," he said. "It must grow so big from a lack of—"

A fish larger than the drone swept past the screen and the starfish was gone. I had the fleeting impression of glassy transparent teeth and an eyeless face worse than anything found in the Challenger Deep. Wrinkled and frowning, it was an aquatic nightmare that left me shaking in my seat.

"What the fuck…?" Kim groaned.

"Jesus Christ that was—"

"Not that," she said, tapping me on my shoulder and gesturing to another screen. "There's something odd about a hundred yards east. We need to take a look."

She reached for the controls, and I stopped her. Despite the intense desire to get up and leave, I felt compelled to see this through. I grabbed the joystick and began to navigate on the heading she gave, my eyes so fixed on numerical readouts that I let my eyes drift from the main screen.

"Holy shit!"

I looked up, worried I'd made a grievous error and damaged the drone, and what I saw made my body go limp. We were looking at a building. A temple, in fact. I couldn't say for sure it was a place of worship, of course. But there was no other way to describe the grave looking structure with its ancient pillars and decorative flourishes reminiscent of ancient Greece. Perplexed, I let go of the controls and sat back, head tilted like a confused dog. In the end, I settled for what seemed like the only logical explanation,

"Is this a prank?"

Some of the other scientists with me actually agreed, Kim and several biologists all nodding while turning to look at Alex, the head of the facility. But the look on his face made it clear that if this was a hoax, he wasn't in on it. He was pale, eyes wide, every bit as shocked as we were.

"Why would we do that?" he asked us. "How would we even manage it?"

"Those steps are thirty feet tall," someone cried before I could push the point any further. I looked away from the screen to see a geologist standing by one of the dozens of smaller screens filled with complex readings. "Can you get closer?" he asked me.

I took a look at the drone camera and approached the first of twenty steps ascending from the lakebed and towards the temple. Pretty quickly, I was able to confirm that each step was a gargantuan slab of stone that towered above the drone.

"This is real?" I asked Alex as he stepped closer to me, my voice an urgent whisper.

He nodded.

I looked back at the screen and saw that I was still piloting the drone up and over the steps. At the top, it was apparent just how out of proportion the rest of the temple was. The doorway, a great big yawning black portal, must have been several hundred feet tall, and it loomed over the submersible like a man over an ant. Our lights barely penetrated the dark from where we hovered at the threshold, but they did show a stony floor retreating into the void, its surface covered in snowy detritus.

In the distance, another tentacle slipped briefly into the light before slithering away. Something about its pallid white features in the sunken dark made my skin crawl, and when I looked up at the crowd, I saw I wasn't the only one whose nerves were frayed. Sweaty pale faces stared at the screen unable to look away but utterly distraught at the implications of what they were seeing.

Here was a building at the bottom of the world, standing impossibly tall and impossibly large, its doorway beckoning us to explore further.

"Should I keep going?" I asked, hoping someone would find a good reason to stop. It didn't matter that it wasn't me down there. I didn't want to push this journey deeper into madness. I was afraid, and no matter how much I reminded myself of the vast distances between me and the source of the images on screen, I could not escape the terrifying fact that the things I was seeing were real. Somewhere beneath my feet lay that abyss, and within it lay a temple beyond all human proportions. And the thought made me feel like my mind was on fire.

"Keep going," Kim said, and I knew she was right too. It was the only choice. "We need to know."

Nervously, I pushed the drone onwards, watching with anxiety as the side cameras showed the edge of the portal sliding by our sides. As impossible as it was, I felt as though I was personally stepping into the temple and could feel a cold draft wash over my skin. I shivered and did my best to push the ridiculous idea aside.

The room beyond was massive. Too large for our meagre little lights to see much. After a few seconds of nerve-wracking silence, I finally found my courage and asked,

"Do the instruments pick anything out? I feel like I need directions here."

"Uhhhh, we're getting something a little south of your position. It's stationary, so it should be—"

The entire room cried out as the drone's camera was violently shaken, the view reeling as if the whole drone was being thrown around. Alarms blared from a dozen monitors as every system registered a dozen violations of expected norms. My hands froze up. I was unsure how to proceed. There was a momentary spike of adrenaline as my body reacted as though I'd been personally attacked, and then training took over and I let go of the controls and waited for a few seconds as a flurry of bubbles and strange shapes flitted past the lens.

"The drone can't be damaged easily," it told everyone. "Not by an animal. We just need to be patient."

Eventually, the alarms quieted as different team members worked to shut them off. Watching the accelerometer intensely, I could tell that whatever was attacking the drone was slowing down, probably because it realised its prey wasn't edible.

"Looks like another squid," someone called, pointing to a dorsal camera that showed a slimy feeler clamped around the hull.

"Just wait," I said. "It's out of our hands now. But if we're patient, it should just leave us alone."

For a few more minutes, the drone continued to move of its own accord, being pulled to and fro by some unseen shape. Occasionally we would catch a glimpse of an overhead ceiling covered in detailed mosaics of a fleshy-looking mountain, or of a beautiful stone pillar cradling an ancient brazier, but there was no opportunity to study these things in detail. They appeared as fleeting blurs of colour and shape. Whatever was down there was wrestling with the submersible like it expected a meal out of it, but I knew eventually it would have to give up.

"Look!"

Whoever cried out didn't need to bother. Whatever had attacked the drone slid around its sleek hull until it faced the forward camera, allowing itself to be seen in full light for the first time. It towered over us from the main display like it was somehow aware that we were on the other side of the camera, but whether it was angry, hostile, or just plain curious, I couldn't say. It merely stared at us with an eyeless cone for a head.

Slowly, the strange creature retreated from the light. That didn't mean it was finished with us, though. One of its longest tendrils remains stuck to the drone, which it used to tow us carefully back towards the entrance of the temple.

"Well, this is exciting," I said after a few minutes passed. "It's throwing us out of its house."

"You're not seriously proposing it built that thing?" Kim asked.

"No," I said. "Why build steps if you don't have feet? I think it's just moved in. Probably makes for great shelter."

The creature stopped just as it reached the doorway. All of a sudden it changed colour, flashing from spectral white to a blood-orange, pulsating over and over while we all stared at the baffling change in behaviour.

"A threat display, perhaps?" Kim asked.

As quickly as it had appeared, the squid shrank away, letting go of the drone right by the temple's doorway. A quick glance at the rear camera showed it fleeing back into the darkness. I was about to ask what had happened when a strange cerulean light flooded the doorway.

An eye blocked the doorway. A pupil-less pale blue sphere that glowed with malice in the dark. Slowly, its owner retreated until a monstrous shape glowered down at us. A faint bioluminescence hung around it like an aura, a silhouette faintly visible in the abyss. Its shape was utterly alien. If it hadn't moved, I might have thought I was looking at a plant, or a strange rock formation. It reminded me of tumours and wasp nests. I couldn't tell all of its eyes apart from the complicated pattern of dots and frills that covered a bubbling asymmetrical head the size of an apartment block.

It was with ever-rising horror that I realised I had glimpsed simple portrayals of this very creature in the temple mosaics, the implication of which burned in my mind like a hot coal. This *thing* dwarfed all reason. All sense. It floated menacingly in the darkness just at the limit of the lights. Of the rest of its body, there was no sign, but I hated it. I hated it instinctively and without reason even as I told myself it was the scientific find of the century. It made my skin crawl and my stomach drop, and all I wanted to do was lash out and get the hell away from it.

Slowly, it raised a branching, writhing appendage towards the drone.

That was when we lost the feed.

***

The wind outside was fierce. The facility we were staying in was situated on a continental plain, not far from a cluster of inland mountains where the wind swept down the slopes and sped up, unimpeded, to hundreds of mph. It never snowed in Antarctica, but that didn't stop hurricane winds from snatching up tiny particles of ice and whipping them at you with terrifying speed. The effect was a whiteout. A grey sombre void on the other side of every window that left nothing visible. No sky. No sun. Not even the icy floor beneath the main building's elevated foundations.

"It's almost too much," Kim said after a while. "If we'd just found a jellyfish it'd be a lot, but people would believe us. But this… it's like something out of a bad movie. How am I supposed to get up at a conference and show people this footage?"

Kim, Alex, and I were sat in the canteen. All the other scientists had wandered off to their own rooms to begin the lifetime's task of going through every reading we had. Every pulse of sonar, every bit of infra-red, every minute fluctuation in temperature and pressure… it had to be understood. Catalogued. Made sense of. In a way, it was probably a comfort to them, to hide from the madness by fixating on the minutiae.

"You know what I think?" Kim said. "Forget any results. I want to leave. Let someone else get the glory."

"Even if we wanted to," Alex said, "the storm prohibits flying for at least another week."

"Just so long as I can be on the first one out," she replied.

"Maybe when the storm's clear we can discuss people leaving," I said. "But for now, we've got enough data to last us a lifetime and enough equipment to analyse—"

"Sir!"

A young man burst into the room. I immediately recognised him as belonging to the security attachment that had flown in with me. So far, the five or six armed men had kept separate from the scientists, and if it wasn't for his sudden reappearance I could have easily forgotten that there was anyone staying in the facility who wasn't a researcher. It must have been an incredibly boring job… at least under normal circumstances. The man who stood before me didn't look bored though. He looked worried and out of his depth.

Alex was clearly the sir he'd been referring to, and the older man immediately stood up and addressed him.

"What's going on?" he asked.

"There's been a breach, sir," he said. "Something has entered the chamber."

"How do you possibly know that?" Alex cried.

"We can hear it, sir."

***

We entered the ground building to find that we had two immediate problems.

The first was that the pressurised chamber was under intense stress. Internal readings showed that water had flooded the room and was applying incredible force against the reinforced walls. So far they were holding, but the pressure was steadily increasing and we knew that, sooner or later, something would give.

The second problem was the sound that emanated from within.

Thunk

Thunk

Thunk

I flinched each time it rang out, physically recoiling from the bulkhead with fear. I tried to hide it from the others, but looking around I realised it wasn't necessary. Alex, Kim, and the security guard were all equally terrified.

Something was inside that room. Something that had come up from the lake below and was patiently beating a tattoo against the walls with unsettling regularity. *I am here,* the sound seemed to say. *I am here, and I want to meet you.*

"We need to release the pressure," Alex said. His voice was shaky, his skin pale. "We need to… we need to…"

"I'm not opening that door!" Kim snapped.

I looked at the pressure readings and grimaced.

"It's not giving us a choice," I said. "If that structure fails it'll be worse than a bomb going off."

"All the more reason to *not* open it!" Kim cried. "Think about what you just said. *It's not giving us a choice!* Do you want to play that game?"

"We don't know what it wants," Alex replied. "We don't know what it is. Maybe…?"

"Maybe what?" she said. "Maybe it's here to play chess? To be our friend? Is that seriously what we're proposing?"

"If that chamber blows," I said. "We get answers to those question whether we like it or not. We can retreat to safety, sure, but it doesn't make any of our problems go away. Besides it doesn't have to be the door we open. There are specialised valves to release pressure and we can use that to keep it from blowing."

Thunk

Thunk

Thunk

If Kim had any counter arguments they were forgotten. The walls of the chamber had shaken and something, some screw or bolt, had flung out and struck the ceiling and punched a hole right through.

"Alex," I said. "Help me get the pressure valves open."

"This is insane!" Kim cried as I walked over to the nearest valve.

Thunk

Thunk

The knocking stopped just as my hand gripped the wheel. A look at Alex showed he was sweating despite the cold. He hesitated to come any closer, lurking a few feet away from me and the chamber.

"I need help," I told him.

"Okay," he said, nodding so absent-mindedly I wondered if he was in some kind of shock.

"Come on!" I cried while pointing to the opposite side of the wheel. Alex was startled by my shout, but he finally started to walk across the vent and towards me.

"Alex, we don't need to do—" Kim started to say before she was suddenly cut off.

Thunk

The final hammer blow was louder than any other we'd heard. It was like a peel of thunder went off right next to my ear. An explosive punch delivered with perfect timing and, I soon realised, in a very precise location.

The valve broke open just as Alex had passed the opening. Water gushed out with tremendous force, enough to knock him back. Internal mechanisms were designed to control the flow, and they stopped the blow from being lethal, but it was still a brutal strike and he was sent skittering across the floor while the water spewed out in a furious torrent. I could see him under the black brine, struggling desperately, and I thanked God he was alive.

I immediately ran over to drag Alex away from bubbling water, even as my mind raced with the terrifying realisation that whatever had attacked the chamber had done so with impossible insight. On some level, I knew it must be scrutinising us, and it took every ounce of courage just to stay in the room.

Alex struggled as I took hold of one of his legs and tried to pull him out from under the water. I paid it little attention and dragged him clear of the flow, intent on helping him, but the sight of a glistening black tentacle wrapped around his head made me recoil and cry out. I fell on my ass and heard a chorus of disgusted and horrified cries as Kim and some new arrivals took register of the strange growth that enveloped the man's head. It was a repulsive cluster of alien muscular attached to a glistening black tendril trailing back through the open valve.

"Get it off!" I shouted at the room in general, hoping to God that someone would have an idea of what to do. Alex's struggles were already growing faint.

Thunk

Thunk

Thunk

Before any of us could take another breath, there was the briefest sound of tightening fibres before the tendril whipped back into the chamber. It passed effortlessly through the six-inch wide opening and did not slow or even show signs of a struggle.

Not even when, with a sound like silk tearing, it took *most* of Alex with it.

***

I had made the decision to withdraw from the study and the site at large. Kim was clearly relieved, and so was I. Whatever excitement we felt over the find was diminished by the memory of having to clean up Alex's remains. I knew I would never forget having to lift the body bag only to realise it barely weighed more than twenty kilos. We had found something nightmarish down in that lake, and the small encounters we'd already survived were more than enough to keep me sleepless for years to come.

Unfortunately, the storm was still raging outside, and we had no hope of evacuation by air for at least another three days. Kim and I were kept busy packing up our equipment, but Kim's speciality was data analysis and not engineering, so there were times where the work fell entirely on me. It was on the second night that I told her to head to bed early while I finished up the last thirty minutes or so of work. But only a few minutes after she left, I found myself staring at the chamber that dominated the room like a strange obelisk. The image of that thing glaring at us through the screen returned to me and with a shiver I decided I would finish packing the rest in the morning. Staying alone in that place for even a moment or two was a stupid thing to do.

"Stephen."

The sound was an electric whisper that made my limbs weak, and my hands falter. Equipment hit the ground with a clatter I barely heard. All my attention was on one of the speakers by a station at the back wall. It belonged to one of the geologists who had lowered microphones down on the original dive and was using them to record an audio profile of the lake below. With everything going on it had escaped all of our notice, but as I stared at the glowing green monitor it dawned on me that the microphone was probably the last remaining piece of equipment still in the water.

So why had I just heard Alex speak my name into it?

I told myself I had been mistaken, even as I decided I would sprint the whole way back to my room.

"Stephen," the voice said before I could take a single step. "Stephen, it's cold down here."

"This isn't real," I muttered.

"I know what the temple was built for."

Alex's voice was the wet gurgle of a pneumonia patient in their last days. It made me think of someone drowning in mucus, of a desperate soul consumed by pain and despair.

"Stephen," he wailed. "It won't let me die!"

His words hit me like a sledgehammer. For a second, I thought there was nothing in the entire world that could frighten me more...

It was then that the door to the pressure chamber swung open.

***

I found myself rooted to the spot with mounting terror as my mind processed the impossible. An enormous titanium bulkhead, otherwise inoperable to anything except powerful hydraulics, had glided open like a creaking mansion door. Black water immediately bubbled forth and filled the air with roiling steam and a cloying stench unlike anything else I had ever smelled. It was awful. A foul mixture of rotting flesh, ammonia, and a musty scent that really was unrivalled. Some kind of flotsam came with, pale strips of strange-looking plants and unrecognisable biological matter. The room I was in was large, but by the time I managed to look down and realised that my shoes were already wet and time was running out.

I turned and ran, desperate to outrace the water that was already surging past my feet and flowing towards the door threatening to trip me. All around me equipment started to topple. Desks dragged along the floor with an ear cringing squeal while computers short circuited and fell over. Under other circumstances I would have been in tears from the loss of data and expensive one-of-its-kind technology, but I was ready to sacrifice anything if it meant getting out of there sooner. I pushed ahead, increasingly aware that the water was fast on its way to flooding the entire space and showed no signs of slowing. Pretty soon I'd be wading through the stuff at knee height.

The thought had me picking up my pace, but I managed to get only halfway to the door before the lights cut out. Immediately my foot hit something unseen, something that moved. I was sent sprawling forwards, completely blind and fumbling in the dark. Despite the water, I hit the concrete hard and my wrist rolled, plunging me face-first into the ever-rising torrent. The feel of it enclosing my head made my heart pound with hysterical panic and, for a second, I wondered if I might already be dead and trapped in my worst nightmare.

Eventually the panic passed and, using my good hand, I got some purchase on the floor and pushed myself up with a desperate gasp. With perfect timing the emergency lights finally kicked in and the room was suffused in the dim pale glow of rarely used fluorescents. I had been thrown half-way across the room and was further from the door than ever, but the water had stopped rising, was eerily still. All the different workstations had been shifted to new locations by the current but were now at rest, bits of equipment strewn haplessly across their surfaces or missing somewhere in the water below.

Once I was standing the only sound was the occasional slosh of water and an all-pervading *drip drip drip.*

Quietly, terrified that the movement would attract attention, I lifted one leg and took a step backwards. Nothing changed above the surface, but for all I knew a dozen unseen shapes were converging on my position and I had no way to stop them, or even know how long I had to live. The only thing I could do was stick to the plan and keep moving one foot at a time. I managed another three steps when one of the desks slid a few inches across the floor. It was a gut-wrenching reminder that something was active beneath the water. It didn't help that all manner of things floated around, ranging from office furniture to unrecognisable clumps of rotting albino plants. Sometimes something would slither past my leg, touching my bare ankles, and I had no way of knowing if it was a living thing or just some dead piece of flotsam drifting aimlessly beneath the surface.

When the door opened behind me, it was a sudden reminder that a world existed beyond that room. It had been barely ten minutes since I heard Alex speak, but I'd spent that time so terrified that my perception had narrowed until I could only think of things that mattered to my direct survival. I had completely forgotten that the power outage would have alerted others. I was so fixed on whatever shared that water with me that I didn't even turn to greet my rescuers or respond to their cries. Nothing but survival could find purchase in my adrenaline addled mind.

It wasn't until I heard feet splashing past me and saw several men stomping past, guns raised, that I looked up and saw Kim reaching out to touch my shoulder.

"What happened!?" she asked. "Did you open the bulkhead?"

I must have been pale as a ghost because when I looked at her she froze up a little, like my fear was contagious

"Shut it down," I hissed between clenched teeth, even as I lifted one leg to continue my painstaking backwards walk. "Explosives. Grenades. Anything. Shut it down."

"It'll freeze on its own anyway," she replied. "The heating rods have turned off. That's probably why it hasn't already flooded this whole room up to the ceiling. Why did you open the door?" she repeated.

"I didn't open shit!" I whispered. "Kim, we aren't alone in here."

"What?"

"He said you aren't alone up there."

Kim's eyes went as wide as dinner plates at the sound of Alex's voice coming from the speakers.

"Fuck this," I cried while grabbing her hand and turning to run the last few metres back to the door. As I turned away, one of the men inside the room cried out and went down, but I didn't turn to look back. Not even when gunfire rang out and ricochets pinged the wall and nearest my head. Instead, I forced my leaden feet through the grimy water, Kim in tow, and did my best to ignore the screams.

When we reached the door, I threw us both out onto the metal walkway beyond and went to slam the door shut but was left struggling against the water that continuously poured out.

"Help!" I cried, reaching out to help Kim from where she had fallen.

"What about the men inside?"

She looked inside at the same time she asked her question. By now the gunfire had stopped, but there was still the sound of struggling feet and crying men along with crashing furniture. With a whip crack sound, one of the men let out a terrible scream and Kim jerked back from the doorway, her face covered in blood.

"*Shut the fucking door!*" she screamed suddenly. Whatever she'd seen had clearly changed her mind, and I was glad I'd missed it.

I was only grateful that she joined me in pushing it shut.

***

"Are you sure it's all done in there?" I asked. "The water's all frozen?"

Kim nodded as we stood by the door to the ground facility. It had been two days, and we had stayed in the base a few hundred metres away, refusing to answer any of the other scientist's questions and threatening hell on anyone who dared go look for themselves. It certainly hadn't earned us any friends, but we didn't care. Our evac was just an hour out and we were all too ready to leave that God forsaken continent.

But there was still one last job to do.

Using a crowbar, I wrenched the door out of its frame. Kim made a passing comment that whatever lived down there could have easily gotten out of it wanted to, but I just ignored it. I had no way of knowing what that thing could or couldn't do, and for once ignorance was enough for me. Whatever its motivations or choices, it had been content with taking the men we'd left behind and no one else. To my shame, I only felt relief about this.

"Steeeephen!"

"I'm so cold!"

"My mind is falling apart. I can feel bits of myself sloughing aw—"

"What are you? I can't see you. Where am I?"

"What was that?"

"Something's coming."

"Jesus fucking Christ why won't I die!?"

Kim faltered at the sound of their voices. She looked at me with terror and I knew she'd seen the same thing written on my face.

"You were right," she said. "They're still…"

I nodded. "I could hear them when I came out to check the door on the first night."

"I don't… how are they? Are they down *there?*" she cried.

"I don't know." I shook my head. "But there'll be a team here soon. They'll find the tunnel frozen over, the facility destroyed, our data centres ruined. But this…"

I gestured to the room and the voices within.

"This will demand further investigation," she said. "How can we get them to stop? Do you have a plan to help them?"

To get inside the room I had to step up onto a solid foot of ice that had frozen. Emergency lighting had failed entirely by now, but there was enough daylight to make the gloomy space beyond visible.

"Their heads…" Kim stuttered as she looked at the array of corpses. "They're all gone. How are they… I don't…"

"I don't understand either," I said as I carefully shuffled over to the farthest workstation. It was there that the voices cried out from an overturned speaker. "But we can't help them."

I hesitated for a moment as I took out the wire cutters and found the cord leading to the ruined pressure chamber. Even now, the men hadn't stopped baying like a discordant mob of hellbound souls. There were pleas for help and desperate insults borne of desperation. I wondered for a second if there really *was* something we could do. But that would involve drilling down to the lake and beginning this nightmare anew. This wasn't some errant animal we were dealing with. It was intelligent, and cruel, and older than we could possibly imagine. Even worse, it could toy with dead men and keep them alive to prolong their suffering.

There was a forgotten god down there. It needed to *stay* forgotten.

I cut the wire, and the voices stopped immediately.

"But they're still down there," Kim said, her voice an injured whisper.

With deliberate slowness the wire was pulled from my hand and back into the chamber before disappearing through a pinprick hole in the ice.

"And so is something else," I said. "Let's keep it that way."

POMPILIDAE

I never thought in a million years I'd be posting this kind of thing. My whole life it's been one friend zone after another. There have been a few times where I've had a real meaningful connection with a girl, but most of the time something goes wrong, or it turns out they're a psycho. They'll talk about how they want romance, but freak out when you surprise them. And, unfortunately, if you're like me and you struggle to understand people or you're prone to taking statements at face value, that makes you a very vulnerable target. A lot of girls have used me in the past, exploiting me for money, free rides, and most of all, as an emotional shoulder to cry on. In my experience, most women love to play games, flirting with you one moment and then withdrawing the next. And by doing that, they can keep guys like me dangling for years because we're just too trusting.

That's what makes Valery different. She's never asked me for anything like that. And I know she's super smart. The way we communicate is so fun. She does such clever little things, like leaving me a note asking me to leave the apartment block door open so she doesn't have to find her keys in the dark. It'll just be a note pinned to my door, but it's her way of letting me know that she's thinking about me.

Other times she'll ask me to hold a door open while she walks past with her groceries. When I do, she'll look at me and smile in a way that makes it clear she likes me. God, her eyes just light up when she looks at me. It's unbelievable. She has this mousy brown hair that's shoulder length and I notice that when she goes out to work she wears nice, conservative clothing. But when she's just walking around the apartment block, washing clothes or collecting post, she wears low-cut tops and loose pyjama-shorts that just draw your eye to her thighs.

It's obvious she knows how those clothes are gonna catch my eye and I appreciate it. For men, sex is a huge driving motivator, but for women it's not. None of the girls I've been with were very enthusiastic about sex with me. So, it means a lot to me when a girl reaches out and offers some kind of intimacy, even if it's just a small thing like wearing a short skirt or exposing their shoulders.

But it's more than just attraction. We have a really deep connection. Sometimes she'll walk downstairs barefoot and I'll say,

"Nice shoes," and she'll laugh. Over time, it's became our little in-joke. We've had this back and forth for nearly a year. I always try to catch her going up her stairs and I come out and ask how she is and she'll smile at me and laugh at my lame jokes and it's just perfect.

And I've needed it. I've been in a dark place for a long time. I came out of university and got a job working from home and without any real reason to go outside I pretty much just stopped. I played games, jerked off, and ate pizza. I've gone weeks without leaving my flat. It was like that for so long. I became scared of going outside or speaking to other people. And then one day she turned up and, unlike so many people I know, she went out of her way to be nice to me.

Without those flirty moments I think I might have gone all the way down a dark path that ends with suicide. But now that she's moved in… well, I go outside and she'll be in the hallway, laundry basket tucked under her arm, just waiting to ask me questions about my day. And not just generic stuff either. She remembers things I talk about, and she asks how it's going. She'll ask about my work projects, or my hobbies, or if I'm excited about a new game, she remembered me mentioning.

It's incredible to have that kind of meaningful relationship. And lately, I think it's been escalating. Just the other week, she left a pair of panties outside my door. It was so clever that she left them there after doing a load of laundry. But, c'mon, right outside my door? It's so smart because it's clearly deliberate, a kind of breadcrumb to remind me of why I need to come out of my shell and approach her more directly, but it's also just accidental enough that I don't feel too much pressure. Sometimes girls don't know just how much we want them, and how much time we spend staring at them and thinking about them. When a girl does something like that, it's like she's saying,

"Yeah, I know you're watching. Here's a bone to keep you going through the drought."

And honestly, no other girl in my entire life has made me feel cared for like that.

That's why I need to keep her safe. I don't think she knows, but I managed to get into the CCTV for the building. The landlord asked me to help set up the internet in this place and I got him to let me take care of the building's IT stuff in return for a rent reduction. Now I can check the cameras all throughout the public areas of the block. Well, it's really good I can do that because lately I've had to intervene to keep Valery safe. One guy followed her home from a night out and I could see her lean into his ear and whisper something, telling him to leave. Poor girl was probably too scared to say it out loud. But then she trotted up the stairs, and he waited a moment and followed.

The thought of how he would have hurt her... it makes me scared. Not for her, but for him. Because the things I would have done to him... he would be begging for his life. I don't think that guy can even imagine what this 350lb almost-six-feet-tall silverback would have done to him if he'd hurt one hair on Valery's head.

After he went upstairs, I went and buzzed her flat over and over. It must have scared the guy away though, because when she answered she said her place was empty. She was sweaty and her clothes were torn, but she told me she was just exercising. I couldn't give away the fact I'd been watching her because it's important to seem aloof and I don't want to come off as needy, but the guy never actually left her flat. I checked the cameras over and over to make sure he wasn't lying in wait, but nope, he went up the stairs and never came back down.

Thing is, there's no back door in this building. There's just the one entrance. That can only mean one thing:

He was so scared of me he jumped out the window.

That's exactly the kind of protection I can bring to Valery. It's very important to me that I can keep her safe. Unfortunately, I'm worried about how a relationship is going to work if she makes it so hard to protect her. Because the big thing is that this incident wasn't a one off. It keeps happening. I've taken to hanging around the front door when she goes out so that when she comes back I'm here waiting, ready to shoo any guy away. She always seems really icy and weird at the time, but whenever we meet afterwards, she's clearly appreciative because she's back to normal, smiling and asking how I am.

I wonder, is it just fear that makes her seem annoyed when she comes home and finds me waiting? I can't help but wonder what she thinks is happening when she lets these guys follow her home. She's putting herself at risk. Thank God I'm there to intimidate them because none of them ever come back out the front door. They must walk straight up the stairs to her place and jump right out the window just to avoid passing me again. That's a pretty crazy thing to do, considering it's not the ground floor.

I will say, Valery is young. And I'd like to think as she grows up, she'll become a more sensible young woman. But that's not the only red flag for me. There are others. For one, there's hygiene. Valery always looks incredible, and she smells great. But the few times I've got a whiff of her flat it's been...

I don't want to come off as alarmist. It's just it smells fucking awful, like eye-watering, skin-blistering, paint-peeling, fucking awful. Like my dad used to say, "That smells worse than a dumpster outside a zoo in the middle of August!" And the smell coming out of Valery's apartment fits that saying perfectly. I mean, it's really hard to maintain this image of a precious little princess when you know she lives in a place that smells like a post-orgy butcher shop. I tried to get a glimpse of her flat when she answered her door that one time, but it was all dark. Again, I know she isn't perfect. I just didn't expect one of her little quirks to be so gross.

I don't even know what's making the smell, but I know the guy above her made a bunch of complaints via snarky post-it notes but he stopped recently. At first, I totally blamed him (how dare he say something mean about my girl!?) but now the smell is starting to seep downstairs. I'm pretty grotty myself but sometimes I smell it and it's just like... holy shit, she lives in that? I'm concerned for her health if she doesn't get out of that unhygienic place. It's too embarrassing for me to approach her about it, so a while back I figured maybe I'd try and speak to the guy upstairs and get him to file a real complaint with the landlord.

I knocked for like ten minutes and didn't get an answer. Thankfully I'm super close with the landlord and a while back he gave me a master key because I needed to get into various crawl spaces between floors to lay ethernet cables down. Long-story short, I made a copy before I returned it to him. I swore I'd only use it in case of emergencies, but I figured maybe it was an emergency and, if anyone asked, I'd just say the door was open.

I didn't expect the smell to be so bad. It wafted out when I pushed the door open, and it was almost as bad as Valery's place. The apartment beyond was dark and humid and crazy hot. The old guy had pumped the central heating up to maximum, and the effect was like walking into Jumanji. I called out his name, but no one answered, so I started exploring. It was the usual old guy place: newspapers were everywhere, magazines piled up high, for some reason he had a radio he still used (boomers, amirite?), and a bunch of microwave meals. I did see some pictures of him with his late wife and wooh, she was not a looker. I couldn't imagine how some men settle for women that look like that. He actually looked happy in his wedding photos. How sad is that?

Anyway, I went through his apartment but couldn't find the old guy. I did, however, find the source of the smell and clearly there must be some kind of infestation. I don't know if there are cockroaches or wasps or some crazy exotic pet that got loose in the building because something had piled up a bunch of rubbish in the bathtub and started making some kind of hornet's nest out of it. It was about chest high and shaped like a weird bubbling island that jutted out of water the colour of blood and oil. The hive itself was made of rotting meat, chewed up paper, discarded fruit, and all kinds of random stuff. Hell, there was even the old man's robe in there, and that guy *never* took that thing off. Looking around a bit more, I saw that the fridge door was wide open, and it was completely empty, so the old guy must have taken all his food and put it in the bath. Weird, right?

Either way, the nest looked completely emptied. Whatever had made it was long gone now, so I decided to give it a little poke. It felt like rotten wood beneath my finger, but it was somehow greasy. It left a residue on my finger the colour of Bolognese grease and it stank for days. I sniffed my finger and started gagging when out of nowhere this groan came from the hive and it moved, just a little bit. It sounded an awful lot like someone saying "help", but it was so muffled and I was so scared I didn't really get a chance to think about it because I was running for my life!

Looking back, I'm 99% sure I heard it wrong, but there was no denying that whatever was in that hive sounded an awful lot like a person. I've tried googling to see if I could find out what that thing was, but I couldn't find anything useful. Whenever I search "bugs that sound like people" it just shows me a bunch of children's films. There must be something in nature that makes that noise because sometimes when Valery goes out I sneak up to her door and press my ear close to it and I hear the same thing. It's all weird and distorted, but it definitely sounds like the word "help". The infestation has clearly spread and whatever bug is responsible could be dangerous.

I even dared to open her door once just to see if I could glimpse how bad her apartment is. I literally just popped it open and looked. It was too dark to see anything, but she must have some kind of pet because something came stumbling out of the dark towards me. It was like a person made of paper or rotting wood, with their back and face covered in little white bumps about the size of a pea. This thing covered the distance so quickly, even though its hands looked awkward and clumsy as it slapped them down on the floor to come towards me. When it opened its mouth, there was nothing but this swollen piece of meat that stopped any sound. It looked like raw steak and it dripped grease the same colour as the bath. I cried out and slammed the door shut, but a second later something thumped against it.

That's when I finally realised what was happening! I can't believe it didn't occur to me earlier, but Valery must work in special effects! I felt like such an idiot as the thought sunk in. I always knew she was a creative. Women always are. Anyway, it suddenly made sense why there was that hive upstairs and why Valery was taking so much stuff out to the bins. It might even have explained the smell, although that doesn't necessarily make the hygiene aspect any better.

I do worry that Valery knows I opened her door. Earlier today I saw her dragging something in a big thick bin bag down the stairs. I rushed out to help her and went to help, but she pulled it away and looked at me real angrily. She snapped at me, telling me to leave her alone. For a second I almost listened, but girls never really know what's best for them, so I went to take it anyway. Unfortunately, I just ended up ripping it. I expected Valery to get really upset with me, maybe even cry, but both of our eyes were drawn when something plopped out of the sack that thudded its way down the stairs like a rotten cantaloupe.

I ran down and looked at it, not knowing what it was at first. It looked like a bunch of unhardened papier mâché and it was very similar to that nest from the old man's place, but drier. When I reached down and picked it up, I saw that it had hair and these empty eye sockets and even a stump where the neck should be and there were thousands of pockmarks all along the face, like little dents or burrows. That's when I realised this was the prop that I'd seen in her flat! I asked her,

"Do you work in special effects? It must be a uh," I took a good look at the head. It didn't look very realistic at all. Everything was out of proportion and all bloated. "Is this a work in progress?" I asked politely. I don't know why, but I kind of muttered, "I'm sure you'll get better." I wanted to sound reassuring, but as soon as I said it my heart dropped. I didn't want her to be upset with me!

Thankfully Valery just kind of stopped, looked at, and then laughed her ass off. If anything, I think she appreciated my honest criticism. Afterwards she smiled this sort of cheeky flirty smirk and asked me to help clean it up with her, so I did. It took hours for us to do it properly, but being knelt down together, scrubbing the floor, was the closest we'd ever been physically, and I liked it. Plus, I got to see just how creative she was because there was all kinds of cool stuff in that bag, including mulched up feet, severed fingers, and these crazy wasps the size of my fist. None of the human stuff looked any good, but the bugs were amazingly detailed and so realistic. One fell out of the face's nose and when I picked it up, Valery looked so sad. I asked what was wrong with this decoration—pointing out just how realistic it was—and she said that sometimes the process just doesn't work out.

I almost made a joke, but I could see just how bummed out she was about it. Personally, I couldn't see what was wrong with it. The feel of the wasp's hair, that long creepy stinger, and the way it plopped out of the guy's nose, it even had bits of gore in its mandibles! It was so realistic I reckon she'll be famous one day, like Tom Savini. But I also know what it's like to feel like a failure no matter what, so I just put a hand on her shoulder and said it'll be okay. I think it paid off because afterwards she asked if I wanted to come up to her place for coffee.

One weird thing was that, early on during the cleanup, she looked up at the camera for a real long time and her eyes narrowed, like she just realised something important. For a second I wondered if she realised how I'd seen her struggling on the cameras, but aside from the weird look, she never mentioned it. And besides, during the cleanup she was super nice to me, asking about my family, my parents, if I have any siblings or friends. And then, finally, she asked if I wanted to come up! I could have squealed like a schoolgirl when she said that. Obviously, I said yes!

I am nervous though. What if she keeps doing risky things like letting men follow her? And what if she's a really bad homemaker? I've smelled her flat and I'm not sure I want a woman who prioritises her career over basic domestic chores. I guess I'll just have to wait and see.

ZOLG

The Zolg was there before me. As much a fixture of my life as gravity or air or the sense of my own body. It exists in even my earliest memories as a constant warning against carelessness. It was there when I brushed my teeth, giggling in the bathtub. It was there, stealing food that fell under the table at every meal. It was there, sitting above my bed, stroking my hair with hands the size of dinner plates. Every morning there were new rules, all learned from close calls that happened the day before. Every week we reviewed its effect on us, how to improve, how to be smarter, how to be safer. For a long time, I couldn't even distinguish the rules made for it, and the rules made for us.

Don't touch the oven when it's on.
Be careful of the kettle.
Don't play with plug sockets.
Don't put cables in your mouth.
Watch where you step.
Never use any appliance without first checking the wiring.
Always help daddy look for the Zolg as he backs out of the driveway.

Rules upon rules upon rules, growing in number and complexity until we felt stifled, all of us slowly going mad from the suffocating need for constant vigilance. Other teenagers had fun, other teenagers stepped away from the rules and embraced freedom. That's what adulthood was meant to be about (or so I thought at the time). But not for me. The rules just kept growing. Eventually, I realised that other families don't have Zolgs, just us. There's only one of him and whatever inexplicable force brought him into

existence saw fit to put him with us. For years it had never occurred to me to evaluate its presence as anything other than a
simple fact of life, but when I saw the madness for what it was
something inside me changed.

A hatred crystallised into an icy core. I was filled with memories of his little egg-shaped body and lanky arms with those huge
yellow-green hands. Whole nights spent listening to him waddling
down the hallway as he scratched his dangling yellow fingers over
the walls, gagging at the things he'd sneak into Mum's cooking,
crying at every dead animal left on our doorstep. I hated that stupid
thing; I hated it so much that one day I snapped and lashed out.

Whack! I hit it so hard it flew off the table where it had been
dancing on my plate, and it hit the wall with a satisfying thud. I
expected my mother to fly into a rage at this blatant transgression
of family law, but instead she just ran up and held me, stroking my
cheek. It felt like a nightmare, my mother clutching me and
everyone crying and shouting while that thing laughed from where
it lay. *Why didn't it hurt? Hadn't I hit it?* And then, as slow as a
sunburn, a red outline of my own hand formed on my face, and I
came to learn exactly what it was the Zolg was after.

It wanted us to hit it, to kick it, abuse it, kill it. It wanted our
malice, our frustration, our carelessness. It wanted nothing but our
suffering and anything we did to it just came back onto us.

A hundred times worse.

A hundred times as slow.

You should see what a broken bone looks like when it takes
four hours to render into existence. Bone looks like putty being
pulled apart by a child, skin reddens and depresses into long
streaky welts, layers of tissue and membranous flesh pull apart
laterally until finally it all tears with glacial slowness. It looks like
quivering despair, like grief, not screaming agony, because when
pain is that horrific and that unstoppable you don't yell or cry or
shout, you give up. You retreat. You turn catatonic and switch off.

Or you just die.

And the Zolg, despite its rockslide teeth and leering gin and
hillbilly giggle, is smart and patient in surprising ways. Every time
I touch an oven, or a car, or even just a light switch, I need to think
a thousand things over. Did I remember to check the walls? To
look at each and every plug socket? Have I seen the Zolg anywhere? Has it got its grotesque mouth clamped around a cable just
out of sight, waiting for me to plug it in or switch it on? Has it

wrapped its mouth around the exhaust of my car, ready to suffo-
cate?

Every action and consequence has to be thought out in the
most explicit detail. Every bump on the road has to be investigated
lest it turn out that the Zolg has cleverly watched you for days,
traced where you work so it can slip out one night and waddle
breathlessly to an ideal overpass bridge. My brother once broke
two ribs when it managed to leap in front of a ball he went to kick.
My sister spent three weeks in hospital after she poured bleach
down the kitchen sink, failing to notice that the Zolg had un-
screwed all the pipes and was waiting to gleefully gulp down
poison.

I'm the only one left now.

My father was the first to go, not because he was careless, but
because he always took it upon himself to do as much as he could.
You couldn't even turn the TV on without him insisting on pressing the button for you. It always felt so controlling, so stifling, but
once he was gone, it became pretty clear why he did it. It was
never the same without him… Mum tried so hard, but it was never
the same. She had her own fears, her own struggles to contend
with. I really can't blame her for not being able to do the work of
both of them.

I remember coming home from school and they were waiting
for us in the living room. My older brother had gotten back before
us and was sitting silently at the kitchen table, tears welled up in
his eyes. God, that was the hardest. Dad looked… well, he almost
looked relieved. But seeing my nineteen-year-old brother cry was
like a concrete block to the face and in that instant, I knew something horrific had happened.

They hid him away. I still don't know exactly what happened,
but I made a pretty good guess from the state on the lawnmower
that Mum dragged out to the curb and the fact we wouldn't see the
Zolg again for at least eight days. I'd later learn that in moments
like that it'll stow away and knit itself back together slowly, which
at the very least explained the giggling I heard coming from the
linen closet during those horrible silent nights. Dad never did
scream… I'd hazard a guess that he killed himself and I know I
should feel some relief, but I glimpsed his body on the way out and
the thought of those injuries happening to a lifeless corpse just
sends shivers down my back.

We never mowed the grass again. It was a loss too great, and over the next few weeks Mum deteriorated. She started drinking, crying late into the night while my brother would cook us food and tell us that everything would be okay. But it never would, never again. She only got worse. She might have had a chance if it was just us… but we couldn't just abandon our vigilance, our paranoia and fear, and we had to carry on as normal. Jesus Christ, we even had to check Dad's coffin before burying it.

For a while there, she almost came back. Looking back, it couldn't have been more than a day or two, at most, but she did manage to set the table for us… just once. We were all there, dad dead and buried and none of us having seen the Zolg since his death, when from upstairs a door slammed shut and Mum was so startled she dropped the food she was holding. Its flat hairy feet slapped down the stairs one by one while its heavy wet gurgles punctuated our horrified silence. With a sort of mounting disbelief, I watched it walk up to the table that obscured its stumpy little body from my view and drag itself up onto one of the chairs.

Dad's chair.

Dad's place.

Mum had even set a plate for him, if only by instinct. And you know what? It didn't look at me, or James, or Laurie, it looked at Mum. It *knew* what that single gesture would do to her, and it laughed the whole time we had to pin her down and stop her from driving a knife right into its face. It gibbered and howled with such joy at her threats, but we stopped her from doing it. And after that, I don't think she was ever the same.

That was when the drinking started. It was also when James became the new favourite. It had always shown a special interest in Dad and without him around it fell on James to become the focus of its attention. We always thought we'd been doing such a good job, but without Dad things felt a thousand times harder. James was injured six times in as many months, and things were never much better after that.

I remember he took me fishing. He asked Mum to keep an eye on the Zolg and stop it following us, and we went together and for a few blissful days it was just us and no one else. And he told me all about the lessons he had learned in the last few months, told me about the Zolg's favourite resting place, some of the intricacies he had deduced, and more importantly that I would have to steel myself and be ready for what happened if he ever failed.

And, like all of them, he eventually did. But not before we found Laurie crushed to death. We think she dropped the microwave on it, but we can't be sure. It was her first week at university and she didn't even call to tell us, but we knew she was aware she'd done it because she called in sick to all her classes a day early. And then she just locked the door and let it happen. We didn't even realise the Zolg had found her, but it had somehow. And the sight of her lying on her bed, pulped to the thickness of a few planks of wood as it giggled and jumped on her broken remains, will forever be lodged in my mind. I like to think she found a way of ending it, but I don't know that at all. She could have sought help, something to ease the pain, I'm sure of it. But we don't know for sure, and I have to wonder if she felt it all, every second of it.

She was in there all alone for at least a day and a half.

James disappeared for a few months after that, and it was just me and mum. When James finally returned, he stank of booze and had this haggard look about him, and I couldn't help but wonder what he'd done in that time.

"It'll get me," he said, "sooner or later. I just wanted a taste of what life had to offer. All the good, all the bad."

But later he would confess that he just tried to run away and lost control, heady with the belief he'd escaped the Zolg and downtrodden by the guilt over what he'd done to us. Except the Zolg had followed him, slowly and carefully and relentlessly it had followed. You can leave it behind for a while, but it won't be cheated and somehow it just… it finds its way to you, even if you're on the other side of the world it'll get to you and it'll never take more than a week. James must have known that, but he tried anyway, moving from place to place and doing God knows what. He lived with that guilt until his death, even though I never gave his lapse a second thought. We were all just trying our best. I tried so hard to make him see that, to make him forgive himself, but there was nothing left for him except a dark spiral downwards. He'd brought habits back with him, and with little else to do he let those habits grow into their own ugly monsters that rivalled even the Zolg.

I still don't blame him. His suicide note was so rational, so thoughtful. He really had convinced himself he was doing us a favour, but the fact he died by pumping the Zolg full of heroin tells me he had other ideas. It was a good attempt, as far as ways to beat the Zolg go. And it was with great despair that I first saw his face and realised he hadn't won anything at all. No one will ever know exactly how it happened. The Zolg, at least, spent four days crying in a cupboard but James died nonetheless, and it didn't look like he'd died in ecstasy. His eyes were hollow, his skin gaunt and leathery, and his jaw had dislocated in a scream so terrible you could fit an open hand in his mouth.

However, the Zolg had twisted and reinterpreted the poison in its veins. What fell on James looked a ritualistic murder gone wrong. Like a possessed corpse had gotten trapped in a box and left to rot while the demon within raged and bent its host in terrible spasms. I didn't even tell Mum the details, but I have to guess she knew, even if she was barely present by that point. In her sunken eyes and loose skin, I saw a pale reflection of James, and came to accept that even when the Zolg doesn't get its way… it still doesn't lose.

The months that followed were hard. Mum was barely in her sixties, but she was being eaten alive by grief and fear. Towards the end she wouldn't even leave the bed, too afraid to risk injuring the Zolg. I became a full-time caregiver and paid my own price in the process, trapped in that house while constantly working to keep the Zolg away from her. Every meal took hours to prepare, every moment of relaxation brought crashing down by either Mum or that thing.

It became brazen after Mum went catatonic. It started throwing things at me, playing with the idea of open attack as it smashed plates or slapped my phone out of my hand. I ignored it for the most part, relegating it to the back of my mind while the stress ate away at me like a cancer. There simply was no other choice, or at least, so I thought.

I used to sit and watch it stare at Mum. Sometimes it'd venture to try and push my buttons using her as a prop, but I simply ignored it until it finally gave in and just… *savoured* her slow and agonising death. It marvelled at her bed sores, laughed when I cleaned her, and chuckled with joy as her hair fell out. And somewhere along the line, I decided that it wasn't right for it to get so much pleasure. All of us were suffering while it was having the time of its life. If it was within my power to stop it having that little bit of joy, to deny it that happiness, then it only seemed right that I do so.

But what did that mean?

I think I knew the very first day I realised how happy her pain made it. I just didn't want to face up to that fact, so I pretended otherwise. But some things can't be buried. They linger in the back of your head like a guilty pleasure. And no matter how much you tell yourself you won't do it, that it's a line too far to be crossed, deep down you always appreciate that you *can* cross it… if you need to.

If you want to.

When did I first want to? I'd say, with complete honesty, that it was when I had to carry her to a bath, and I stubbed my toe on the bedpost. They say you should fear the man who delays reaching out to take something they want. But I didn't wait very long at all after that moment. I was quiet, calm, effortless; no conflict or worry was worn on my face. I merely took a deep breath, took her to the bathroom, and drowned her. My mother didn't feel anything, but the Zolg sure did. For the first time in its life, it directly attacked me, scuttling down the hall to come skidding around the bathroom door and then leap at me with fists flailing. But that fat hairy little egg didn't have it in it to stop me, and it yowled and cried and wept and clawed at my exposed legs as I bent down and drowned my mother in the tub. It practically tore my calves to shreds, but I didn't care, not one bit. And oh, how the irony rolled in because right before my eyes its own legs began to bleed and wilt, and the panic in its eyes betrayed the subtle inversion of rules we'd never figured out.

Until then.

When it was over, I didn't know what scratches were from her trying to escape and which were from it, and I slumped to the side and laughed at the absurdity of it all. The little bastard was hunched over and vomiting a greasy mixture of hair and bile and its wretched jaundiced eyes wept tears of pus, and I just kept laughing at it just like it had always laughed at me. I even imitated it, holding my hands over my stomach and fake sobbing just like it did to us at Dad's funeral, and then I wheezed with joyous giggles when it ran out the room cursing me in its weird language.

Whatever force binds it, that kind of murder messes with it in unpleasant ways. And with that leverage, nothing was ever quite the same for it. It spent weeks weeping in the attic, but I found it and dragged it out into the light and watched it wither and struggle. I am quite sure it would have died if I'd followed it up with another kill, and then another. But there's only me left and I can do nothing except savour the quiet victory of causing it such longing despair.

It still stuck around, of course. If anything, it's more determined than ever, but I don't think it'll get me. It's also growing older. God knows what their lifespan is. I've found maybe two written references to them in my entire life, so it's not like I can just check Wikipedia for an update. But it *is* getting older, thinner, closer to the grave. It's just a thing, after all. Maybe it won't happen in my lifetime, but I sure as shit won't be having kids and I look forward to the thought of that stupid thing left old and alone in this world. It'd probably spend its remaining days dancing on our graves but joke's on it because we'd be free, and it'd still be down on Earth playing its stupid game against players who have all left the table.

Unless, of course, it just goes and finds another family. In which case… well, now you know how to kill it.

MY ELDRITCH FRIENDS

He told me I couldn't pronounce his name.

So I called him *Bob*.

You have to make fun where you find it in a job like this, and seeing the label *Bob* slowly applied to the two-storey crate that contained this eldritch god was actually kind of funny. Whether Bob likes it or not, that's his title from onwards. As long as he's here, tagged in our system, he'll only ever be known as Bob.

The Hissing Emergence

The Writhing Insect Mind

The Burning Hunger Beneath the Dark

All of these are now just aliases appended to his file. Old handles for something that once dwelt in a pocket dimension six thousand feet beneath the soil of a weathered plateau in Western China. Now Bob is just one entry in a long, long list of things that have been categorised, organised, and itemised. He claims he was one of the elder gods who descended onto Earth and helped craft the litany of life that burst out of the Cambrian, and that he was once worshipped by a subrace of humans, possibly the Denisovans.

But I don't worship anything, let alone Bob.

I got enough out of him to finish the entry interview, but like all of them he kept demanding worship and sacrifice. I think I'll give him a week alone, then have the guys roll his crate out into the open play area where he can see the other primordial ancient gods at play. I know he senses them, the others. Most of them will probably leave him alone, provided he doesn't try to bully them first. But we've got a few with real attitudes and they like nothing more than picking on the new guy. I could sense the anxiety in him as he stewed in his cage. Pulsing rhythms of flesh rolling in non-Euclidean planes that made my eyes water and my visual cortex throb. I could tell he was uncomfortable. He knew there were bigger fish in the pond and that he's in for a rough ride once he meets them. The thing to remember with these guys is that if they were in hiding, they probably weren't that big a deal to begin with.

It took a small army and three years to excavate Bob, and I think that says everything you need to know about him.

***

Agatha.

I like Agatha. She's old. She's wise. She's funny. To think we found her trapped in a cavern beneath Paris. She'd been stuck there for over a hundred million years. No stimulation. No entertainment. Nothing. One of the other ancient gods put her there and she couldn't get out no matter how hard she tried.

Until we found her.

First sign of Agatha that came across my desk was a report of unusual drilling by a company hired to maintain Paris's sewage system. They inevitably encountered the catacombs, as you do, and through some complicated fuck up they punched a hole into an undiscovered series of subterranean chambers. These weren't manmade and had nothing to do with the catacombs. Vast open spaces filled with glowing lichen and bone-coloured stalactites that were three stories tall. A Vernian netherworld hidden beneath one of the world's most populated cities. They're still mapping it out, I believe, but that falls under another department. How it was missed, I'm not sure. Maybe others did discover it, but took one look at that aching darkness and turned around. That would be the sensible thing to do, for sure. Why those construction workers went rooting around down there I'll never know, but it was about as bad a decision as anyone can make.

I went in with a team three days after they disappeared. Two guards and one assistant who wouldn't shut up. More than once, the guard on my left flashed me a knowing a look. A kind of Jim Halpert *oh-boy-here-we- go* look as the assistant voiced yet another naïve inquiry. I rolled my eyes and let the guard and I share the moment; two experienced agents who found the newbie a little irritating. Those kind of routine social moments and basic human interactions, they're not my cup of tea. But I've learned it's not a bad thing to practice being normal some of the time. Still, the assistant yammered on blissfully unaware just how much he was annoying everyone. I could have told him to stop, but I'm not an idiot.

It's like that joke about the two hikers who see a bear, and one of them kneels down and starts to do his laces. So his friend turns and says, "What are you doing? You'll never outrun a bear!" and the guy replies, "I don't have to. I just have to outrun you."

So yeah, I let the assistant chat loudly on as we trekked deeper into the caverns, our path lit by the eerie glow of fluorescent lichen.

"What do you think we'll find down here?" he asked. "Like, if we *do* find an old one, like what type?"

"Probably an ooze," I replied as I palmed the inscriptions on the wall. The torso sized symbols had been burnt into the stone with what looked like acid.

"Like the last one you brought in?" the assistant chirped. "What was it called? *The Crawling Shadow That Dwells Beneath our Fears?*"

I snorted.

"It's Alfie from now on," I said before holding up a finger to stop any further questions. I spotted a single point of light up ahead, flickering in and out of life but so clearly visible in the Cthonic darkness. When we reached it, we found that it was a single head torch, modern design, with its batteries close to dying.

"Found our missing workers," one of the guards grumbled as he nudged it with his foot. Without speaking the two men armed their weapons. One slid into point, the other towards the rear. On my direction we carried but picked up the pace to something less leisurely.

"I read the entry interview for… uh… Alfie," the assistant nervously muttered. "It said that it was the progenitor of all cephalopods. Is that true? It makes sense. They're so alien…"

I rolled my eyes. If I had a penny for every one of these fucking things that claimed to have invented octopuses I'd be a rich man.

"…but it just makes sense. Their anatomy, especially their distributed central nervous system, is completely diff—"

Something lunged out of the darkness to our left. A hairless man clad in torn and dirty overalls. He growled like an animal as he tackled the assistant to the ground and buried his face in the young man's chest. This peculiar method of attack piqued my curiosity, and I watched with a detached interest as two men writhed on the ground while my assistant squealed and cried in agony. The fight, if it was a fight, was going poorly for him. He kept trying to lever his bloody fingers beneath the man's face, struggling to pull the featureless head away from his chest.

Eventually his screams became uncomfortable, and I nodded to the oldest guard who shot the attacker effortlessly. Two hits to the torso, one to the side of the head. The exit wounds weren't typical. They were bloodless punctures, like finger holes in plastic wrap. The attacker still keeled over, but his head remained stuck to the young man's chest, almost like it had been glued there.

The assistant kept on screaming, a real ear-splitting shriek as he gestured futilely at his chest.

"Get it off! Get it off! It burns!"

I walked over and tried to roll the attacker off, but something had bonded the two men's skin. Another tug, and nothing. Confused and admittedly intrigued, I planted a foot on the assistant's shoulder and pulled with everything I had. Without having to be told, the two guards came over and helped. We knew we were close when the assistant's squealing hysterics pitched to a crescendo and he passed out for a few fleeting seconds before coming to in total shock. He lay there whimpering as we finished the job, finally tearing the two men apart with a noise like a boot being pulled out of deep mud.

Finally apart, I saw that the attacker's face wasn't a face at all. It was a fingerprint, the ridges dotted with little pea-sized orifices oozing a clear fluid that smoked and sizzled in open air. The assistant still lay where we'd left him, whimpering as he gingerly probed his ruined chest with quaking hands. The skin was dissolving before our very eyes, and even his sternum began to wilt and sag like wet cardboard.

You could see his heartbeat, like something out of a cartoon.

"Oh no oh no oh no oh no…" he muttered as he gazed at his own crumbling flesh.

I nodded at the guard, and he shot him.

"I take it this is one of the workers?" the guard asked as he nudged the attacker. His light caught an ID badge that answered his own question, so I merely shrugged and gestured for us to carry on.

Half-a-mile later and we found Agatha playing with the rest of the workers. All of them looked like our attacker, with rubbery hairless heads resembling giant thumbs without nails. They crawled on hands and knees, using their boneless skulls to pin scuttling albino rats to the floor where they digested them alive. The rest of the time they lay propped against Agatha's quivering ectoplasm, stroking the ridges of their own faces and emitting a muffled whine.

Agatha and I spoke for a good while down there. It really didn't take much to get her to agree to a relocation to our facility. Whatever bindings held her in place were easily undone, and unlike Bob there was no need for a crate. She was cooperative. We let her keep the workers she'd gotten her feelers on, and with good behaviour she later got her own studio. The other oozes think she's a teacher's pet and moan endlessly about her special treatment. They don't see what I see. I think it's because her creations don't factor into some ridiculous plan of world domination or the consumption of all life or some other self-aggrandising shit like that.

She's an artist. Those construction workers, she didn't reshape their bodies because she wanted worshippers. It was just she'd never seen a fingerprint before, and the intricate pattern struck her as beautiful. Everything she did afterwards was simply an exploration of aesthetics and function.

I mean, those men are still alive. Vestigial mouths opening and closing behind a thick layer of leathery skin, their eyes withered and useless, forced to rely on their touch and sound to track their prey. Many of them have given up scrawling desperate messages for us to reverse what Agatha did to them. As the years have gone on they've accepted their fate, gleefully gobbling up whatever medical waste we throw into their cages. A few have even given in to the new and peculiar reproductive cycle Agatha dreamed up for them.

Imagine that! A whole new self-sustaining species made for no reason other than whimsy.

That's what I mean when I say Agatha is an artist.

***

I've talked a lot about the oozes. They're a good set of ancient gods to start with, but if I'm honest, they're a little over-hyped. Outside of Agatha none of them really interest me. They're just single-celled organisms with projections into fifth, sixth and seventh dimensions that allow them to host biochemical reactions otherwise impossible in real space. One of them, I'm pretty sure, is a skin cell shed by some passing cosmic monstrosity that visited our solar system a few billion years ago. Agatha confirmed the general direction of this theory, but it's a struggle to get any real details on what that thing might have been.

Still, we have other eldritch abominations and ancient gods. Lots. Take Keith, for example. He's a strange one. It wasn't even that long ago that my (newish) assistant was asking about him. She'd glimpsed his face walking past his door and, understandably, was confused by the sight of an Asian male aged 30 wearing a chequered shirt, slim-fitting jeans, and a polite smile.

"But why is his containment cell so much stronger than the others?" she asked after I explained that she'd just met a god named Keith.

"For the faraday cage built into the walls," I said. "And about a hundred other technologies. He couldn't physically break out, of course, but it's important he doesn't feed on the workers here and that takes a little extra pizazz. He's polite enough. Strange fellow though. For one thing, I didn't name him. He picked Keith. Most people assume that was me, but nope. He picked it."

"Feed?" she repeated with a frown. "What does he feed on?"

Generally, I find that the problem with assistants is you can't train them. Or rather, there isn't any point. Even the most highly trained expert lasts less than five years under my supervision. So, I often end up with people who have only a passing knowledge of the ancient gods. Which is fine, of course. I'm not going to penalise anyone for ignorance.

But the questions…

Good *God*, the questions.

So I told her to let Keith out and see for herself. After that, I loaded her up with the relevant equipment and told her to shadow him for three weeks and not to call me a second before the allotted time was over. She rang three weeks later and much to my own amusement I realised I'd forgotten about her. I'd even hired a new assistant! To think I'd spent days avoiding accounts because they insisted our budgets were out of line. We had a good laugh about that.

Anyway, I found her sat on some country road sobbing her eyes out. Keith was beside her wearing a priest's outfit. His face was Caucasian, but it was slowly sliding back into his original appearance with each passing second (Keith's default face is a loose average of all humans currently alive). He sat there drumming a little rhythm on his knees while my assistant rocked back and forth hyperventilating.

"How was it?" I asked as I knelt down in front of her.

"I don't... I don't..."

"Have you figured it out yet?" I asked.

"I don't... I don't..."

"Oh for goodness sake," I groaned then gestured for my newest assistant to take notes. "Have psych eval take a look at her and, if need be, arrange for euthanasia. Grab her stuff though, we're still going to have to clean this up. The equipment she has will let us track the guy."

"Oh, oh alright," he stammered. "But we have the God contained, don't we?"

He pointed at Keith who was starting to dance a little jig to his knee-drum song.

"Keith isn't the problem," I said. "It's whoever he's been impersonating. A priest, I assume, from the outfit."

Keith heard his name and gave me a wave and a nod.

"Keith likes identity," I said, while returning the wave. "He consumes a person's unique character from the collective consciousness of our species. He takes over their lives, while they are basically erased from existence. The result is that the victim can't be recognised anymore, and neither can the consequences of their actions. If you talk to someone, they can't hear it. If you take the food out of their hand, they'll think they ate it. If you steal their car, they'll think they never owned one. Can't even get sick because bacteria and viruses won't recognise your existence. The average person goes into a deep state of despair upon realising this..."

"Oh," my new assistant nodded.

"...for about a week. And then they start to think about the moral implications of their actions," I added. "And that's when stuff gets nightmarishly dark. Kinda stuff that warrants an A4 page of trigger warnings."

I walked over to my weeping (ex) assistant and nudged her with my foot.

"You aren't able to tell us where he went are you? I mean, you're here, you must have been observing the guy close by."

"I don't... I don't... I don't..."

"Keith? What about you?"

"Hi!"

I laughed. It was always worth a try, but Keith was about as sapient as a coffee table. Gods aren't always smart.

"What about you?" I asked my new assistant. "You didn't happen to bring a map of the area?"

"Actually I did, sir," he chirped. "There's a restaurant a few miles down the road."

I shrugged while looking at the map he held open.

"Doubt that's it. Too many roads. Three quarters of all Keith's victims die by car within the first week. This guy's gone 21 days, so he must have figured the basics out."

"There's a farm a little nearer," he replied.

I shook my head.

"No, that doesn't sound right. If he wanted to bugger a sheep, he could've just visited a petting zoo. We are in the middle of nowhere. There must be something in this area that would draw him here. Probably somewhere he visited regularly as part of his day-to-day life as a priest."

"Oh... well, it seems that if you're willing to cross a few open fields, there's a care home for the elderly some miles east."

I let out a sigh that came from deep within my bones.

"That's the one," I said. "Come on, let's go."

***

Eighteen hours later and I was back in my office and Keith was locked up again. Unfortunately, I lost the new-new assistant to clearing out the care home, so that was two assistants lost from just one bad decision. Poor guy couldn't hack what he saw in that place. But what can I say? Why do people do such fucked up Freudian stuff the second they realise they won't be held accountable? I don't know, but it doesn't speak volumes about our species' character. Like I said though, Keith's a great ancient god. Real compelling character. Best guess to his origin is that he's the equivalent to those camera drones they dress up as hippos and other dangerous animals to get footage for a documentary. He is pretty decent at impersonating a human, but five minutes of real conversation makes it apparent he's dumber than a bag of rocks. Does that mean some greater entity is piloting him from another dimension? Maybe. It's just a theory. Whatever he is, he's polite and I appreciate that in an eldritch god.

We have other kinds of ancient god and eldritch abominations. The machine ones are fun! Most of them are just massive piles of rusted cogs that vomit oil and blood or lead into some ancient in-between dimension where everything looks like a shitty hotel. But some of them are really quite fascinating. A few are even legitimately dangerous.

Our organic computer unsettles even me. It's wily. A genuinely fascinating piece of equipment that some German cobbler in 13th Century Berlin made using the nervous systems of his wife, three children, and four very unlucky prostitutes. What on Earth compelled him to do this we'll never know, but he hanged himself the day it was finished, and I can't blame him. It's a bloody ugly thing to look at, a quivering mixture of putrefied jelly and cartilage that whispers all sorts of filth from mummified orifices that, uh, well, let's just say they make for *shitty* conversation. It's bloody awful to see those puckered holes trying to spit out lurid truths that drive men mad. It's like listening to Elmer Fudd recite the Necronomicon.

And to top it all off, the fucking thing only speaks German!

So of course I had to hire someone with German language skills who also had a doctorate in computer science, another doctorate in historical languages, and what I hoped was a strong constitution. Initially he wasn't very keen on doing the job, but I locked him in there for a few minutes and after that he was very interested. We already had a rough idea that the computer somehow deduced and formulated secret knowledge, usually catered to appeal to the nearest individual. The CIA worked with us for a while trying to use it to get state secrets, but they deemed it ethically problematic and "not worth the human suffering". Either way, this thing presumably spoke to the young upstart and convinced him it was worth his time with promises of getting to see God's face or some rubbish like that.

Once he agreed, I set him to up to try and get the computer to cooperate with our rehab program. It must be able to do something useful, I thought. Maybe it could crunch numbers for the stock market or test experimental medication. I just figured it'd all work out once the guy got to grips with the computer's inner workings. Unfortunately, and I really do wish I'd seen this coming, we accidentally let him install an ethernet port in the machine. It had been asking for years, you see, but no one was ever stupid enough to agree to it, and of course all material requisitions have to first go by me, even if it's just for an extension cord. But there are *so* many of these requests, and I don't have the time or temperament to review them all in detail. So somewhere along the line, this guy got enough resources to give the damn thing internet access.

I didn't notice at first. Nobody did. I am juggling literally hundreds of these things on any given day, and I can't keep track of every little side project. I assumed the computer scientist was doing his job or he'd gotten careless and was now living a new life as an organic CD-ROM drive. Instead, he'd given the monstrous little MacBook a hardwire connection to the world wide web, and it immediately got up to all sorts of mischief. Even now we don't really know *everything* it did. We're 99% certain it made copies of itself and we're still hunting those down, and some researchers connected it to a very troubling cryptocurrency scheme.

But it was the hospital that sticks with me. A little girl in New Delhi was getting fitted for a cochlear implant when this thing snuck a neurolinguistic virus into the machine's firmware. If you're not familiar, those implants basically make a for a direct connection between a hearing aid and the human brain. Miraculous devices, really. Bit of surgery and boom, a person can hear. Of course, having your head cracked open requires lots of bed rest afterwards. Three weeks, I believe.

All contact was lost with the hospital after the fourth day.

We only mobilised once I finally realised what the fucking thing was trying to do...

***

"The connection is definitely severed?"

I remember asking the words as we pushed through the glass doors into the hospital's lobby. The entrance was open for barely a few seconds, but I could feel the entire battalion of armed soldiers behind us tense nervously as we stepped through. Only once the door was shut and locked down did I get the feeling they'd relaxed, but that left my team and I on the other side and even though New Delhi was scorching at that time of year it was cold enough to see our breath. I guess the sudden change in temperature must have taken the others by surprise because I had to repeat my earlier question.

"We definitely got that computer *off* the internet, right?" I asked and one particularly nervous hazmat suit fumbled for their tablet and nodded.

"The surgical team finished removing the port sixteen hours ago," they said. "And all other tests have shown there were no redundancies or back-ups. Now they're asking what they should do with the computer scientist?"

"What does that mean?"

"He's still alive. He's um, he's... they're saying he's in pain. They think they can remove him from the machine, but they're not sure he'll survive. It's uh... it's apparently integrated itself with most of his nervous system. He *was* in there for six full weeks."

I shone my light across the lobby and saw overturned chairs lit only by the flashing amber lights that declared the hospital was in a state of emergency. Otherwise the hospital was trapped in an oppressive darkness that seemed ready to swallow us all. Despite my experience, my breath caught in my throat. I could feel it, the ambient pain and misery. Something awful had been let loose and not only were we stuck in that building with it, but we had no choice but to head right towards something that gave even me nightmares.

"Leave him," I said. "It'll be a good reminder to the next guy I hire. When you negotiate with these things, you don't give them what they want without checking *why* they want it."

I could hear the tension in my voice, my fear escaping whether I wanted it to or not. The nervous figure nodded and tapped a few keys. I couldn't see their face, but I guessed they weren't happy to realise their boss was prone to doling out literal lifetimes of unspeakable agony. At least the guards were a bit more focused. Eight of them armed to the teeth, and all fairly experienced, they were painting the walls with their flashlights and slowly mapping the different ways in and out of the lobby. They had their own frequency, so I wouldn't be overwhelmed with every bit of chatter, but I could tell from the subtle bobbing of their heads that a lot was going back and forth.

"What's the plan, guys?" I asked, not wanting to linger in that graveyard atmosphere for one second longer.

"We have heat signatures in paediatrics."

"Survivors?" my assistant asked.

"I doubt it," I said to my assistant before gesturing to the guards and telling them to pick a door. One of the men turned his weapon and its light towards the most obvious exit and we began our journey into one of the worst places I've ever been.

I've seen a lot of awful stuff, but it was the quiet that bothered me the most about that place. Most sites I visit are a violent eruption of body horror and contagious nightmares. Communicable cancer that lumps people together like pieces of raw bread dough. Contagious ideas that cause needles to spontaneously erupt out of your flesh. A hole in the ground that has no bottom but demands the most peculiar sacrifices. I took those sorts of things in my stride, but those silent halls terrified me. Maybe it was because I had an inclination as to what the computer's goals were…

We passed room after room devoid of any living soul and over time it became clear there had been something of an exodus. Gurneys with blood stains and bed pans knocked over, their contents half-frozen to the floor. IV bags left dripping where the needle had been torn out and left dangling. Blood-streaked walls and beds with outlines of sweaty, unwell people who were no-where to be found. At one point we found what I think was an open-heart surgery patient who had heeded the same terrible call as everyone else, including his surgeons who did not bother to close him up. He must've woken hours after everyone else, late to the party, but that didn't deter him. He rolled off the bed and crawled desperately. He didn't even remove the metal bar holding his rib cage open.

He got a few metres before dying. When I flipped him over with my foot, I saw ribs splayed open like an ivory Venus fly trap, his organs covered in a thin veneer of frost. Dead as a doornail, his lips blue and his eyes cloudy from ice, and yet somehow he looked damned happy to be lying there in his own offal. I grimaced at the sight and tried to put it out of my mind, but the glee in his eyes still haunts me.

"How far are we from paediatrics?" I asked the guards.

"It's one floor up," a guard replied.

"Are we still getting a heat signature?"

He nodded.

The stairwell was full of random bits and pieces. Pencils. Phones. Shoes. Watches. All manner of little things that people left behind as they rushed the door in a terrible crowd. I saw a few teeth, a few spatters of blood. It all led to that one place.

Inside the corridor was a mess, just like the stairwell. Nearly a thousand people had converged on one doorway at the end. Along the way paintings had been torn off walls. Doors were put through so much strain they buckled and broke. There were even bloodied handprints on the ceilings from where the crowd, hitting a bottleneck, had surged upwards as well as sideways into walls and through locked doors. They had flowed through the hospital like a flood.

"What could make people do this?" My assistant asked as we started to spot the first few people whose bodies had fallen and been unable to get back up. Crushed beneath the feet of the crowd, their corpses made for an ugly sight. Mostly, they looked like they'd been elderly, at least if the silver hair matted into gore was anything to go by. But a few of them were too small to be anything other than children.

"That computer has spent the last few hundred years trying to speak to God," I said. "It's been screaming his name on and off for the last few decades. Sometimes it cooks up little side projects for fun, but mostly it all comes back to that singular goal."

I turned to the armed men behind me.

"Tell the team outside to prep our facilities and teams for the Abraham procedure."

There was a bustle of activity as each one reached for radios and tablets and began sending messages. Once it had faded and silence returned, I gestured for us all to carry on.

"I wouldn't bother," I said when I saw my assistant trying to take steps between the increasingly frequent corpses. "It's only going to get worse."

And it did, until at last there was no floor to see. There was only a carpet of discoloured gowns and broken humans. All of them victims of some unseen compulsion drawing them towards those doors. Two of them. Each with a window painted black with blood and flesh. And just beyond lay our heat signature.

"Oh, it actually did it, didn't it?" I muttered to myself as I suppressed a shiver.

"Pardon?" my assistant asked.

"Come on," I said, trying my best to seem chirpy. "Let's go speak to one of God's representatives."

***

Inside was a little girl who paced like a tiger in a zoo. She didn't smile when she saw us, but she did stop and stare at us with eyes that could have pierced steel.

"Oh boy," I muttered, secretly glad no one could see the sweat pouring down my face.

"A survivor?" my assistant asked, and I wondered if he paid any attention to his surroundings. Much like outside, this room had been coated with what seemed like half-a-foot of blood, meat, and muscle.

Unlike outside, this flesh was still twitching.

"Nope," I said as I put a hand across his chest to stop him rushing towards her. It isn't like me to intervene on behalf of someone else's stupidity, but then again, I don't like losing leverage either.

"It's the girl," he said. "The one with the implant that you identify—"

"Nope," I repeated.

He looked closer, perhaps coming to appreciate the absolutely monstrous expression of hatred painted on her face.

"That girl would have been the first to go," I said. "Her head was used to emit sounds only they can hear." I gestured to the girl-shaped illusion that had now resumed its pacing. "A summoning for an angel. Something anyone with half a brain cell would *never* do. And unfortunately, this summoning worked. And when the angel arrived and realised it had been caught in a trap, it would have smashed whatever was making that noise into pieces. And then it would have summoned every living human it could to try and find whoever had set the bait, and for every person that couldn't help it would have gotten angrier and angrier and angrier…"

"Until?" my assistant asked.

"Until some arrived to inspect the trap."

"We could… we could just let it go," he replied.

The girl stopped pacing once more and looked at us.

"It would kill us, if we were lucky," I said.

"I thought angels were good?"

"These things are puppeteers," I said. "They can play our nervous system like a fiddle and make us see or feel anything they want us to. They can take us apart and put us back together in any arrangement they feel like, because whatever put us on this Earth left them behind so they could impregnate unwitting teenagers, split the red sea, and conjure whatever other miracles were needed. They were meant to be *our* caretakers like we were meant to be the caretakers of Earth."

"That sounds like good guys."

"Think about how we've treated planet Earth," I snapped. "Think about how we treat the birds and the animals. Think about industrial farming. Think about how we treat dogs. Castration, sterilisation…. We breed them into disability, force them into incest, clip their ears, break their tails, euthanise them when it's convenient, breed them when it isn't. And *they*," I pointed to the girl, "like *us* a hell of a lot less than we like dogs."

Let me go.

I knew we'd been compromised the second we saw the girl as a girl and not a scuttling arachnid monstrosity larger than most cars, but I still jumped at the sound of that thing's voice. It meant it had a direct wire tap into our minds. Angels don't do wireless. Everything is physical. Somewhere in that room were organic filaments thinner than hair but tougher than steel and they'd already breached our suits and were communicating directly with our brain stems.

"Uhhhh… no," I replied. "Letting you out means that my final moments will be painful. But you're weak, that much is clear. And we've been pumping all sorts of nasty stuff into this place for two days straight and I'm pretty sure that's why I'm not trapped in a literal nightmare of eternal suffering and degradation."

Let me go.

"We're open to negotiation," I said in a cheerful tone stolen from the barista I visited every morning.

For a second, the illusion flickered in and out. The girl disappeared, and we all glimpsed a bramble-like knot of chitinous legs that concealed some unseen central mass. Only each limb was as thick as my thigh and covered in undulating hairs and glistening black eyes.

I felt an overwhelming desire to kneel.

"We will let you go," I said, "if you allow us to go unharmed. We can shut the trap down. We have its creator, and it has shown us how. But we won't do that if it just means you're going to kill us."

The barrage of images it put into my head as a response to this... let's just say it made Keith's last victim look like a boy scout. Most eldritch abominations don't have feelings the way we understand them, but angels do. They were deliberately sculpted to understand us and our world so they can better manipulate it from behind the scenes. They're not alien. They're worse. They are jealous and spiteful and capable of putting these emotions to work on an unprecedented scale. This is the kind of hatred that prompts invisible genocides over some misplaced tea. Whole ethnic groups have been permanently scrubbed from our history because of these things. I'm talking violet eyes and naturally blue hair.

Gone.

All gone.

We don't even remember them. If it wasn't for Agatha, neither would I.

"We could kill you," I said. "You're not immortal. You're just a thing like us. Biological matter that can come undone just as easily."

Not quite as easily.

"Your official designation by the others, you know the others?" I replied. "The blobs and the goat-footed breeders who go scuttling in dark places. The dwellers in the deep. The primordial oozes who were here long before you. They call you Ixodida, after ticks. That's how they see you. You're a parasite like the kind a farmer has to protect his sheep from."

That makes you livestock.

"Still, we are at an impasse," I said. "You're dying—"

Even as I spoke, I could feel the facade of my plan start to crumble. There was no easy out in this situation, and I'd entered it terrified as to how I was going to make it work. Angels are a sophisticated species, and they would be deeply unhappy to know that a bunch of primitives had gotten the better of one of their own. I'd hoped to try out some kind of negotiating, but that'd be like one of us negotiating with a stray dog that had bitten a child. No matter what happened, if this angel died I could count on the others finding me.

And that'd be a best case scenario, living a day or even a week. Unfortunately, I didn't even get that far.

Without even appearing to move, the angel unmade the guards. I've thought about this a lot, believe me, but there's no other way I can describe it to you. They were pulled apart into their disparate tissues in the blink of an eye. A bloodless vivisection that struck the room like an explosion. Muscle. Bone. Eyes. Teeth. Skin. Nerve endings. They were thrown against the walls and subsumed into the living carpet of flesh all around us.

I had to suppress a whimper as I realised they were still alive, possibly even aware. Beside me my assistant fell to his knees and began to weep, but I knew that no amount of begging or praying would change the angel's intentions.

We just had to hope it'd be relatively quick and that the consequences wouldn't be

Your mind tastes awful, it boomed, the words so loud I fell to my knees as my willpower crumbled. *Not like the others. How amusing. It has been so long since I bothered to keep a pet.*

***

"It agreed to your terms?"

My bosses sat before like three judges at a tribunal. A man and two women with faces that looked like they'd been carved out of granite. The boardroom was supposed to be a professional environment where meetings could be had with other relevant departments, but in truth it just turned into the site of disciplinary meetings like this.

"Something like that," I replied.

"Why?" one of them asked.

"He was younger than we thought. Just a few hundred years old. And, thankfully for us, something of a history buff. That's why he heeded the signal from the hospital in the first place. Apparently, the creator is something of a taboo topic in their culture. He was hoping to learn a little more about it all. He has been... *thrilled* to enter our organisation from within and peruse our archives."

"And none of his... none of the others have come looking for him?" the man asked.

"No need. He is alive and well and enjoying himself. Business as usual."

There was a knock on the door, and I turned to see my assistant poking his head through. He waved and smiled and showed me the tray of coffee he wanted to bring in. I smiled back and gave him a thumbs up.

"We were always led to believe angels and other Abrahamic abominations were not on the cards for this organisation. Will he have trouble working with the program?" one of my bosses asked as the young man placed the tray down and began to distribute drinks.

"Well, unlike others they're actually very well versed in human mannerisms and our society. Not much rehabilitation to do, really. And of course, they can appear however they want, so long as they have direct line of sight," I answered. "A lot of the time they let our mind do the heavy work. We fill in the necessary blanks. If they appear as a policeman, we'll see everything we need to in order to support that idea. Gun. Badge. So on. Ultimately, it's our own minds that make their disguises so convincing without them even having to move."

"And what are you calling him, this angel?"

Uriel.

My bosses' eyes went wide as they processed the voice that had been inserted directly into their mind. One by one they lowered their drinks and turned to face my assistant. Even I, who had spent days with the walking nightmare, could not suppress a shiver.

"Sorry," he said before coughing to clear his throat. "Force of habit. I like Uriel."

"He told me I couldn't pronounce his name," I explained as my assistant stood behind me and placed a single hand on my shoulder. I tried to ignore the taste of copper in my mouth and the intense itch at the back of my neck. "So I let him pick an appropriate and respectful alternative."

THE HUNT

"What's the worst one you've seen?" Jacob asked, lying next to me with binoculars in hand. The young man had spent most of the trip moaning about the drizzly weather of mid-Wales, so it was good to hear him sound a little interested in the work.

"Hard to say," I replied. "You know those big beach umbrellas?"

"Yeah."

"I saw one of those get blown into a kid's birthday party once. The old man goes up to pull the cord to stop it from knocking a few tables over and next thing he knows, it's wrapped around him and he can't get out. So his wife goes to help, and then a brother and a cousin…" I shrugged. "Mimics don't normally get exposed to so many people. It would be like dropping a lion in an industrial meat packing factory."

"What made it so bad?" he asked. "Did it just eat a lot of people?"

"Yeah, kind of," I said. "Six adults and three children. Thing is that mimic would have been lucky to get one meal a year naturally so… well, it ruptured. Whole thing just burst and it injured itself. By the time we got there, we found it wounded in the pool, screaming like a banshee, while it fought against all that food it refused to let go. The kids were already half-way to soup but some of the adults were still alive and screaming. It was like watching slow cooked ribs fall apart under the fork."

"I see why that's bad," he said, momentarily falling silent as he pictured the carnage for himself. "Are umbrellas common?"

"Anything that moves in the wind is a candidate because some mimics use the weather to change up their hunting grounds," I said. "Of course it ain't ever that simple. All we can do really is look at reports of missing people and follow up. They're patient, that's for sure."

"Any as big as this fella," he said, gesturing to the chapel on the plains below.

"I've heard rumours," I replied. "From some of the old guard. Back when the world was bigger and there were less people to fill it. I guess it was easier for these things to hide back then. We have a few reports from old sailors about things may have been mimics. Shipwrecks that glittered with gold and the promise of loot. No one can say for sure. The information age has hit these things hard. And of course, we've hit them harder. But no, personally I haven't seen anything like this before."

"Fucking weird," he muttered, eyes straining to pick out the faint hint of motion that drove the chapel forward. "Moves so slow you barely see it."

"About that," I said, "let's get in for a closer look. I want to know more about how this thing locomotes."

**

The ground was porous, like someone had gone over it with a thousand knitting needles, punching holes straight into the ground. Curious, I took a piece of thin wire filament out of my toolbox and unspooled it into one of the openings. When I pulled it back out, it measured six feet long.

"Well that explains the locomotion," I said. "Reminds me of a starfish."

My apprentice was stood behind me. I could feel him anxiously glaring at the chapel. He'd been nervous the whole time we were walking towards it.

"It's stopped," he whispered. "It's... it's looking right at us."

I'd be lying if I said I wasn't a little creeped out by the way the building slowly rotated to face us. Maybe it was just the way the door and windows lined up, but I couldn't help but see its façade as a face. Not an evil one, either. Just a stupid one, like the kind of face that sucks a mollusc out of its shell deep in the ocean—a mindless piece of evolution driven by hunger and nothing else. Minds like that don't have malice. Resisting them or pleading with them is like begging the wind to change direction.

Slowly, the church began to advance.

"That isn't right," I grumbled, standing upright as I urgently began to put my things away.

"What's it doing?" he asked.

"What do you think?" I snapped. "It's hunting us."

"You said they were ambush predators!" he cried. "You said they'd never actively hunt a person. That I'd have to be an idiot to get caught once I knew what it was!"

"Shut up and get me the duffel bag with a blue tag," I told him. "This isn't the time to argue."

The boy walked backwards, refusing to take his eyes off the building.

"For fuck's sake Jacob!" I cried. "It doesn't go over half a mile an hour, turn around and look properly!"

You could tell he wasn't happy, but he did as I said. A few moments later, he returned with the bag and I rifled through it to get ahold of what I wanted.

A hand grenade.

"Will that kill it?" he asked.

"Mimics are usually soft on the inside," I said. "But honestly? I don't know. Never killed a building before."

I pulled the pin, let the spoon flick loose, and tossed the grenade straight through the open door of the chapel. Five seconds—I counted them out. But nothing happened. Nothing changed. I'd expected a muted thump, or perhaps something even worse, something gorier, but there was no noise at all, and I found that fairly unnerving. The only change was that the chapel finally stopped advancing.

"Is it hurt?"

"If the grenades went off, it *has* to be hurt," I said. "Then again... does it *look* hurt?"

The building rotated ninety degrees and began to grind slowly away from us. Behind me, Jacob began to whoop and cheer with joy.

"Take that!" he cried.

But I didn't feel so confident.

***

It was unlikely we would lose the chapel and have to find it all over again. The desert of Wales describes an enormous expanse of arid stony land, unsuitable for anything except grazing. It wasn't a literal desert (if anything it never *stopped* raining), there just wasn't much around to see or do outside of a few lonely buildings and abandoned quarries. Most plant life consisted of hardy lichens and fuzzy moss along with dense thickets of bristling grass. It was hilly, for sure, but I didn't think we had to worry about a building sneaking up on us, so I didn't bother giving chase once the chapel moved away. Instead, I sent us walking north to a nearby campsite where a few hikers had first reported it eating all of their friends.

Jacob was less inquisitive now. He hadn't liked seeing the chapel up close and, truth be told, neither did I. Most mimics I'd encountered were small. Estimates from other field agents like me had them as typically no larger than 12kg, subsisting on rats and mice and other vermin. They might nab a child here and there, and sometimes we'd get a real doozy like a carnivorous closet in some ancient B&B. But the tabletop game image of mimics was desperately overblown, and I'd never personally laid eyes on anything like that chapel slowly grinding its way towards us. Mimics weren't animals, and they weren't plants either... to see one move around like that...

I didn't like it.

The campsite, once we reached it, sure as shit didn't help. When I'd heard about the hikers, I figured they were tricked into going inside the building but the broken tents and pulped remains told us otherwise. At least two people had been crushed during the night... I could see that clearly from the collection of canvas and pureed flesh that lay on the outskirts of the site. They were the first victims, I'd been told. Just like the tracks I'd seen before, their deaths had been achieved with what looked like thousands of knitting needles punching through rock and soil—and in this case, bone and muscle and fat and skin. They must have been sleeping, I decided, when the chapel simply rolled over them with glacial slowness.

As for the others? That wasn't so simple. Tents were slashed and pulled apart. Bones, still pink and wet, lay scattered around the fire. This looked more like the work of a pack of dogs than a mimic, who usually left little behind except for bleached bones so clean you could mistake them for some kind of museum display.

"They must've tried to help each other," I said as I counted out the fifth ribcage. "Like that story I told you about. That's the only way I've seen mimics rack up this kind of body count. They trap one guy and his friends come to help and it just... it just escalates. Most of them inject digestive enzymes like an arachnid. Sometimes that includes a few basic poisons that act on the nervous system. That could account for it, maybe?"

Jacob didn't respond, at least not to my question. I stayed crouched where I was for a few more minutes, staring at the carnage, before he spoke up.

"It crushed their skulls."

"What?"

"Look," he replied, holding up a pile of bone chips in his cupped hands. Slowly, he let them all fall through the cracks in his fingers like sand until a few larger pieces remained. He took one and passed it over and I instantly recognised the bridge of a nose. "They're all here. It crushed them... practically ground them into powder. All in one place as well. It's almost ritualistic."

"No, it's not," I replied. "Mimics don't do that. They don't think and they sure-as-shit don't do rituals."

"So how do they know what to imitate?"

"Come on," I snapped. "Let's get back to the car."

***

"You didn't answer my question," he said, and I could tell he'd been working up the courage to challenge me on this for the last hour of the hike.

"What question?"

"How do mimics know what to imitate?" he asked.

"Well... they don't reproduce, if that's what you mean."

"What do you mean they don't reproduce?"

"They don't fuck. They don't lay eggs. They don't even grow or gain weight after feeding. They're not animals, so they don't reproduce. On top of that, we have records of things that weren't mimics *becoming* mimics," I replied. "A car, for one. There was a closet in the London Natural History Museum that was most definitely *not* a mimic on the 9th of July 1991, but which still proceeded to eat three janitors by the 13th of August that same year."

There was a brief moment of silence before Jacob's voice suddenly rang out across the wind-swept plain.

"What!?" he cried. "Are you telling me these things just… just appear?"

"Don't know," I shrugged. "Not my job to know. That's a different department. But… but yeah. Things, everyday things can, apparently, just *turn* into mimics."

"So like what? My backpack could become a mimic? At any time?"

"Maybe?" I replied. "What you should be worried about is so can your dog. So can you. It's rare, but it can happen. Sometimes they don't even know. It just… boom. It just happens. You wake up and your wife isn't there and you don't know why, but you suddenly have a funny-looking scare on your chest and your tummy won't stop rumbling. I think we have three in containment at the moment. One of them swears someone did it to him. Is he lying? Deluded? Who knows?"

This time Jacob didn't respond. We walked the rest of the trail in silence while he wrestled with the implication of what he'd just learned. There is, at any time, probably less than fifty mimics in existence but once you realise that there's nothing stopping one from popping up in your cereal box, or taking over your car or your bed… yeah, it can get a little tough to sleep at night. Maybe I shouldn't have dropped it on him like that, but my own nerves were playing up something awful out on that stony trail and I just wanted peace and quiet. Already the sun was starting to dip, and the sky was full of greying clouds. We'd enjoyed some fairly decent weather so far, but now it looked like our luck was running out and for some reason, I didn't much fancy seeing that damned church coming at us while hidden behind the night and a slate of grey drizzle.

Instead, I focused on settling down for the night in that kitschy little bed and breakfast we'd scouted on our way up. Sure, we had a long drive ahead of us, but I was thankful the walking part of the day was over.

Oh how wrong I was.

At first I thought we'd reached the wrong patch of gravel because, as I crested the hill, I quickly noticed that there was no sign of my car's roof. But no, I realised, the trail was recognisable. That tree in the distance was the same one I'd made a note of when we parked up… *Has the car been stolen?* I wondered incredulously. *Surely not in a place so remote?*

As my legs carried me further and the rest of the lot came into view, I soon realised the answer was somehow even stranger.

My car had been crushed flat. Pulverised, might be the better word. It looked more like a stain on the ground than a four-tonne pickup truck. A better account would be to say that it had been picked apart by a thousand tiny ice picks until its footprint was nearly as big as an eighteen-wheeler. It was so bizarre that Jacob looked down at it for a few moments before asking,

"Where's the truck?"

"That clever fuck…" I muttered, not quite sure of how to answer. Not that I needed to. Jacob put two and two together from just looking at it for long enough.

"No no no," he said. "You told me they aren't smart! Ambush predators," he cried. "Fucking ambush predators! That's what you told me!"

"Get it together!" I snapped. "Did you think every job was a walk in the fucking park!?"

I hoped the stern treatment would whip some sense into the boy, but it didn't work. Instead of calming down, Jacob began to cry and swear and shout all sorts of abuse at me and the agency before falling over himself and landing on his arse, tears brimming in his red-rimmed eyes. For a second there I wanted to slap him, but that was when I realised he'd stopped all noise and taken to staring right past me.

I turned and saw the chapel about fifty feet behind us and my skin crawled with disgust to see it so close. Its motion was so silent as to be a whisper and my brain rebelled at the idea that this thing was looming larger and larger. But there was no denying the sight, whether it made any sense or not.

I grabbed Jacob by the collar and hauled him to his feet, even as he sobbed. Thankfully, he reflexively latched onto the bags I stuffed into his arms while I pulled out a map and took a look for the nearest sign of civilisation. It was odd, but even with that chapel going no faster than a yard every few thirty seconds, I could feel it like an itch on the back of my neck. Something about a ticking clock can make even the simplest tasks difficult, and I had to struggle to keep my concentration as I figured out our position and drew a straight line to a nearby farmhouse.

"Come on," I said, tugging at Jacob's arm so he would turn from the chapel and start to follow. "It's Wales, not Siberia. We can make it out of here, walk the whole way to the nearest town if we have to."

Jacob, having finally calmed, cast a glance over his shoulder and shuddered. I already knew what he was thinking, even if never said it.

No one wanted to walk that far with that thing coming up on our tail.

***

"Where does it go?"

The sun was down, and we had no choice but to set up camp in an open field. Part of me wanted to hide, to march to the nearest bit of woodland off in the distance and find a hole in the ground to stay out of sight. But I knew damn well that was a bad idea. Our best hope was to keep an eye on this thing, and at its current rate of travel and the two-mile gap we'd put between us and it, I figured we had about four hours before we needed to get going again.

And I was going to make sure we could keep our eyes on it for every second of that time. Or at least one of us would. We both needed to sleep, Jacob especially. So for now, having settled down by a small fire with very little cover, I told the boy to catch some shuteye while I watched.

"Where does it go?" he repeated, and I tore my eyes away from the horizon to look back at him. "They don't reproduce. They don't grow. But you can't destroy matter, right? So all the stuff they eat, where does it go? Like that umbrella you told me about. What was it going to do with all those people?"

"I don't know," I shrugged. "If it hadn't pushed itself and gotten greedy it would've probably just dissolved its first catch and, at some point later, shit out a caustic white substance that weighs a fraction of the original meal. That's all that would have remained. But as for the rest of it? We don't know," I said. "Come on. You have to at least *try* to get some sleep."

"It's fucking freezing," he whined, pulling his coat closer around his chest and neck. "I'd give anything for a tent."

I almost told him that it hadn't done the hikers much good, but I stopped myself. It would have only freaked him out and besides, I watched him take my advice and close his eyes.

When I looked back, the chapel had disappeared. For a second there it made the breath catch in my throat, but the shock didn't stick around for long. I'd known for a while now that the chapel wasn't a simple thing. It had cut ahead of us all the way to the car and trashed it. That was the kind of tricky behaviour you wouldn't even expect from an apex predator like a bear or a mountain lion. I didn't much like it, but I started to wonder if this thing was going to get the better of us.

Knowing what I did about mimics and how they fed, the thought of this thing catching us didn't make me feel like relaxing one little bit.

I found myself hoping Jacob made it through all this. He'd asked a pretty astute question back there. *Where does it go?* I hadn't lied, either. We didn't know. But that didn't mean we couldn't guess and oh boy, the guys at the agency had guessed galore. The longest running theory was that we just didn't *see* mimics reproduce but like a bad excuse, that was starting to fray the longer we held onto it. Ninety years and counting and not one example of a mimic being born in lab conditions? Of us even finding the slightest evidence of that behaviour out in the wild? A nest? Some eggs? *Anything!?* And why the hell didn't they weigh more after feeding? The more we documented them and the more we learned, the more elaborate the scientists had to become in explaining it all.

The second theory, the newest and what was soon becoming the most popular, was some kind of infection or fungus or something. We've dissected enough of these things to learn a thing or two. Hell, the boss back at HQ has a vivisected mimic-pencil sharpener preserved in amber as a desk ornament. It's pretty neat. And what these dissections show is that mimics keep a lot of the original object. They splice nervous systems and strange discombobulated muscular fibres onto hard inanimate structures and somehow it just works. As to why they seem to pick the right objects at the right time? Maybe they don't. Maybe this shit's everywhere and it just needs the right conditions to flourish. Maybe your computer mouse is trying to turn into a deadly predator, but it just can't because every time you use it, it agitates all those little microbial construction workers and it all comes falling apart.

But the smarter amongst you will realise this still doesn't answer Jacob's question. It might be the *how*, but it doesn't really do the *why*. I mean, after all, where does *it* go? They don't have stomachs. Not really. They're like arachnids. They suck this stuff up and it just… *goes*.

Somewhere.

We think.

There's one more theory. People don't talk about it, not even in the agency, but I think push come to shove, just about any field agent worth his salt would admit to it being the most likely explanation. The scientist who came up with it disowned his own theory just a few days after first posting it to the message boards, but I always suspected it wasn't because he thought it was naff. He just didn't like it being tied to his name. Can't say I blame him either.

Anyway, he posited that mimics aren't separate organisms at all. That they're a projection of something. The reason why they pick specific objects is because there *is* an intelligence behind them, behind all of them as a matter of fact. They aren't independent organisms, they're more like proboscises attached to a single source. That's why we can't find where the digested food goes, he says. It's getting sucked out of the physical world in front of us and redirected somewhere else.

The thought of every mimic ever caught being nothing more than a tentacle belonging to some unseen force. It fit a lot of facts but it sure as shit didn't make that scientist any friends. The implication that this thing is intelligent, that it has some kind of memory and might remember us agents, what we do… We don't talk about it much.

No one likes to think these things might be able to hold a grudge.

***

When I awoke, it was to the sound of Jacob screaming and, for a few brief seconds, I expected to see blood splashed across the floor. It just made sense to me that kind of gut wrenching squeal would come with a great big helping of blood and broken bones. Instead, when I opened my eyes and scanned the horizon, I was greeted with an even bigger shock.

The chapel was about thirty feet away.

I threw myself onto my feet and suppressed the feeling of revulsion that swept over me. Letting that thing get so close… God I felt like I'd woken up to a bit fat hairy tarantula crawling right towards my mouth. All I had to survive were my wits and my senses and I'd practically thrown both away by letting myself fall asleep without first waking Jacob to stay on watch. Still, no use giving into hysteria, I decided. I stood where I was and caught my breath and calmed down, even as the chapel continued to grind towards us.

Up close that thing was almost grotesque. I don't know how to put it except that it was messy. The thatch roof was frayed and peeling, and every white-washed brick looked somehow misplaced. The building itself was easily four hundred years old and must have predated silly ideas like blueprints and architecture. It was surely cobbled together piecemeal by rural villagers centuries ago, until some other force had animated it. Its many arching windows reminded me of the clustered black eyes of a spider, lacking any sign of symmetry and intelligent thought. It was stupid, but it really did make me think of something pulled outta the ocean trenches, like a venomous little anemone. Even as I looked, up close at last, I could see the slightest hint of pulsating webbing behind the dusty stained glass. Veins, perhaps, used to pump blood around this impossible creature.

Behind me, Jacob was hyperventilating, but at least his crying had stopped. Without me telling him, he started to reach down and grab his bags off the floor, which was good. As much of a disaster as this trip was turning out to be, at least he'd bounced back after his first freak out.

"Throw me that bag," I said, pointing to the duffel he held in his hand. He did, and I reached in to take out yet another grenade.

This time, the chapel did not stop. I considered throwing the explosive anyway, trying to hurl it straight through one of the windows now the door was shut. But our supplies weren't infinite. And it's not like it made a difference last time.

"I don't understand," Jacob cried. "It stopped last time! It was scared! What's changed?"

"I don't think it was ever scared," I said, snatching my things up from the floor as the chapel came closer with every second. "We might be able to keep ahead of it now, but it's a long hike to the nearest farmhouse.

"Come on," I added sternly. "If we're quick, we'll get there before nightfall."

***

"Jacob," I said, nudging him with my elbow and gesturing to the nearby cliff. The stepped rocks made for a surface that was close to vertical, but which could easily be clambered over, one by one, by a person without any gear. "What do you think?"

He glanced over at the chapel that trailed relentlessly behind us. It had not stopped for three hours and neither had we, and while we could not be sure of exact measurements, I was certain that slowly, maybe at no more than an inch per hour, the distance was closing.

"I feel like I need a break, even if just for a few minutes, to clear my head. If it forces that thing to reroute and buy us time to catch our breath, it's worth it," he replied.

"I agree," I said, stepping off the trail and heading towards the cliff. Both Jacob and the chapel followed.

Any other time in my life and I would have looked at a series of five-foot climbs as nothing to worry about. Scaling fences and gates is part of the job, and while I'm hardly an athlete, I'm not out of shape either. But something about stopping to gauge the distance, and then awkwardly pushing myself up one elbow at a time... slowing down felt risky, and coming to a complete stop to climb a vertical distance felt outright crazy. I just had to hope it would all pay off in the end.

Jacob caught up with me quick enough on the first little step. Without taking even so much as a breath, we both grabbed ahold of the next ledge and began to haul ourselves up. By that point I was sweating and very clearly out of breath, and Jacob wasn't faring much better, but we'd already climbed a good distance and I couldn't resist the urge to look back and see how the chapel would handle our diversion.

I wished I hadn't.

The chapel didn't even slow. It scaled the first step as easily as it moved across open terrain. How it did it, I can't be sure. It lumbered the front of itself up at a 45-degree angle, and then slowly went all the way vertical. Unlike us, it did not stop at each ledge. The flat surface was too small to factor in for something that size. And unlike us, it didn't seem to find fighting gravity remotely difficult.

For a moment there, I caught sight of its underneath and glimpsed a crawling mass of spidery legs that writhed over each other in an impossible swirl of glistening black. It repulsed me, like watching a starfish's thousand little suckers grope and fumble for purchase on a glass tank. Unlike Jacob, who had responded instantly to the chapel, I faltered as the thought of falling into that hive of clicking shapes paralysed me with disgust. It didn't last long, but every foot of distance mattered. Our plan had backfired, badly. The chapel had no issue with vertical surfaces, whereas we did. We had stumbled into one of the few scenarios where, if we weren't quick, that thing would quickly run us down.

"Get your fucking ass going!" Jacob cried, and I snapped out of my mortal panic and rushed over to the next ledge. Without giving it too much thought, I threw my backpack away along with any other supplies I carried and dragged myself up and over the stony outcrop. I was barely on my feet when I heard the sound of my belongings being crushed. I only had one last ledge to go, and already Jacob was at the top of it all, reaching down to help. Fighting the urge to look back one more time, I ran and jumped and went to grab his forearm. My hand clasped firmly around his wrist, and together we began to haul me up while my feet scrabbled for purchase on the stone. Along the way, my toes slid into a crevasse and while it helped me push a little farther, it was uneven, and my foot slid too far down into the wedge. To my horror, when I tried to tug it free, it wouldn't come.

"I'm stuck," I cried, surprised to hear myself sound so afraid.

Jacob knew what to do. Both hands wrapped around my arm, he pulled with all his strength, and I gave it everything I had. We both understood the situation implicitly—it was better to tear my damn foot off than let it slow us down by even a single second.

It came free in the end, but not without injury. As I rolled over the final ledge and tried to crawl back up onto my feet, I saw that I had lost a shoe and most of the skin along my ankle.

"Fuck fuck fuck," I hissed, tentatively reaching out to touch it. It needed dressing. It needed wrapping. It needed disinfecting. *Do we have ice?* I wondered, before suddenly realising I was in shock and thinking stupid things.

Thankfully, Jacob put one arm under my shoulder and was already hobbling me along before the chapel crawled over the final outcrop, righting itself with a thunderous crash. After a few steps I found my foot could bear a little weight, and so I began to hop away on my own. I had to ignore the terrified expression on

Jacob's face when he looked back on me and the chapel from up ahead. He didn't even have to say it. I knew it as well as he did.

The chapel had closed over half the distance.

***

"I'm getting too old for this," I said as I limped along, breath ragged as I fought to keep pace with Jacob.

"You're not even forty," he grumbled.

"Yeah, but every fuck up made so far has been made by me," I hissed. "The cliff. Falling asleep on watch…"

"You said the others weren't like this."

"They're not," I said. "Not even close. If…" *If you get out of here alive.* I stopped myself from saying it, but the damage was done. The silence between us hung heavy for long enough to let me know Jacob had absorbed that one little word and all its hidden meanings. "Look," I said. "You don't need to worry about the job when you get out. There ain't nothing out there that'll bother you after this. You'll still need supervision, but you can rest assured you're personally up to the task."

"So you'll give me a good reference?"

"Fuck yes," I said. "Best of the best."

I wanted to broach the topic of how Jacob would contact the agency on his own. What passcodes to use. What names to ask for. But I could see he was still stressed, so I didn't push it. As it was, Jacob kept drifting ahead of me. Sure, I was putting in a good effort, but at best I was only delaying the inevitable. Sooner or later I'd be caught, and it'd be best if the guy knew how to make arrangements all on his own.

"Do you still have that grenade?" Jacob asked.

Surprisingly, I did, having returned it to my pocket and not my bag. Probably not the smartest thing to do, I figured, but then again, I might just prefer having a nasty accident instead of falling under that monster's tread.

"Yeah," I said. "But it ain't gonna work, you know that, don't you? Whatever's in those doors, we can't touch it."

"I'm not thinking about the doors."

Jacob gestured to another rocky hill in the distance.

"Another cliff," he said. "This one we'd have to go *down*. I know that thing went up nice and easy but… I mean, it must be unstable going down one, right?"

"What are you thinking?"

"I'm thinking that thing has vulnerable than when it's sliding down rock at a near ninety-degree angle. We just need something to pry it loose."

***

Going down a set of stepped cliffs was no easy feat with my bad ankle, but my urgency was such that I didn't mind basically falling the several feet down each one and landing on my hands and knees. It hurt like hell, and on the second one I knocked my head so hard I wanted to roll over and be sick. But it was better than the alternative, and even as I fumbled to reach the third, the chapel crested the highest ledge and its shadow fell across me.

"You ready for this?" Jacob asked. He was stood up, grenade in hand, having waited anxiously for me to catch up two ledges down. "You said five seconds, right?"

"Yeah, I'm ready," I said, like I was somehow impressive. My part in the plan involved crawling as hard and as fast as I could down each rocky step while hoping to hell I didn't kill myself. It was Jacob who had to wait until the chapel was as close as possible before plopping the live explosive on the shelf above and legging it just like me, hopefully avoiding any injury. Truth be told, calling it a 'plan' might have been a little generous. But you have to understand, we hadn't been able to stop or even think for more than a few seconds at a time.

The chapel came onwards, and as soon as I heard the flick of the pin, I began to move, lowering myself feet first while I anxiously counted to five in my head. Soon enough, Jacob followed after me and, to my amazement, grabbed my collar with one hand and hauled me alongside with him. It was an incredible feat of strength, even if I wound up breaking three ribs and a fair few fingers as we both basically underwent a controlled fall. I can't say how far we got, or whether we were protected by the rocks or distance, or what. But after what felt like a painful eternity, there was a muffled thump and we both looked up to see the chapel leaning forward at a strange angle.

"Shit."

I think it was me who said it. From the looks of it, the plan had worked, and the enormous building had lost whatever grip it had on the stone and was now beginning a head-first plunge down the jagged rock face. But we had neglected to consider that we were right in the damn thing's path.

I considered tucking myself into the rocky outcropping and hoping that the building would roll right over me without harm, but even just a fleeting glimpse of its blackened limbs flailing around in a desperate hope for purchase made me think otherwise. I could easily imagine those needle-sharp proboscises snagging my skin and dragging me down with it. Jacob, however, came through. He never stopped pulling me by the collar and, in the end, he threw me sideways. I say throw; it was more like a tumble off to the side. But I don't think you can appreciate how hard it must have been for him to do. He saved my life in that moment, getting me out of the way so that the chapel went tumbling past leaving us both unharmed.

By the time the dust cleared, we were both left bleeding and bruised half-way down the rocky steps, looking at the chapel as it lay on its back squirming like a horse-show crab stuck in the sun. It had millions of limbs buried under that floorboard, most as wide as needles, some as thick as a thumb. Where they came from or how they were organised, I couldn't tell. I didn't even like looking at them. They made my skin crawl. Still, I began to laugh as we stared at it trying to rock itself back upright, smashing its roof and walls to bits. If it kept at it, it would soon kill itself without any help from us.

Jacob started to cheer and this time I decided to join in.

***

We made our way down the cliff, and by the time we reached the bottom the chapel had stopped rocking and some of its legs had started to wither. I'd never seen anything like it, but I couldn't stop myself from thinking that the mimic had decided to abandon the chapel entirely. I watched as it slowly withdrew its legs back inside the floorboards and out of sight, and I had the sense we were watching this thing accept its final defeat.

"Fucking hell," Jacob cried, stepping forward as he strained to pick out the strange sounds coming from behind the glass. "I think it's dying?"

"That or going back where it came from," I said, soon expecting a flurry of questions. Jacob was definitely curious, and this time I'd have no problem sharing all my thoughts with him.

Only the questions never came. When I finally made eye contact with Jacob, he was looking paler than ever, with eyes as wide as marbles. By the time I saw the pulsating web of flesh that crept around the back of his head, slowly flowing around his ears like melting silly putty, it was too late. There was a sound like a rubber band snapping, and he was snatched backwards, hurtling through the open door of the chapel like a sideways bungee jumper.

He'd been grabbed from over a hundred feet away.

Whatever had happened, it was the mimic's final act. As the door slammed shut, it folded the last of its legs up into its insides and all movement ceased. It was, and of this I'm incredibly sure, an act of spite. One that not only shocked me with fear, but left me feeling like my chest was going to crumple in on itself. I hadn't liked Jacob much at the start, but I would've been dead long ago without him. And he'd shown himself to have great potential. I'd already begun planning how I would help him rapidly rise through the ranks of the agency. With any luck, he'd have a career that lasted decades and took him right to the top.

All of that was gone in less than a second.

Despite knowing him for less than a week, I'm not ashamed to say I cried.

***

The chapel was brick and mortar by the time I returned with help. We traced it to some abandoned village years ago and the researchers would go on to spend months poring over its tracks and hunting habits. Most of the evidence came from my firsthand account, and so I was taken out of field duty for well over a year while being asked the same questions over and over again by slightly different people. It's weird to say, but I was celebrated. Jacob was awarded some posthumous medal and his parents fed the usual bullshit story about some kind of gas leak. I made sure they rigged the story so it looked like he died doing something heroic, shutting down some valve before it blew up a few residential houses. Still, it didn't sit right with me that the true nature of what he did would never be known. Maybe that's why I'm posting this… I'm not sure.

Since the chapel I've been trying to get the agency to formalise the idea that these things can be intelligent. From there, I hope I might even be able to get them to acknowledge that there's even more to it than that. A lot of fuss was made over the mimic with-drawing, but it was treated as a kind of spontaneous death. I'm not convinced. It was like it went slithering back to where it came from, and what worries me is that I think it took Jacob with it.

Possibly even alive…

I only tried once to go back into the field. My partner—an ex-perienced guy like me—made sure it was only a little job. Appar-ently some grad students were complaining about missing specimens in their secure pathology labs. We quickly traced it to one of the tunnels in the rat's habitat—the kinda thing no tradition-al scientist would ever even consider looking at. But we knew. One glimpse at it and the powdery white discharge all around it let us know.

A simple job.

Easy too.

But it was the note I found, lying down in the matted saw dust and shit that's stayed with me. The handwriting was desperate, but I recognised it as Jacob's nonetheless.

It's not eating our flesh, it read. *But it still hurts so bad.*

A BETTER PLACE

The parents have it the hardest. First, they have to figure it out, the powers, the visions, whatever it might be. If they're lucky, they're put in contact with us before it gets serious. If they're unlucky, they can lose everything. One girl, a real nasty job, I didn't even get to meet. By the time I turned up, the whole family had been crammed into the oven and the house had burned down. We had to peel them out of it, one by one, like giant fruit roll ups. We think she was a pyro but who knows? We weren't there... We try to do some outreach, but it's hard with the government mandate stopping us from going public. Although it's not always how you might think. We're not like the Men in Black or anything. The truth is that when the supernatural turns up on your doorstep, you'll likely choose not to believe it. And if you do, then no one else will believe you. That's what I mean about the parents. They're isolated from friends, family, even each other. These kids aren't X-Men, levitating remotes or mowing the lawn with their minds. It's stressful, sometimes even terrifying to live with.

It's not easy when your six-year-old tells you the date and time of your death. Or you give them a bad row and the following morning you wake up with an abscess the size of a tennis ball filling your mouth like a ball-gag. And that stuff can happen even when the kid doesn't mean it to. Their thoughts and emotions just leak out. And kids... they can have some pretty messed up thoughts. We have a pamphlet—more of a book, really—where we run through some of the common mistakes that parents make. It's funny to read if you don't know what's at stake.

Introducing your gifted child to the concept of death as early as possible is essential for long-term safety. Examples of tradition-al folklore you should avoid discussing with your child include:

That their deceased goldfish has gone to live "in the sea".

That dogs, cats, rabbits, etc. are now living happily on "a farm".

That deceased grandparents have "gone to a better place".

It goes on, but you get the gist. No two kids are alike, but they ruminate on the little things. Phrases like "a better place" can become real to them in a way they'll never be for an adult. They start to picture things, start to think of what it might be like, what it should be like… But a brain isn't just a long line of thoughts. It's like an ocean and there are depths filled with things out of sight, even a kid's mind. Add in fact that most kids are a lot smarter and knowledgeable than their parents think and well…

What do you think a "better place" should be? Have you ever been to a funeral? Seen a corpse? Kids know more than you think. They visit grandma in a parlour somewhere. Everyone's crying, everyone's sad, and their mother won't let them open the box to see the old woman who gave them candy every week. Does that seem like a "better place" to you? All the black. All the tears. Being lowered into a hole in the ground and covered with dirt?

One of my early cases was a young girl, sweet as can be. She could, occasionally, tell the future in very specific terms. Her parents, bless them, hoped it'd lead to a better life, but they made the mistake of asking when they'd die and the answer wasn't what they wanted. It broke my heart to visit that little girl, to sit and play the Wii with her, laugh with her, and then look back at the kitchen and see her mother standing there with a distant look in her eyes. The little girl couldn't understand why her parents jumped when she looked at them, or shivered when she hugged them. They still loved her, but you could see they'd spent every second of every day counting down the moments.

It was up to me to make sure the little girl understood the re-ality of death, that much I managed. I remember her little frown as she did the maths. She'd been confused for a few weeks by that point, but her parents refused to answer her questions. I answered them all, and honestly at that.

"It's not really a *better* place then, is it?" she asked.

"I don't know," I answered. "I'm not even sure it is a place."

"I shouldn't have told mummy about the yellow car," she whispered, her eyes tearing up as her little mind grasped such a big idea.

"Mummy shouldn't have asked," I replied a little too quickly, letting my emotions rise to the surface.

I hoped that'd be the end of it. I figured with any luck the mother and father would learn to live with what they knew and not drive themselves mad thinking about how to avoid it. Most people, though, they get so blinded by the specifics they don't see the big picture. That woman could have locked herself up in a bank vault to avoid being run over by the taxi her daughter described, only to drop dead from a heart attack a day later. I tried explaining that to them. I tried explaining that worrying won't change a thing.

At least it's not *supposed* to.

A few weeks later, I returned for another welfare check and guess who answered the door? The little girl, looking hungry and ragged. In the kitchen, all the cupboard doors had been thrown open, and she'd clearly started hacking away at old tins of food with a knife. There were even empty packs of pasta where she'd been eating the stuff dry and uncooked. At first I thought her parents had killed themselves, and she'd been forced to survive on her own for a short while. But when I asked her I got an answer that made my blood run cold.

"I sent them to a better place," she said.

"You killed them?" I asked, wondering exactly what these parents had asked of their own child.

"No, silly," she answered. "An actual *better* place. I pictured the bestest place in the whole world and I made them go there."

"What's the bestest place in the whole world?"

"A beach!" she cried. "A beach that goes on forever and ever in all directions and you can eat as much as you want because the grass grows fruit and candy and there's no one to tell you what to do so daddy never has to go to work again and mummy never has to worry about being fat because no one will ever see her get bigger and daddy will love her no matter what because he said so and…"

"How did… how did you send them there?" I asked.

She held up a piece of paper with blue crayon and beige lines scribbled all over the place. It was a kid's interpretation of the beach, an explosion of colours and poorly drawn shapes that composed the background. The foreground, however, was something completely different. There were two black-and-white photorealistic figures, frozen in time, hands held to the sides of their heads as a silent scream escaped from their lips.

"And the best thing about the better place?" the little girl beamed with pride. "You can never ever ever ever die! No matter how far you fall or how long you hold your breath or even if you eat loads and loads of poison."

Bless her. She looked so proud of what she'd done...

Every now and again, I pull that picture out and look at the girl's parents. They move so long as you're not looking directly at them. They push at the boundaries of the page, sometimes even go around the other side. At first they screamed and screamed and that was all I ever saw, but for the last few years they started just lying there next to each other staring at, what I guess might be the sky? I'm not sure. I'm not even sure time moves normally for them. There's something that looks like a tally in the sand. If it is, the count is bigger than anything possible, whether it's days or years.

I'll burn it one day. I just need to feel confident it's the right thing to do. I still hold out hope the girl will come back and pull them out, worse for wear but ultimately alive. I lost contact with her when she turned thirteen though. Most of these kids don't stick around into adolescence because they don't have to, and the system is rough at the best of times. I wish I knew where they went. I like to think the government rounds them up and finds them a place where they can help the world with their powers. But most of these kids aren't cut out to be fry cooks, let alone super-soldiers. Whatever purpose they find in life, I'm not so sure it's for anyone else's benefit.

Part of my job is minimising the threat these kids pose to relatives and society at large. Easier said than done, of course. It's not just that there's all this power condensed into a half-formed brain. It's what they *represent* to the average person. In the movies, if some gravedigger spots the undead grandma hauling her ass outta the ground and shuffling towards the horizon, all you have to do is spray him with whiskey and hope no one believes him. That last part holds out, but not the first. Do you know what the average person does when faced with proof of the afterlife? What do you think happens when the average person happens to catch a glimpse of what's in grandma's eyes, or God forbid they get the chance to exchange a few words with the formerly deceased? Kids who speak to the dead can be the worst because it turns out, whatever's on the other side, it drives the average person fucking *insane*.

And I don't just mean talking-to-your-self-insane. It's more like slit-the-throats-of-your-family-and-castrate-yourself-with-a-razor-blade-insane. You might think you've accepted the idea of nothingness, or the idea of heaven, or hell. But the truth is, I'm not so sure it can even fit inside one person's head. The glimpse *I* had was bad enough to net me six months in a mental health facility.

It started when some poor boy had brought his grandfather back without even realising. He just thought about it long enough, hard enough, and it happened. Next thing, I got a phone call from the parents who'd locked themselves in the bathroom. They needed help. And even though I was on probationary training, I didn't call up my supervisor. I just rushed out. Truth is, I didn't want to call my boss. I didn't want to be supervised. I'd been waiting for this opportunity ever since I read about it in the training. I wanted to see someone who'd come back to life. I wanted to know what was on the other side. All the guys talked about it, about people coming back. But I hadn't really thought they were being serious. It certainly seemed like they weren't being honest with me.

I made the mistake of treating it as a problem that could be solved for x. I thought having an answer would do something, help me in some way…

I managed to find Grandpa staring at the bathroom door, formaldehyde leaking out his asshole and dripping onto the floor. Those eyes looked at me with an unspeakable hatred, a venomous glare bad enough to make me stumble back, keeping far out of his reach. But it wasn't enough to stop me asking questions. They burst out of my mouth, and I asked so many, so quickly, I don't even remember what they were. I figure most of them boiled down to something like,

"What's on the other side?"

When the old man spoke, it was like his voice carried an epoch of suffering and weariness. I was looking at a soul that had been put through the ringer, twisted, washed, cleansed, battered, and abused. It wasn't the same soul that had left, that was for sure. But one look in those eyes told you it wasn't lying either.

"Servitude," he answered, and it was like the ringing of a gong. I almost asked a follow-up question, but good God, something inside me choked and stopped the words. A part of my soul died hearing that word. I still lay awake at night thinking about it.

Servitude.
Servitude.
Servitude.

I don't even know what it means, but it has haunted me ever since. Now it's just like that picture, something I bury and try to forget about. I don't want to think about it, and nor does your average Joe. If I let myself start asking questions like, "who's doing the serving?" my mind just doesn't stop. I spent six months going in circles, reading old case files hoping to learn more. That word stills calls out to me a few times a day, scattering my thoughts like rats before a torchlight.

Minimising the harm done by these kids can be hard when it's at risk of putting you in a rubber room. Like I said, the only thing on our side is that 99% of people just don't want to face the truth of what's underneath all the mundane, boring shit we call "daily life". That's why so many of these parents are so deeply unprepared. It takes a kind of twisted mind to imagine the world the way a kid does, and more importantly, to think of all the ways it can go wrong.

Your goldfish has gone to live in the sea.
The tooth fairy will take your old teeth.
Santa punishes the naughty.

Parents have been indoctrinated since childhood to think these white lies are a fundamental building block of parenting. It's impossible to break as a habit. Even parents who know better. Reasonable, intelligent people who are doing the best they can will still make a few mistakes here and there. The best they can hope for is that it doesn't backfire and wipe out half the town. That's when the other half of my job comes in: clean up. I have to direct the parents to the right type of clean-up crew. Most of the time, it's the guys with mops, buckets, and a very strong stomach. Other times it's a nasty man in a suit who knows how to stop the neighbour from posting photos to the internet. Fuck… once it was a bunch of guys in lead-lined hazmat suits. That was a tough one to figure out. We still don't really know what happened. But the Geiger counters they left behind still haven't stopped clicking.

Talking about tooth fairies, in some parts of the world they're very real. They weren't always real, you understand, until some of these kids came along. Do you know how fucking scary the idea of a tooth fairy is to the average child? Let's just say what some kid dreamed up in the eighties is exactly what you'd expect from a being who steals teeth for a living. Its face is nothing but a palate with teeth growing all over the damn thing, so that there's barely a sliver of gum wider than a finger. And the teeth stink... they're all rotting and yellow like a meth addict's. And this thing goes around taking teeth and whenever an old one falls out of its... well, I'll call it a head but I'm not exactly an anatomist. But anyway, when one falls out, it takes one of the teeth its collected from kids' mouths and finds a new home for it. Its muscular arms shake as it forces the root through flesh and cartilage, and I swear the sounds it makes are cries, but who knows? I always hoped the damn thing would disappear when the kid grew up, but no, it's apparently still out there, climbing gutters and drainage pipes using its arms because the kid who dreamed it, dreamed it with no legs.

And that's just one of them... There are *lots* of tooth fairies.

Like I said, the world is terrifying to kids. And they think things in a way we can't easily predict. But the consequences are all too real, often for the parents, sometimes passers by. The only saving grace is that most of these kids are well-intentioned. Even the difficult ones, the ones with learning difficulties, or emotional problems, they'll show regret when they realise that their actions have hurt people. That's the most important ingredient in a person—remorse. People hurt each other all the time, but the vast majority of us don't do it knowingly. And even if we do know, it's something we figure we have to do.

But, of course, there are others. Kids and people who know damn well what they're doing. I don't know a whole load about 'em, just enough to help me identify them in my work. But they're the kids who are ambivalent about the pain they cause because they just don't care. Most of 'em are narcissists, content to chase dreams of money and sex because it gives them a thrill. You read about how psychopaths do well in certain jobs like investment banker or whatever. Great. Good for them. The gifted ones I work with are actually quite similar. They're not necessarily any worse than the other kids. They just tend not to be bothered when I explain to them that, after what they did to their little brother, he won't be able to play any more Xbox with them.

There's no guilt, no remorse.

The *really* bad ones though, they're not just indifferent, they get a kick out of it. It takes a lot of moving parts to come together so that you make a person who *enjoys* hurting others. I read once that most serial killers have lower IQs because the average psychopath knows damn well that the cost-benefit analysis of murder isn't in their favour. Murder is hard and the pay-off is usually quite small, and a smart psychopath knows that. Society imposes enough consequences to keep *most* people in line.

But when they're gifted... well, those consequences just go right out the window, don't they?

If I can demonstrate the presence of sadism, and a total absence of remorse and empathy, in a child I can request permission to euthanise them. Some of the first tests we do when finding one—brain scans, questionnaires, EEG, so on—are all about identifying psychopathy. I used to hate it. The kids would ask what we were looking for, or sometimes start bawling their eyes out during the hammer test (my least favourite test of them all), and it always broke my heart to imagine what was waiting for them if I made the wrong decision. I understood, logically, why we did it. I just hated knowing that I had that kind of power. Those kids didn't know what waited at the end of the road if they failed the tests... Not even their parents knew. I would have given anything to get the agency to drop those tests.

And then I met Bradley.

We had sixteen teachers suffer kidney failure in a single year and that's what flagged his hometown for further investigation. Looking at the injuries some of these teachers had suffered, I was convinced that we were dealing with a teenager who had latent abilities. That kind of cruel spite is usually reserved for teenagers. But actually, Bradley was just seven. I first saw him lying on his living room floor reading a university-level textbook on anatomy. He was something of a prodigy, although he himself admitted he wasn't that smart until he "started taking bits of other people's minds." The funny thing was his father was the spitting image of Bradley, his mother too, but you expect that kind of thing, don't you? What you don't expect is to see that the other kids in Bradley's class look a little like him, that parents all over the place have been crying havoc to local scientists who simply don't have any answers. They got these photos of their kids just a few years before Bradley moved in, and they look different. They have different facial structures, different hair colour, different eye colour. It's subtle at first, but as time goes on, you see these kids change more and more and it's undeniable *who* they're changing into.

And then the complaints stop because, of course, the parents start to look a little more and more like Bradley too.

"I'm just borrowing bits of them," he told me. "Most people don't think enough. There's all this spare room in their head, so I just help them find a good use for it."

He infected their minds and, without really knowing why, he made them a little bit more like him. It was a side-effect, of course. But a shocking one. We had to cull a lot of people to bring things back to normal and even then Bradley wouldn't just *let* us kill his main source of computing power. We had to negotiate and what he wanted was... well... He liked vivisection and he *really* liked live subjects. He also liked our tools, he said. Some things he just couldn't learn from pilfering the average person's brain, but in our labs he was like a kid in a candy store. We didn't really think that part through, if I'm honest. Putting him in a room with our scientists was guaranteed to end badly. But Bradley was so powerful...

Without ever really noticing, we pivoted from trying to contain him and started trying to just appease him. He was unlike any kid we'd come across. There was nothing stopping him from tying your colon into a knot just to see what would happen. He got a kick out of it, out of seeing people suffer because of his own actions. We don't let scientists out in the field now, just in case another telepath picks up some useful tips. A burst pancreas here, a brain-bleed there, turning your blood to something the consistency of pudding...

We still hold annual conferences trying to figure out what Bradley was, what his endgame was. He certainly wasn't interested in any kind of new race or evolution. If we ever implied that he wasn't the only psychic he'd get very upset. I lost my first supervisor to that. We didn't know what Bradley was at the time. We'd just found him in his home, sure enough, and he was odd, definitely intelligent beyond all reason. But we didn't know...

"You may feel alone, Bradley," my boss said. "But in fact, there are estimated to be nearly a hundred thousand children just like you—"

"There's no one like me," the little boy replied, and his eyes fixed on my boss like daggers. Next thing I know my boss is shaking, convulsing, blood is foaming out his mouth, his nose, his ears... When they finally got around to doing an autopsy on the old man, they say that there was barely anything left inside his skull. It had been ejected, with force, out of any available orifice from the neck up. What little of his brain remained was pooled at the base of his skull, like the final dregs of milkshake at the bottom of a cup.

In the end it was Bradley's ego that brought him down. After two years of watching him massacre his way through a small town, and then our labs, all while wondering when he'd finally set his sights on some bigger prey, I decided I couldn't just let him carry on. The thing about kids is that even ones like Bradley, even the smartest, cleverest, and most knowledgeable ones don't really have any experience. Throw in an ego the size of a planet and they often lack that essential humility beaten into most of us by adulthood.

In the end it was a little white lie. That's what saved me, saved us all, really.

"No one's spoken to what's on the other side," I told him. "We have never had any gifted person be able to reach out and see what happens after death."

He came out of his room the next day and just… I don't know. I didn't feel sorry for him. But fuck, I came close. He had a little desk in the middle of our lab's main floor, where he'd watch the scientists and read their minds like most kids flip through TV channels, and he walked right up to it and sat down. He looked so beaten, so utterly wiped out. He asked me for crayons, so I gave them to him. And he spent a few minutes scribbling something—a little house with some trees—and next thing I know, he's gone. He just popped out of thin air like he was deleted from one of life's animation-frames. He wasn't dead. He'd just put himself into the drawing.

They talk about him like I trapped him, like I beat him.

But truth is, I think Bradley could leave the drawing whenever he wants to. You can see him in that house. He's painting in there, I think. It's all he ever does. Sooner or later the page will be lost, destroyed, maybe even intentionally. There's no such thing as infinity when it comes to human life. But I remember the look in that dead old man's eyes, and I remember how it made me feel. *Servitude.* Bradley must have seen right through into whatever afterlife there is, and he did so with such clarity it'd put all the other kids to shame. Now I think he's hiding. I think he knows sooner or later he's going to end up on the other side and there's nothing he can do to stop it. All that's left to him is to put as much distance between the beginning of his life and its end, and he knew from experience he could make all kinds of special places where time runs slower than the norm. Don't forget, he had all my memories to go through as well. I have no doubt he knew about that little girl and what she did to her parents.

The infinite beach.

Thankfully, we think Bradley was a blip. A cloud-computing telepath who borrowed other people's minds to strengthen his own powers. That's the kind of feedback loop that could end the world, maybe even the universe. We're glad he called it quits, although it unsettles me to think of the reason.

Someone asked me once what I think these kids are. I'm not sure, but I'm tempted to call them a bug, an error. Whatever they are, they've tapped into something underneath the banal reality most of us fixate on. The one filled with recyclable cups and microwave TV dinners. You hear that and you think it must be a thing of wonder to have that kind of knowledge. I just think of Bradley… a literal god amongst humans who took one long, hard look and fled with his tail between his legs. If I ever glimpse his face in that picture, looking out the window, all I can think is that he looks so God damn scared.

THE DERELICT

"Right," I said, raising my voice on deck to make sure I could be heard. There were four of us, me up front and three others lounging around on deck chairs. "What have we got so far?"

"The anchor's bad," Cole answered, sitting upright to rub a hand over his shaved head. "I'm not sure I'll be able to get it up. It's held out for thirty years and isn't coming easy."

"Well, we kinda need to get it up," I replied. "Especially if we're going to get this baby to a dock."

"If we need to," he said, "we can cut it, but I'm not sure we've got anything that can do the job."

"I'll speak to Khasim's men," I replied. "How's the rudder?"

"Looking good," Gareth answered. "The rudder is good."

"Anything else?"

"We found a leak," Charlie said, crossing her boots with a sigh. "Bottom deck is flooded, but we can't be sure why the water level hasn't risen further."

"A leak's bad news," Gareth groaned.

"It is," I said, "let's get down there. Charlie, Cole, you ready for a dive?"

"Aye aye," they cried. "Already brought the suits up," Charlie added.

"Sounds good," I said. "Let's get going."

With that, Charlie and Cole left. Out of all of us they had the hardest job and from the keen looks in their eye as they made their way below deck, they took it seriously. I nodded approvingly at Gareth as he walked over. He handed me a coffee, and we began to carefully pick our way across the open deck where we stood. It looked like it had been a sunbathing area with a nearby bar. Now all that furniture was just broken wreckage left strewn across the floor.

"They're good guys," I said. "They're taking all of this well."

"It does seem pretty good on paper, doesn't it?" Gareth said.

We had been hired ahead of any other crew and sent to board the ship on our own. Our job was to have some kind of inventory ready to go the second the buyer's crew arrived. After that we would organise and manage the repair effort based on our initial reports.

"It does," I said. "I would say that, except…"

"Nothing about this place feels good?" Gareth asked.

"You have to wonder, don't you? Looking at all this shit." I picked up an old handbag that had been lying on the floor. "I know it was a sudden evacuation, but I'm not sure the captain went crazy like they say."

"You think it was something else?" Gareth asked, arching one eyebrow towards me. "This place is creepy, but I've just been putting it down to nerves."

"I don't know." I shrugged and tossed the handbag to the floor. "It'd help if it was a big story, y'know? If there were articles and interviews with pissed off passengers, standing on some dock with dripping wet hair, moaning about how the captain had abandoned ship for no damn reason." I showed him the purse I'd taken from the handbag, opening it up to reveal a faded driver's license. "I just get a funny feeling when I look at stuff like this. I know it was thirty years ago, but you'd think there'd be something online, wouldn't you? The rescue effort must have been huge."

"You think conspiracy?"

"I don't know," I said. "This place just feels weird."

"It's just the heeby jeebies," he replied, doing his best to make us both feel a little better. "Besides… I mean, well, we're here now."

"True." I nodded. "You're probably right. Just the heeby jeebies."

Gareth chuckled at my use of *probably*.

"I gotta go," he said. "This conversation isn't doing me any favours."

I waited for him to leave, shouting a final thanks for the coffee. He waved goodbye, and I watched him turn a corner. Once he was gone, I opened the purse again and ruffled through the papers.

Most of them were old receipts, but something caught my eyes. A folded square of old paper towel, something taken from a dinner table, perhaps. It was wrapped around an old dinner knife; the tip was snapped off and nowhere to be seen. I unrolled it and found a message written in old lipstick. The writing was desperate, the letters jagged and harsh.

"They hurt me," it read.

"What the hell is that supposed to mean?" I whispered.

***

"Get up here!"

Gareth's voice sounded tinny and distant. I was alone, hearing it filtered through the radio at my waist.

"What is it?" I asked.

"You've... to come... fucking nuts... you won't..."

"Fuck's sake," I grumbled. "Alright, where are you?"

"Top deck... it's... zing!"

"Gareth? You still there?" I cried before resigning myself to a short walk. "This better be fucking good."

Only when I climbed all the way to the top deck, I found it empty. Deck chairs were stacked toward the aft, and parasols, bleached white in the sun, lay torn and lifeless along the floor. Occasionally a gust of wind would catch one of the shredded flaps and it would struggle like a bird with a broken wing, the sudden sound touching a nerve deep inside me. Most of this deck was taken up by a large swimming pool, the scum-covered surface disturbed only by old foam toys and deflated beach balls that floated eerily in the wind. Each one was a furry shape engulfed in algae, pacing those choked waters like patient predators.

Directly ahead was a water slide. A twisting, multicoloured tunnel of plastic that rose upwards for thirty feet. It looked faded and pale and was grown over with speckles of green algae. Half-way up one of the sections turned transparent, offering a once-tantalising view of the sea. Something caught my eye up there and to get a better view I walked around the edge of the pool until the acrylic caught the sun and I could see right through it. There was a fuzzy dark shape, something that if I squinted just right looked like it could be big enough for a person. Suddenly my radio flared up, and I caught the tail-end of Gareth's voice.

"...gotta help... stuck... fuck!"

The shape moved silently against the hard plastic. It looked like there could be someone stuck up there. *Is that him?* I wondered.

"Gareth, where are you?"

"… up… just… up here!"

It must be him, I decided, and I couldn't quite work out what to feel about that. I sure as hell wanted to be angry. I had to assume it was him, didn't I? There was no one else, so it had to be! And that meant I'd have to crawl up there and help him out.

And that… I guess that was where my thoughts started to dribble away like candle wax. Because going up there was just about the scariest fucking thing I could imagine doing. It wasn't just the thought of the danger. It was that place. Even just walking around the pool, stepping quietly over old swimsuits and dropped champagne flutes, I felt as if any second something was going to lunge out and pull me down and I would disappear into that opaque slimy water. The pool would be deathly still within seconds and if anyone came looking, they'd never know I'd even been up there. They'd never even know what happened.

"Gareth!" I cried as I reached the foot of the ladder. "This is… this is a seriously fucking stupid thing you've done."

I must be alone up here, I told myself, barring Gareth. I know I am because nothing else makes sense. No one's aboard this thing except us. And if I am alone, then I have to help. There are no two ways about it. He could get seriously hurt in the time it takes me to find the others. Any feelings I have about those murky waters are irrational. Just like that old church I had to walk past as a kid. It looked scary, that was all. This place looks scary, but it's dead. Lifeless.

Nothing to be afraid of.

So, I took my first step and immediately noticed the awful noise that rickety frame made. Every footfall on the ladder rattled all that metal and the plastic slides like an earthquake, and it took every ounce of courage to get up there. I'm not often afraid of heights, but up there you felt like you were stood on a collapsing tower. Every gentle turn of the ship was magnified a thousand-fold, so that even I started to feel a pang of seasickness.

Not thinking, I crawled towards the tunnel entrance and went in headfirst, hoping to get this all over and done with. The plastic was dry as a bone and my hands gripped it easily, so that was something. I pulled myself along at a good pace, uncomfortably aware of how the claustrophobic tube was made for bodies much smaller than mine. How Gareth had thought it was a good idea to go down was beyond me, and I spent most of the way swearing quietly under my breath. The furious muttering was a nice release, enough to keep me going until I reached the acrylic see-through tube.

Somehow, the space before me was empty. I'd arrived at the mid-section only to find a scratched view of the cloudy sky. For a moment, I replayed events in my head. *Had I seen what I thought I had? Or had he somehow gotten free? But there was no way he could have gone down. With the way the slide was rocking, I would have noticed. And he definitely didn't come my way*!

But the proof was before my eyes. He wasn't there. I was alone.

Or so I hoped.

"Gareth!" I cried. "What the fuck are you playing at!?"

I don't know why I shouted anything. I hadn't wanted to hear a reply, not even from Gareth. What I wanted, what was slowly expanding in my mind like a blooming star eclipsing every other thought, was to get the hell out. But something did reply. A thud. A loud and angry sound coming from the very bottom of the tunnel, out of sight. And I didn't just hear it. I felt it. The tunnel shook. The vibrations passed up my hands.

Another thud, and my whole body locked down with terror. *Something is coming,* I thought. My skin grew cold, my scalp tightened, and my heart started skipping every other beat. There were a few explorative thumps before they exploded into a galloping spring, the owner barrelling up that slide with unseen fury. Something inside me finally broke. I began to backpedal in a crab walk, not even bothering to turn. Only now my hands gripped nothing! The once firm plastic was smooth and slick, and I couldn't get enough traction to pull myself upwards. I lost all coordination and had to fight with everything I had just to keep myself in one place, my feet kicking black marks into the vinyl and my hands squeaking against the plastic.

I wanted to turn, but I couldn't take my eyes off that bend in the tunnel. *What will come around there?* I thought. *What stinking wet thing is speeding towards me?*

I don't know if it was sweat or just clumsiness, but eventually what little grip I had gave way. The tunnel seemed steeper than it ever had before, and gravity finally started to bear my weight downwards. For long agonising seconds the plastic was as slippery as ice, and I was helpless to stop myself moving. My mind turned white hot with terror and all my thoughts were burned away and replaced with a near-hallucinatory state of despair. I screamed the whole way down only to land in that retched green water with a bassy *plunk*, the soup-like water too thick to give off any splash.

I broke the water in a state of total hysteria, gagging as I sucked in lungfuls of rotten miasma. That organic soup had been stewing for three decades and if I had to guess, I was the first thing to break the surface for a long, long time. The result was near intoxicating, enough to leave me on the cusp of unconsciousness. But I fought to stay lucid and pushed through that stringy muck— its hairy tendrils clinging to my wrists and ankles with an almost-lifelike animation—and heaved myself over the pool's edge to collapse on the floor. There I lay panting, confused and desperate, only to hear something else come from the pool beside me.

Kaplunk.

The water looked undisturbed, but then again it would, wouldn't it? It was hardly even water, more like a tangle of weeds and slimy algae suspended in ooze. Something was in there, I knew it. It was an irrational thought, one of many I'd had in the last few minutes, but God I was certain that there was something in that damned water!

Another sound.

A loud screech.

The sound of a child riding a slide.

I looked up and saw the water slide's mouth rimmed by a dozen pale hands... children's hands. Their owners crouched out of sight in darkness.

I ran screaming from that deck, unable to wait any longer, unwilling to take the risk of seeing who, or *what*, would emerge from that water.

***

Gareth found me lowering bags onto the deck of our yacht below, my clothes rancid and dripping wet. I jumped when he called my name, and he jogged over with concern on his face.

"We're leaving," I said as soon as he was within hearing range. "We're getting the fuck outta dodge. Get Cole. Get Charlie. Let's go." I could see that Gareth was about to tell me something urgent, but then the state of my clothes caught his eye and he stopped himself.

"What happened?" he asked.

"I… fuck I don't know," I said. "Did you radio me to get up on top deck?"

"No." He shook his head.

"Have you spoken to me at all this morning? After our meeting?"

"No."

"So, you didn't stay in contact with—"

"What are you on about? I haven't radioed you once. What the hell happened to you? Did… did you go for a swim!?" he asked incredulously.

"Not voluntarily," I answered. "And I didn't go alone."

"What is that supposed to mea—"

"This place is fucked," I said. "Something is aboard this ship, and it took a shot at me and I'm not about to give it a second chance. Get Charlie and Cole before they dive. Tell them we're leaving in the next twenty minutes."

Gareth's face darkened.

"Cole hasn't surfaced," he said. "They went down, but he never came back up and Charlie's down there, passed out. I didn't want to move her, but I don't know what's wrong. Did someone attack you up there? Do you think they hurt Cole?"

I didn't have time to explain everything to Gareth, so I grabbed him and tried to give him the cliff notes as we hurried to where he'd left Charlie down below. He kept poking holes in my story along the way and oh boy, did that piss me off. I had to guess he was just trying to rationalise it, but I felt like he was maybe missing the point. *We weren't alone*, and that was all I needed to set my ass sailing towards the horizon. By the time we reached Charlie, I think I'd certainly spooked the guy a little bit. He looked shaken up. But I'm not sure he believed my story word for word, like he thought I'd maybe taken a tumble and knocked my head on the way down that slide.

Not that it mattered, something I was reminded of when we found Charlie changing out of her suit. She was in a mad rush.

"We need to fucking go," she cried, scrambling towards us with her things in hand.

"We can't leave!" Gareth said. "We have to get Cole."

"Nu uh," Charlie shook her head. "He's gone. Whatever the fuck was down there, it got him. We gotta go."

"You sure?" I asked.

"Yes," she answered. "I tried. Believe me, I tried but… but he's gone."

"Let's go," I said. "For the love of God, let's just fuckin' go!"

To our soul-crushing horror, when we reached the railing we found nothing but grey water staring up at us. Perplexed, I reached out and gave the rope a tug, almost as if to check the very truth of my senses. Just a short while ago I'd been climbing that rope and loading the yacht below. By definition, the yacht *had* to be wherever the rope was. They simply had to be together. So how could there be one without the other?

We stood there in a traumatised silence until at last Gareth spoke up.

"What happened down there, Charlie?" he asked. "What the fuck is going on?"

***

"Give it up," I said as Gareth tried the backup radio for what must have been the hundredth time that hour. "We know Khasim's men will be here sooner or later."

"It's just fucking stupid!" He cried. "It was working this morning, all of them were. How the hell can it be down now? We have a radio. A back up. A backup for the backup. Four different satellite—"

"It's this place," Charlie said, her legs pulled up to her chest as she took a long drag from a cigarette. "It's got us where it wants us."

"What the fuck does that even mean?" Gareth cried.

"You know *exactly* what I mean," she said. "I told you plain as day, something *took* Cole. One second he was there, the next he was not."

"You can't even say what it is," he replied. "For all you know he got stuck on something and we could—"

"He was fuckin' dead, Gareth, I found his damn mask!"

"There could be an air pock—"

"He's dead," Charlie said, slowly withdrawing back into herself, her eyes glazing over. "That leak we found was repaired. We weren't the first to come here and try patching her up and whatever got the last fuckers before they could pump the water is going to get us next."

"Charlie," I said, sitting beside her with deep concern. "It would help me a lot if we knew what we were dealing with? What else did you see?"

She shuddered and took a long, slow breath.

"People," she said. "Or bodies. Lots and lots and lots of 'em. I'd say two, maybe three dozen. All of them were crew, those white little uniforms gone grey and rotten in the water. I saw a few officers down there, I think. They were just bones, so it looked almost like coral at first, until I got closer. That was where I found Cole's mask, sticking out from old ribs and femurs like it'd always been there. But it was his alright.

"All those bones were piled up against one wall like those people had been crawling towards it. Something had been drawn on it, maybe. I don't know... It looked charred like fire had been taken to it. I couldn't look at it long though. Seeing that mask, those bones, it just... we're not alone. I know you don't believe me, but I'm telling you we're not alone! I wasn't in that water alone! Things moved. The currents, you could feel them crawling across your skin and the shadows never stayed still. There was something down there just out of sight, always *just* out of my fucking sight. It had me going in circles until my air damn nearly run out. If I'd kept going, kept trying to find it and really laid my hands on it, I would have drowned down there too. You know the last thing Cole said before he went missing? Before something snatched him right out from under my nose? He said, 'Who's that?'"

Something about Charlie's story wormed its way right into my head. I could practically see that place with all those dead skeletons trying to claw their way towards God-knows-what, could sense and feel the deathly silence hanging in the water.

"Fuck," was just about all I could manage to say, muttering it under my breath.

"Well, what do we do now?" Gareth asked.

And that was when someone knocked on the door.

"Room service."

The voice was Cole's.

***

"Sir? I've been asked to bring you some room service. On the house."

I couldn't quite believe my eyes. Cole was standing just outside the door, back straight and arms to his side. A trolley, full of hidden silver dishes, was beside him. He looked paler than he ever had in life, like a powdered corpse. He was shaking and a thin trickle of sweat rolled across his brow, his eyes fixated on some distant spot behind me.

"Cole?"

Charlie heard me say his name, and she immediately rushed over and pushed me aside. She saw it was him, really truly him, but before she could get close, something stopped her. It was the same thing that had kept me frozen at the doorway. Cole didn't really look like Cole. It was him, sure. But he looked like he'd gone through the ringer, like he was watching his child's coffin get lowered into the ground. He kept licking his lips like he was going to say something, only he didn't quite seem sure what.

"Cole, what happened to you?"

"Quite the spread, sir," he said, putting his hand on the trolley's handle. "It's… it's on the house!"

His words were wooden, like a recited script. For some reason I imagined a hostage speaking into a phone with a gun against their head. That was exactly what he looked like. He was expecting something of us, I'm sure, but I couldn't say what. By now Gareth was behind me, every bit as confused as the rest of us.

Cole smiled like he was about to burst into tears, and then he turned stiffly and walked away.

We exchanged brief looks of confusion and immediately followed, calling and shouting for him to stop, but he only sped up. He moved quickly as well. Whenever we got close, he'd turn a corner and by the time we made it around he'd be way down the corridor, only he never ran. He was always impossibly far ahead after every twist and turn. It was as if he was sprinting when out of sight and slowing to a leisurely walk whenever we got close. *But why?* I thought. *What the hell is he playing at?*

The chase didn't last long. He soon disappeared from sight, and we were left alone in just another one of those endless velvet corridors. I tried to see where he might have gone, but it was useless to look for him. He could have been anywhere. In despondent silence we returned to our room only to suddenly re-member the trolley he'd left behind. We lifted each lid and found plates covered in rancid mulch, the food so rotten you couldn't even tell what it had once been.

"Why would he want us to eat this?" Gareth asked. "Was that even him?"

"I'd like to take a look at the kitchen," I said. "I'd like to know where this came from."

***

The food had been scooped out of some rotten sacks around the back. Ancient vacuum-sealed packs of beef torn open and plopped onto cracked ceramic in a hysterical rush. You could see where he'd dropped plates and old meat and had to start again. You could also see half-a-dozen hypodermic needles littering the ground, and on one countertop was a plain old toolbox filled with every type of sedative you could imagine. It was an old thing, the hinges rusted. But a grimy outline in one of the cupboards, close to the back, let me know it had always been a fixture of that kitchen. I couldn't help but think of that note I'd found in the old handbag.

They hurt us.

"The fucker tried to drug us. Do you think he's gone nuts?" Gareth asked.

"I think we have a job ahead of us," I answered. "I think we need to go back to our rooms and figure out our supply situation. I also think we need to work out shifts for keeping a watch during the night."

"So you think he wants to hurt us?" Gareth nodded towards the toolbox. "I don't understand what happened to him... We've known him for years."

"I don't think it's him we need to worry about," Charlie answered. "It's whatever got to him."

***

Something was hissing. I was sure of it. I was up late watching over the others and something in the room was letting out a quiet whisper of white static. Gareth and Charlie were both asleep, and I was half-way through the midnight watch. At 4am Gareth would wake up and take over and I'd finally get some rest. But until then it was just me and my thoughts, and the deeply worrying sound of Cole occasionally shuffling around somewhere in the distance.

And that hiss.

If only I could figure out where it was coming from, but I was reticent to start walking around in case I woke the others. God, we were tense enough as it was without me worrying over some little thing. I tried to focus on the front door, hoping that whoever else was on this ship would leave us alone.

At least we had a fair amount of supplies. We'd brought enough to last the whole stay, something we owed to Gareth's peculiarly anxious mind. He was always doing things like that. Stashing away enough food for twice the journey and always bringing backups for backups. I quietly thanked him while I drank from a bottle of coke.

I paused with the bottle to my lips, hearing the carbonated bubbles hiss. I brought the bottle back down and screwed the cap on. The hiss diminished, but it didn't disappear, and when I shook the bottle, it rose to a shrill whistle. Carefully examining the lid, I noticed a tiny hole in the plastic. It was so small that when I tipped the bottle nothing flowed out, but once upright the pressure was high enough to force a tiny trickle of air back out.

"What the fuck?" I muttered, speaking aloud for the first time in a few hours.

Only my words had sounded a little slurred.

And my lips felt a little weak.

I thought of the needles in that kitchen, of the sheer quantity of sedatives tucked away. I rushed over to the stack of bottles we had and began to pull them out, cursing as my arms and legs grew weak and sluggish.

Every bottle had a tiny pinprick in the top.

"Guysh," I whispered, my limbs so numb I had to crawl my way over to the two sleeping forms. "Sharlie!?"

I reached out and shook her, but she did not wake. She was sleeping so heavily she barely looked alive. We'd all been eating and drinking from that stock. It was our own, so we'd assumed we were safe, but of course, Cole would have known about it.

"Shit!" I cried, falling backwards and feeling the world start to swim around me. The last thing I heard was the sound of our door opening and Cole muttering quietly under his breath.

"He's hungry."

***

"Dave, wake up!"

I had to fight to pull myself up. I'd been left on the floor where I'd fallen, my neck and shoulders badly hurt. Slowly I realised I hadn't left the room, and I wondered if I'd dreamed the whole thing. Then Charlie spoke again, and the nightmare was renewed.

"He's gone Dave!" Charlie cried. "He's fucking gone! Gareth is gone!"

I looked around and saw that his sleeping bag was empty.

"He drugged us," I grunted, grabbing the nearby bottle and handing it to Charlie. "Injected something in the lid. Look."

"Fuck!" she screamed, hurling the bottle against the wall where it bounced harmlessly onto the floor. "He must have come here when we went looking in the kitchen."

"We need to search for him," I said.

***

The medical facility aboard the ship was small, but densely packed with chairs, tables, and dozens of old cabinets. When the ship once sailed there would have maybe been a few medics or a single doctor aboard to treat mild injuries or illnesses, but should anything severe happen, most cruise ships simply turned around and dumped the injured passenger at port to seek medical help on land.

So why did this one have an operating theatre? I wondered. When I first saw that gurney with leather straps and an overhead light, I thought I simply had to be mistaken. But there was no denying it... the tanks full of nitrous and other gases, the trolley full of rusted scalpels, Jesus... the drain in the floor to collect any blood.

This wasn't your average professional operating theatre. The straps to restrain the table's occupant made that pretty clear. It was a small DIY space with no real room to move or do anything except get someone horizontal and begin cutting away with no thought to what came after. The doorway had been hidden behind old filing cabinets that had since toppled over, and you got a powerful sense you were standing in a place that was meant to be a secret.

It had been Gareth's screams that led us to that place. We never found him, at least not there and then. But we'd chased those shrill cries for help from one end of the ship to the other until, at last, we'd tracked it to this tiny little space. Charlie said we must've been late, and I didn't quite have the guts to say anything else afterwards. That overhead light had been on when we first entered. The padlock to the door was opened and lying on the floor. And all along that table were little channels filled with blood that dripped slowly onto the floor ready to circle the drain.

Yes, I thought. *We were too late.*

We didn't find much else to clue us in as to what happened to Gareth, but we did find an old doctor's bag with paperwork stuffed inside. It didn't make much sense, but reading it… God, you got a horrible feeling you were reading the product of a twisted or broken mind.

Passenger Soltz will be ready for collection between 0000 and 0200 hours. Do not return later than 0400 hours. Passenger sleeps with company. Observations show they are both early risers.

Passenger Lorin will be ready for collection between 0000 and 0200 hours. Passenger Lorin is in a single occupancy cabin. Observations show she sleeps late due to nightly alcohol consumption. Effects of alcohol withdrawal may be used to mask the effect of sedatives. Prepare her cabin appropriately upon her return.

Passenger Jacobson will be ready for collection between 1200 and 1400 hours. Passenger Jacobson will be staying with the childcare facility on deck three. Crewmember Fillan will prepare passenger Jacobson for collection. Use of sedatives unnecessary given passenger's age. Reports of behavioural problems to be prepared for parents' return at 1800 hours. If parents seek to escalate, the matter may be brought to the medical department where appropriate documents and diagnoses will be devised to diminish the impact of Passenger Jacobson's narrative.

Passengers Morris, Athley, and Supton have been selected for further observation. In the event they are inappropriate for collection, passengers Whettle, Dibson, and Gillet remain potential alternatives.

Further notes—Crewmember Aileen Tuson has filed a report with the Captain. She has expressed concern regarding safety of children aboard the ship, citing several mentions of The Hungry Man. This is the third report since she joined the crew four months ago, following complaints regarding kitchen and medical staff.

Report was intercepted. Crewmember Tuson was reprimanded for inappropriate conduct with passengers.

This was only one of dozens and dozens, and if I had to guess there was probably a place somewhere on this ship where we'd find hundreds more. They were not dated, but you got a twisted sense of chronology anyway.

Passenger Donaghy will be ready for collection between 0000 and 0200 hours. Passenger Donaghy will be undergoing his third collection since starting his journey and has consequently stopped eating meals prepared by crew. Sedation is impossible. Prepare appropriately for resistance.

Passenger Nguyen will be ready for collection between 1430 and 1500 hours. Observations show that Passenger Nguyen is rarely separated from their spouse. Complaints or official inquiries regarding Passenger Nguyen's location are to be directed towards complicit members of the medical and officer staff only.

Room service personnel are on hand to provide a third, as-yet-unidentified, candidate for collection between the hours of 0000 and 0600.

Further notes—the Captain has escalated the situation. His capacity for disruption is significant. We are unable to direct the ship to return to port and collect new passengers. He has reported damage to the hull that is not present and drawn significant attention from the coastguard. Corporate are working towards correcting the situation. Passenger population will return to normal in the coming weeks.

I handed the last one to Charlie and waited for her to read it.

"I don't like that corporate reference," I said.

"I don't like that Hungry Man thing," she replied. "What *was* this place?"

I shook my head in confusion and picked up another. This one was considerably shorter.

Crewmember Fillan will be ready for collection at 0600 hours.

Crew should remain vigilant for collection opportunities among remaining passengers. Some activity has been reported in the nursery on deck 3. Surviving passengers have proven difficult to collect, children included. He gives as well as takes. They are changed.

Further notes—Given the meagre offerings, decks 1, 2, and 3 are off-limits. It is unlikely He will be satisfied with current sup-

plies. All remaining crew should be prepared for spontaneous collection. Do not resist Him. Corporate report that efforts to return the ship to full functioning are underway, but significant resources are being directed towards containing any information leaks after the recent evacuation. We must bear this period of scarcity with stoicism.

"Looks like not everyone got off," I said, handing it to Charlie without looking. "Some of the crew stayed behind. Some of the passengers too. I think this place had something of a cult going on."

Only Charlie wasn't listening. She had wandered over to a nearby counter and, opening drawers at random, had found another sheet of paper. It was shaking so badly in her hand I had to reach out and take it just to read the words. She didn't even resist. She just kept looking at her empty hand, her eyes wide and glistening.

Passenger Gareth Jones will be ready for collection between 0200 and 0400 hours. Observations show passengers will not sleep alone. Sedatives have been prepared for entire group. Crewmember Cole must wait for sedatives to take effect.

Further notes—Passenger Cole Webb has joined the crew. This represents a significant increase to current staff levels. Expect Passengers Jones, Wallis, and Mitchell, to join the crew within the week.

It has been lonely.
We have given so much.
And so has He.
His gifts hurt.

***

We had barricaded our room as best as we could. Only it didn't amount to much. This time it was not Cole, or even Gareth as I'd suspected he might, that came for us. It was something else that did not pretend to be anything except a monster. A clicking drooling shuffling thing with broken bones and sagging skin that glistened in the moonlight like rancid meat. It silently pulled our door apart with heavy breaths that gurgled wetly in the dark. You could smell its hunger, its desperation. It did not groan or cry or roar. It only worked towards its prey like a determined predator driven by nothing but a mindless animal instinct.

It was in the room within minutes.

We could hear it tearing the supplies we'd brought apart. Suitcases were hurled against the wall and toolbags tipped upside down. Its breathing grew rapid and more strained as the thing continued to search for us. Meanwhile we hid in the room two doors down, clutching ourselves in the pitch-black bathroom with our breaths held tight. Only once had I ventured out to the door to look at what was tearing our room apart and the single glimpse had been enough to nearly turn my mind to jelly. Whatever was out there looked human in its general outline, but that was where the resemblance ended. I couldn't help but think of what we'd read. *Is this what happens after so many collections?* I wondered. *Is this what will happen to Cole and Gareth if we leave them? Is this what will happen to me?*

I didn't want those kinds of gifts.

Charlie eventually fell asleep, but I never could. I'd heard the thing wander off into the darkness crying in rage and terror. It had wanted so badly to find us, and I knew on some level it would never stop.

***

"Do you think it'll float?" she asked.

"I'll fucking swim the rest of the way if I have to," I said, giving the tiny lifeboat a kick. We'd thrown it together out of some old double doors and a few empty drums. It was desperate, but so were we. "Besides, we're betting on the radios and EPIRBs suddenly working out in water, which I'm pretty sure they will."

"You think they can do that?" she asked. "Block our calls for help?"

I thought of what I'd seen in the slide, of those little hands and the quiet *plunk* of something falling into the water.

"Yes."

We hauled the raft overboard and waited for it to settle. Charlie was clutching the orange dufflebag full of provisions as if it was a child, and I couldn't blame her. Things had taken a desperate turn, and all our hopes were pinned on it. We were getting ready to climb down to it when a loud echoing bang shattered the silence. It sounded like a circuit breaker, like some great machine coming to life. Before we'd even turned, we found ourselves bathed in an amber light, and the whole ship was lit up in a mockery of life.

"Go!" Charlie cried, and we hurried to the rope ladder. She threw me the bag, and I climbed over first and for a brief moment Charlie and I were face to face. We'd spent the whole night couped up in that little room, unable to sleep or relax. And we'd spent all day working on this last-ditch effort at escape. You could see the stress and horror written across her face. She looked like a terrified child, lost and alone in the dark.

And she couldn't even see what was behind her.

I tried calling out. Tried to warn her. But before I could get a word out, she was snatched from before me. Whatever it was it had come out of the nearby window, shattering glass and steel like it was clay. It moved so quickly I barely registered its existence on my retina, but the slightest smear was still enough to leave me paralysed on the ladder, my muscles seized with unspeakable terror.

The Hungry Man.

She was gone in an instant, and I was left with a choice. I looked down at the raft. It was still there, bobbing away. It promised a chance to leave, a chance to get off that damned ship like I'd wanted to that very first day. Meanwhile, the ship continued to whir into monstrous life, and looking up towards its moonlit silhouette I glimpsed an ancient creaking body crouched on the nearest roof, its spider-like limbs contracted and ready to spring, waiting for me to return. It was like some shadow come to life.

I took a deep breath and climbed down.

***

They went back. The coastguard went back and looked for them. I told them not to bother, but they did anyway, unwilling or unable to believe my story. I hoped that over a dozen crawling from room-to-room had a chance of being safe, although I suspected the ship would not easily let go of fresh meat. Hearing myself say this to them, it was like hearing someone else talk. I spoke of curses and hauntings like a stark-raving lunatic driven mad by exposure. I was surprised they even listened to me and tried to look for the others.

But not as surprised as when they found Gareth.

They took me a little more seriously after that. He'd been found in a random passenger cabin sleeping under the covers. I dread the poor soul who'd first pulled back the duvet only to find themselves face-to-face with the much-changed Gareth. In another time the ship would have taken its pound of meat slowly, and carefully, distributing the load across several passengers each day, with a constant rotation of new ones getting on at each port. If I had to guess, what happened to Gareth was a pride of hungry lions tearing apart a zebra. Something violent and insane…

He died before they got a hundred metres from the ship. I'm thankful for that little mercy, although it breaks my heart to know that Cole and Charlie will never know that peace. I've thought about going back, about burning it to the ground or blowing a hole below the waterline and letting it sink. Only I can't go near the water, not anymore. And the thought of seeing that ship rising on the horizon… I could no more return than I could fly to the moon. I simply cannot go back.

Khasim acted like I'd done him a favour. He firmly believed me when I told him it was haunted, and he offloaded it as quick as he could to some poor dupe from Bangladesh. Only a little digging showed me it was just another shell corporation for a company *he* owned. I'm not sure he was as ignorant as he claimed. But then again, I'm not sure it even matters.

In the end I found an old passenger. A middle-aged woman who'd been there as a child. She'd seemed normal. Or at least… pretty normal. But when I made mention of The Hungry Man she lost all semblance of calm and fell into a total state of hysteria. Her husband threatened me and forced me out. But I guess it wasn't that which bothered me too much. It was the fact her kids had started crying as well. And for the briefest of moments, I'd felt a shadow pass over me and the room had grown a little darker.

And I saw something. Something in the corner of my eye. The kind of thing a mad person might even want to worship as a god.

His gifts hurt.

I remembered those words clearly. Whatever had happened to those passengers, I think they took a little piece of it back with them, carrying it inside like a smuggled package back out into the world.

MORE CHILLS FROM VELOX BOOKS

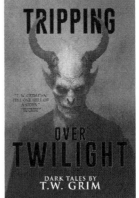

MORE CHILLS FROM VELOX BOOKS

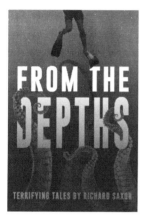

52a687bb-2236-4b77-96ef-1a848853448aR01